THE BOOK OF YAEL

THE BOOK OF YAEL

DANIEL LIVNY

To order additional copies of this book, contact:
Xlibris Corporation
1-888-795-4274
www.Xlibris.com
Orders@Xlibris.com
38057

Dedication

Dedicated to Gen. Rafael Eitan, former
Chief of Staff of the Israel Defense Forces.
a man who changed my life.

Acknowledgements

My thanks go to a few
special people who helped my story
become realized.
Yael Livny
Vince Briggeman
Jennifer Sleezer
Anika Moje
Bruce Barrett

Prologue

The following work is the diary of my sister Yael. It covers seven weeks of her life as an agent for the Mossad, the Israeli Secret Service. The writing itself was part of an assignment from her boss, Gideon Marcus. He was responsible for providing Yael with the demanding tasks recounted in this diary.

My job was to put together her notes from this mission. She knew I would have the time and patience to comb through her often cryptic scribbling and random computer files. Three months after the mission ended, I received final clearance from the Service.

Yael's accounts are sometimes incomplete and disjointed; one can perceive the great weight and pressure she worked under. For an inexperienced chronicler, asked to document the material from which spy novels are made, she accomplished nothing short of amazing work. Her reluctance to write at first obviously stemmed from the insecurities about the process. For the sake of authenticity, I left it unchanged.

So is this a novel or a diary? Yael was aware that others would read her work, and she made an effort to be funny, inventive, and exciting. She wanted to represent the life of an agent, which is the only life she knew, and not an easy one. Excitement comes with the job, but so does death for the unlucky—or, as Yael would see it, the ill-prepared. This is a record of a very significant chapter in Yael's life. It's intended to be more than that, however. It speaks for many of us, in that it provides one perspective on what it means to be Israeli.

There were unique difficulties in putting together this text. Although most of it was written in English, the narrative from the time in Germany is partially in German. In California, after one particularly trying event, she reverted to Hebrew. In the translation I tried to stay true to her style. Parts of the diary were written on notepads, parts on the backsides of crumpled computer paper. Some entries are dated, some are not, and I've had to supplement the text a few times with the accounts of her former colleague, Matthew Patterson, and her superior, Ari Baram.

This story is not just Yael's story. It is also the story of her partners, especially her closest partner and brother-in-law—my husband, Harel Marom.

In Israel, all men and women must join the military by the time they reach eighteen. Before their introduction, all draftees are tested and evaluated to find out what role they will have in the army for the next two to three years of their lives. There are three major selections: high school students from the city are drafted in August; students from the kibbutzim and villages are drafted three months later (which allows them to work the harvest before departing); and non-graduates are taken in February and May; in Israel, less than half of the children attend high school, which is not mandatory and is only designed for the academically gifted.

Combat officers are usually chosen from the August and November pools of draftees, although talented recruits can join later. The army's most valued draftees, however, come from a special draft held on July 21st. Draftees of the highest physical and mental caliber are recognized on this day. Although these candidates initially go through the same branches of the military as the rest, they are scrutinized under a different lens. And from that group comes the final selection.

No more than twelve of some thirty-thousand draftees annually end up in a special division of the Israeli Secret Service. Yael was one of them.

Yael refers to a quote by King David at the start of her tale. I would like to add one, too, after having read the whole story. Golda Meir, the former Israeli Prime Minister, once said:

"I can forgive our enemies for what they have done to our children, but I can never forgive them for what they have forced our children to do to our enemies."

My sister is one of those children. This is her story, a sometimes beautiful, sometimes starling account.

Naomi Marom
Kibbutz Gilboa
July 19, 2002

1

Ye mountains of Gilboa,
Let there be no dew nor rain upon you,
Neither fields of choice fruits.
For there the shield of the mighty
was vilely cast away,
The Shield of Saul, not anointed with oil.
From the blood of the slain,
From the fat of warriors,
The bow of Jonathan turned not back,
And the sword of Saul returned not empty.
—II Samuel, Chapter 1

I've rested my head on the computer table for ten or fifteen minutes now, and I stare sideways out my window at the mountains of Gilboa. My gun lies here next to the keyboard—for private effect, for I shall write in the glamorous fashion of all those famous writers-spies, I tell myself not being able to name one. If Eric walks in on this scene—me, the mountains, the gun, his writing table—he'll be "confused and hurt," and I can't deal with that right now.

He'll be "confused" because I never sit down simply to write creatively. He'll be "hurt"—an American term for angry—because he finds my open love affair with guns distasteful, especially when one has been so rudely thrust upon some pages of his poetry.

His work is inspired by these mountains, and now as I look outside, the peaks are barely discernible in the evening light. I should shut the gingham curtains. My work is inspired by everything outside and under the mountains: the state, the songs of war, Auschwitz, the Arab voices outside our kibbutz, the wailing rabbis crouching in front of shrines—all providing a photo opportunity for tourists.

But Eric, my American husband, who has lived in Israel only two years, he is still one of those tourists, and Israel's landscape and its neurotic people are still mere pictures for his photo album and poems. In his album, we are pictured at the Dead Sea, caked in that stinking sulfurous beauty mud. My calves and thighs were enormous then; I was running five miles a day that year. My lips were red from the Popsicle I had just eaten. And there we are at Fort Massada, fingering the relics left by a rebellious Jewish tribe.

When I was in the army, my platoon was bussed to Massada to take the pledge to defend our country. Although none of us was religious, they gave us new Bibles, and we stood taut as a girls-and-boys choir, and sang the national anthem. Then we soldiers sang a few more songs and tried out our new binoculars on the sprawling Negev desert.

Just a few days ago, my slave-driver boss, Marcus, ordered me to keep a journal of a mission. "A personal record," he said, "with some history that would be useful for the national security archives." I suspect our superiors are developing psychological profiles of their elite troops, but since they've trained us to manipulate psychological tests, we are problematic research subjects. I'm guessing Marcus and his psychologists concocted this assignment. I'll be looking for a new job soon and maybe this assignment will lead to a career and eventual fame as a journalist. Working for the tabloids, if necessary, or even better, . . . writing a best seller. Then I could buy Eric his own library and a nice Canon camera. Our kibbutz is quite poor, and they won't give us any money.

Screw it. Marcus will probably seize whatever I write and file it in the archive, where gentiles are not allowed—except for Matthew. But Matthew never goes into the Mossad archive because Harel says Matthew can't figure out the computer cataloguing system. Our hackers imported some Kafkaesque German system from the Berliner Staatsbibliothek (the Berlin public library).

I go to the window and open the curtain a bit. The Gilboas are a shadowy, hulking presence, waiting for night to fall. Israel is a land of extraordinary beauty, with rolling hills of orange and olive trees, smelling of heat, citrus, and sweet mule dung; but I don't have time to consider that now. I limit my gaze to the walls of my kibbutz bungalow, shabby, but clean. Then I eye my gun, and a snapshot of Eric, who hates my job. My attention returns back to the pages in front of me. So I will write until I become a writer; maybe not a writer like Eric, but enough of one to make a living.

Okay, those first paragraphs weren't bad for a start, perhaps, too heavy on the landscape stuff. I feel more at ease writing the short research papers we have to do. I need to be vague here. Let's just say that I have to report on information that may directly affect our areas of responsibility—in Germany and the west coast of the United States.

Let's face it. Writing an intimate volume like this is not my cup of tea. I've been trained to keep secrets, not to puke them out on paper. But Marcus wants me to keep a diary of a mission. Who knows what for? Again, it is probably the psychological angle. Or maybe it's part of the peculiar Jewish obsession with remembering our history. Biblical Joshua, no doubt, assigned someone too with a similar task on the way to Jericho. On the other hand, if this diary distracts me from my missions, or if some Libyan reads this and figures out my tricks, there will be no future generations. I have been trained to protect little Hebrew babies, not be Saul Bellow.

Let our pale American Jewish cousins write and paint in Brooklyn while I sing the praises of a grenade. They have it good, those relatives of mine. No wonder we don't fit in the world they created for themselves. It was bad luck that my grandparents missed the last boat to New York and had to come to this barren desert to farm.

Anyway, I'd rather write an essay about my dogs than one on what my deeper self sees in my line of work. My dogs are here beside me now, trying to help the best they can. The cuties, how I miss them when I leave on trips. After two tedious years in the army and nearly four more in our tiny covert organization, I fear what little artistic talent I had, has been stifled. We'll see how this goes, Marcus.

2

This past week was rough. After grueling workouts that left our muscles throbbing, Harel (my partner and brother-in-law), a couple of young boys (some talents from the Navy), four more colleagues from the Department, and I headed north along the coast toward Lebanon. The highway smelled of exhaust from old Fiats and of fermented road-kill. A group of shirtless young soldiers waited along the shoulder of the road hoping to hitch a ride. We stopped somewhere near Jaffa and convinced agents Ron Nahar and Mordechai Schulz to climb a fence and throw us some oranges. We gobbled up the sticky sweet fruit and were able to forget about the road for a few moments.

Ten miles after Haifa, we arrived in the port town of Acre. We maneuvered through winding streets, past Arab vendors selling baskets, and housewives in flip-flops carrying onions, tomatoes, and okra in plastic bags. Harel softly nudged me and pointed out the window at a line of tourists in front of a mosque. The tops of the mosque walls were tiled with white porcelain covered with electric blue Arabic calligraphy. The air smelled of seawater, fresh figs, and burnt rubber—from the teenagers' mopeds, which zoomed past our Suburban like fast little fish.

We put our diving gear on the beach and got suited up. One of the Navy boys stopped and stared at a decrepit iron canon that stood a few feet away from us. "Oh yeah," he remembered out loud. "Acre is where Napoleon's Navy invaded. I think the last time I was here was on a field trip in the third grade." The 200-year old cannon was slick with algae and blue seaweed, and I hung my sunglasses around its neck so I would not lose them. "Why do you think Marcus loves this place?" I almost said to the kid, but quickly remembered he wasn't in the Department. He wouldn't understand that Marcus wanted to creep us out with the watery ghost of some dead Frenchmen. The place is special to the Orthodox Jews as well. They believe the whale swallowed Jonah somewhere near here.

We didn't encounter any whales or dead French soldiers, although some dolphins came to greet us. We played with them for half an hour in the deep sea. I swear their eyes were smiling.

Right now, however, it's almost midnight and I wonder how I'm supposed to write in this little oppressive kibbutz kitchen. Damn my parents—frugal socialist Jews with their bad taste. Look at this linoleum, yellow with green triangular designs. Should I try to describe the nasty feel of bare feet on aging, cracked linoleum?

Last November, Harel and I did a mission in Europe, where our boss arranged for us to stay with a rich family in the Provence. "A crash course in taste and manners," Harel joked. Their eclectic collection of 200 year-old Flemish furniture, delicate Japanese screens, and Tudor beds was something of a contrast to the simple trappings of my bungalow, with its huge gray metal fan, a rickety wicker bookshelf, this peeling, wobbly table, and my bed, which dates back to my high school days. I look at pictures of my great-grandmother in Berlin, who sits at her piano among her beautiful pre-socialist furniture, her face framed by an elaborate hairstyle. I have a mirror of hers, a gilded fin-de-siècle affair (a woman with flowing tresses somehow draped around the glass). I've come to think that to possess beautiful things is a luxury, not only because of the price, but also because so often their owners live in what appears to be a very sheltered world. Their focus is on aesthetics, not survival.

My grandfather always told stories of the time when Israel was still occupied by the British Empire and the British officer-gentlemen who hung around Jerusalem in the forties. To my refugee grandfather, a Prussian German Jew with big soulful eyes, these men were the epitome of civilization—*pukka sahibs* (In old Indian English—*authentic gentlemen*) with pomaded blonde hair who sat and smoked, dressed in their crisply pressed shorts. "We are going to bomb your club," I can hear my grandfather saying into an old telephone. The British gentlemen laugh and say, "Nonsense, my good man, and if you really must, do come down and have a drink with us first." The first Mossad agents had charming enemies. They sure get less charming as the Mossad gets older.

My boss, General Marcus, is charming too—and fairly civilized, although he didn't grow up on a kibbutz but in Tel Aviv. He is really not a General to us, since we don't use military rank, but he is the head and brain of the department. If this sounds like I'm taking him lightly, don't be fooled.

I remember once during a closed conference, my attention drifted away from the briefing and towards Marcus. He was listening deeply, heavy lids closed, some dark purple veins running down the side of his jowls. He sometimes looks like the love child of Henry Kissinger and a cat—smart and cruel. After a presentation, Marcus always waits until all eyes are on him, and at the last possible second, before the silence turns awkward, he begins his commentary. He speaks fluidly, but monotonously. When he speaks, he is wiser and older than those around the table who are supposed to be wiser and older. Unlike Ari or other colleagues, he never whines, barks, or gesticulates; his thick arms stay at his sides or on the table like patient, loyal pets.

This man, who gives me direct orders, is the most powerful person in the Middle East. At least I think he is. I've seen him thump the backs of some of our most celebrated government dignitaries, including our esteemed prime minister. I've witnessed Marcus giving the latter an actual tongue lashing. The details of that reprimand are not only classified, but extremely boring. I can assure you of that. I'll just say that courtesy has its place, but that place rarely seems to be near Marcus.

I think it is safe to presume that Marcus has a soft spot in his heart for us—Harel and me. We are the Department stars. We are the dynamic duo from the hinterland, the girl and the boy from the most remote kibbutz, who have shot guns at Arabs and hyenas since grade school. We never actually aimed at the hyenas. We like animals. We just chased them away from our sheep. We are in good shape from all the organic food, and clever from all the liberal socialist schooling. Once when we visited him at his home, I saw a photo of Marcus' murdered daughter, and whispered, "Harel, come here. I look like her! That's why he likes me." But Harel did not think so. "No," he remarked. "She looks like the actress from the Matrix film. She is cute and gentile looking." But that is exactly what I am. Harel is an idiot but he's my brother-in-law and co-star, so I have to be tolerant.

Marcus probably fosters some hope that we will renew our contract, due to expire in a few months. Not in a million years! Sweet dreams, Marcus. I say to you and to all: It has been great, but in three short months, Harel and I are out of here. OUT OF HERE! I like the sound of that. *Es klingt gut.* That is German for "it sounds good," and I like the sound of that, too.

3

Reading reports about our dead agents is one of the more macabre aspects of my job. You can't help, despite yourself, wonder who might read yours. I wonder how Marcus will be able to evaluate the merits of this diary. I should ask my husband Eric or my sister Naomi, the two intellectuals and amateur literary theorists of our kibbutz. It is easier to do concrete missions in which hard stats are involved.

Every time a job is done, we meet with Marcus for debriefing before we can go home. It is moments after a fatiguing transatlantic flight, when all what a girl wants is a smoothie and an iron pill.

Picture Harel and me encircled by Marcus and his department cronies, those elderly pseudo-experts and armchair defense virtuosos. We are given the third degree for real, usually in some stuffy office with bad lighting. When the questioning ends, we're told how things could have been done more competently. As Harel and I sit speechless, feigning interest, they squint and growl at us. How dare we risk entangling our beloved State of Israel in a potential diplomatic embarrassment. Are we not, provincial rubes, aware that Israel is already condemned and ostracized by the nations of the world? Don't we really care?

Of course, these jousts are nothing more than Jewish ritual. When the unproductive inquiry is finally over, they beam and kiss our feet because we are good. Then with no shame they beg us to renew our contract. We are told, in no uncertain terms, that we are without doubt the finest living human beings the Jewish people can offer.

Well, they might only mean the finest of those from the Galilee. Then again, the best of our nation has traditionally been from the Galilee. Gentiles agree: every spring, they descend like locusts upon Nazareth in tour buses and pastel shorts, paying homage to Jesus, one of the region's better known Israelis.

Our kibbutz is northeast of Nazareth, in the hot shade and solitude of the infamous Gilboas. The days are so hot the air shimmers. The nights are full of the disgusting little creatures of the desert—bats, snakes, lethal mosquitoes, and wild cats that screech and prowl around the electric wire fencing of the kibbutz. The winters are cool and breezy, dreary like vast tundra. The vegetation turns to ugly bushels of dirty looking straw. The kibbutz itself has moist black soil and yields luscious figs, red grapefruit, and pomegranates—mostly for export, and we have a reputable veterinary clinic. The surrounding area is accursed and dangerous; it's probably the most remote and secluded place in Israel, barring a few settlements in the Negev Desert.

We have very few trees and bushes, but an abundance of yellow scorpions. Even the Bedouins and their camels don't dare cross the Gilboas. They believe in the curse of King David, who uttered, "No more rain," three thousand years ago. For the last three millennia, those words pretty much describe the situation. Cursed or not, the inhospitable nature of this terrain is a striking contrast to the otherwise lush area of the Jordan Valley and the fertile plains to the west. The Gilboas are our refuge. No enemy is crazy enough to scout us out from this treacherous range, or so I always hoped as a child.

As children, we wandered the mountains trying to find the shields that, according to legend, Saul and Jonathan flung down here. Most kibbutzniks are secular, but on this eerie, vast playground, biblical stories are hard to dismiss. Of course, these are myths we would tell ourselves, but as we ran over the parched hills, it seemed like David had just made his dire pronouncement.

Once, when I was eleven, Harel and I had to carry Naomi three miles back to the kibbutz because she had fainted from dehydration. The next week we forced her to return to hold our map for us. These mountains gave us our first lesson in reconnaissance.

Oh, yes—and the scorpions! Big brown ones with monstrous pincers patrol the mountainside. They are ugly, but not half as dangerous as the yellow ones. As children we dared each other to hold a yellow scorpion with bare hands. It is not as difficult as you might think. We are not their natural enemies. As long as you act tender and loving towards them—that is, make no sudden movement—they will not hurt you. In fact, their stomachs are surprisingly soft, an erotic shock to the fingers as they stroke the golden shell. We get lulled into thinking we are bonding with these creatures, but last year a tourist was killed after running into one of their colonies. Some teenagers from our kibbutz go to the big city of Haifa and come back with little tattoos of scorpions on the inside of their ankle or in the small of their backs. Then they spend the whole summer hiding their tattoos from their grandparents, for whom tattoos have a toxic connotation.

What will people say after reading my story? That I have forgotten that my theme is espionage? Well, I hope they, whoever "they" are, will like hearing about scorpions. After all, they played a part in the making of this agent.

4

Today, the sun greeted us huge and powerful.

Our large kibbutz swimming pool is crowded with fruit-fueled children, all bent on splashing the pool empty. Near me, in the meadow, Eric is practicing Brazilian jujitsu, his new favorite pursuit. He's trying, without much success, to introduce Harel to the marvels of that form of martial art. The adolescent boys of the kibbutz couldn't be happier. They have corralled the two within a semicircle, cheering on the action—and their idol, my brother-in-law.

You would think Harel has an "S" on his chest. Since he and I joined the Secret Service, an open secret in our kibbutz, everybody worships him. Even though, I'm one of the first women to receive this plum of an assignment, even though I am making history for Jewish women, nobody is looking my way. It is damned annoying. I guess people still think that women in the Mossad only get to screw disgusting Arab sheiks and dirty IRA (Irish underground) boys.

Well, Harel is everybody's hero save for me and my sister. Noami is clearly the worshipped one in their marriage. Harel adores her, ever since she smashed an egg in his eye in the middle of our kibbutz dining room. She was six years old then, and no one in the room that day thought she would live to see another day. He walked up to her, yoke dripping off his chin and a large piece of shell still clinging to his nose. I was already on my feet, geared to protect her from Harel's wrath. Instead he smiled and asked her, "Why did you do that?"

She looked at him and answered flatly, "Because I love you." Pretty intense discourse for a six-year-old. I swear I saw it happen.

"Then I am going to marry you someday." Harel responded,

They have been together one-way or another ever since. He has become the star of the kibbutz, and she is pregnant with their third child.

Maybe because of Harel's Superman image, nobody messes with him. You had better not hurt my sister or me—or any other member of our kibbutz, for that matter. Harel is smart and strong, at least the strongest man I have ever met. Even our karate instructors are careful around him. Not my type though. Too brawny. He has big almond-shaped eyes, caramel-colored, wavy brown hair. His idea of dressing up is an old, fake Lactose

T-shirt. A good-looking guy, but I prefer Eric's type: not so beefy, ash blonde, a hairless chest, aristocratic nose, and steely eyes, Prada sneakers, hooded Levis sweatshirt. You know a little class and a little taste. Harel, on the other hand, did not know what deodorant was until age twenty-two.

Harel and I have spent our entire lives together, competing fiercely from day one. In the kibbutz we were raised together like brother and sister. Sharing, sharing, sharing, everything: our goddamn toys, the sleeping hall, books, you name it. After that, romantic love is out of the question. Children on the kibbutz are cultivated in patches, like flowers. My sister Naomi, two years younger, was raised in a separate patch, which I suppose is what made it possible for love to blossom.

Our collaborations also began early. In karate training, Harel easily overpowered all of us. Together we stole watermelons, by night, from neighboring villages. In high school, I wrote his final exams in Jewish history and Hebrew composition in exchange for comparable help on the chemistry final. Our teachers, oblivious city folks such as they were, didn't notice a thing. We were collaborators, as well in our obsession for guns and our Rhodesian Ridgebacks. It wasn't a mysterious obsession. We loved the dogs for themselves, but they were also our guardians, as were our guns. On the remote kibbutz, we were constantly targets for assaults by our neighbors across the border. They came and they came for the kill. The dogs made defending the area considerably easier, but still we were forced to learn to use guns when kids should be learning gymnastics or trying out for the swimming team. Target practice was our daily ritual, so proficiency came quite readily to us. We easily outperformed the few soldiers the army sent to protect us. Those guys spent more time eyeing the healthy, confident kibbutz girls than they did watching for Arabs.

Finally, there was a public outcry against gun use on our kibbutz. A delegation with their "fact finding" mission arrived in two blue and white buses, flanked by a platoon of armed soldiers. They were all city people—officials, experts, psychologists, and maybe even a few rabbis. They had made the one-hundred and fifty mile trip from Jerusalem to see if our kibbutz really allowed children to play with guns.

Harel's father, an old warrior and still the head of our kibbutz today, pointed out that we were the only border area that had never lost a life. He gave them some water to drink and ten minutes to vacate the area.

At the moment, I am more interested in our future, or rather in ensuring that we have one. Harel and I were selected at the same time for the service with the Mossad. Marcus put on a charming façade, playing up his wise, 'I've-seen-it-all', demeanor tb court us. We were dazzled by those melancholy Diaspora eyes. And when he said, "The fate of the Jewish people lies with your unique talents," We were his. What can one say after a statement like that? To serve five years did not sound like much in that room, that day.

Naomi wanted to kill us after she found out. She nearly beheaded us. Judaism and the nationalistic stuff mean zero to her. Harel was worried she might leave him, although he would not admit to that now. He was a broken man until Naomi was persuaded into believing that he had joined the service solely to protect me. I had to swear it was true. Thus, our first mission—an act of deception and victory.

I didn't have that spouse problem yet, because Eric and I hadn't met until our second mission to the United States—three years ago next March. Imagine how Eric felt when I waited until after the wedding ceremony to tell him my line of work. Actually, I didn't tell him, Naomi did. She likes to manage my life and unfortunately she is not exactly an expert on American hang-ups regarding truth and disclosure.

When we met in Seattle, Eric was a grad student in comparative literature at the University of Washington. Harel and I were there under our usual guise—exchange students. I think I was in Forestry that time. As things progressed between Eric and I—well, when Eric first discovered me carrying a concealed weapon in public, the sort of secret that is hard to keep in an intimate relationship—I had to give him a story. I told him I was a security officer for El Al, Israeli's national airline. We had a deal with the U.S. Government to provide us with concealed weapons permits—for our own security, of course. It was a weak story, and Eric was too smart to buy it forever, but sometimes it is easy to use Americans' ignorance of Middle East matters against them. Not many in the U.S. know how close Israel and the U.S really are. Although, conspiracy theorists and other crazy people right or left, beat their heads together over the issue.

My rationale was why to burden him. Eric was livid when Naomi spilled the beans. "Do you fucking assassinate people or are you just plain fucking people?" Eric shouted, full of rage. And then, "Are my parents and brothers in any danger—not to mention me? Jesus, Yael, what else do I need to find out about you and your godforsaken tribal rites?"

In brief, it was quite a shock for a man who has never even stolen a towel from a fancy hotel. Not a nice surprise dowry. Eventually, he began to adapt. Back in Israel, he got used to Duncan and Fiona, our Rhodesian Ridgebacks, who sleep in our bed. It took him longer to adjust to Harel barging into the room to wake us in the mornings. Privacy? Not here.

Eric, in his gentile-ness, had trouble with all this. There was plenty about Eric that the members of the kibbutz couldn't grasp either. When I brought him there for the first time, everyone gathered around to take a closer look. He stared back at them through half-closed lids, raising a Styrofoam cup of espresso to his gritted teeth. "See," I said in Hebrew to the camp of grandfathers and grandmothers, "he is not only American, but he is a real gentile, yet he loves books, writes poetry, and does other things that are quite Jewish." So the grandfathers and grandmothers smiled and patted Eric on the back. An auspicious beginning, and now everyone thinks he is precious.

5

It is the day after my twenty-fourth birthday. I am awake and already on my feet at 5:45 a.m., thanks to Harel's wake up visit a half-hour ago. After yelling in my ear that I don't have to get up for another hour, Harel then bent over Eric's face and breathed, "welcome to Starbuck's coffee sir, how may I help you?" Eric responded, "I'd like some rain and a real espresso machine. And get the hell out of my bedroom." I couldn't tell if he was tired or still grumpy from yesterday. Instead of leaving, Harel watched me watch Eric with a wry smile. "Get out", I mouthed and kicked him in the ribs. He grabbed my leg and twisted it until I burst out laughing, then quickly fled as Eric sat up with a scowl on his face.

I can hear the buzz of the blender now. My sister is already hard at work in our tiny kitchen and in a minute the aroma of freshly crushed mangos and oranges will fill the house. This kitchen is a haven for health nuts—we are all vegetarian except for the Ridgebacks—because being in top shape does not hurt your chances of staying alive—in any business, but especially ours.

Naomi has the tendencies to mother us all right along with her two children. She is not a tomboy like me, but there is a lot of steel in her. We both take after our father—brown eyes and all. My hair is cropped short—straight and black; hers is lighter, longer and wavier.

I still wonder why only I received a call from the Mossad. Naomi was also an IDF officer and is also proficient with guns. Of our generation on this kibbutz, it is Naomi who is the most knowledgeable about the arts. Did the Organization consider her too cultured to engage her in the sort of work we do? Are people who know Bach and Kierkegaard less qualified? Or did they know that she is too shrewd to fall for their smooth talk? I can hear her scoff at the suggestion that the fate of the Jewish people might lie in her hands.

This job has turned Harel and me into something different from Naomi and Eric. The few illusions we still had after our unsheltered childhood soon left us. Let's be real about it, one doesn't have to read newspapers or even grasp human history to understand human nature. I look around. I see the way married partners treat each other: vows can quickly be returned to the wonderland from whence they came. Two people will hurt each other, abuse and neglect their children, then rip their own siblings apart if inheritance money is at stake. I am not even mentioning what unrelated people, let alone nations, do to each other.

Professionals in our world seldom return to a more benign view of human nature. But we recognize that there is a sunnier world out there as well, and it is good to be around Naomi and Eric, who are still able to see it.

I am jolted back to reality and realize after I put this diary down, we will do a routine gun check. The list starts with the Colt .45, a small model that fits into our leg holsters. It is not the greatest gun, but it is small and dependable and great for general use. We maintain our firearms religiously, since some of the components were made specifically for the ammunition we use. The high-velocity, high-density bullets will penetrate even a car engine.

I hate this ritual because I know Eric hates watching us do it. I can't think about that now.

6

Our department headquarters is spread out over several renovated, inconspicuous buildings a few miles north of Tel Aviv. An old British military base chosen by Marcus. It must have taken time and money to fix those age-cracked Jerusalem stones. Nobody builds houses like that anymore. The Arcadian feel to the land around our headquarters, as well as the unimposing buildings, successfully diverts the mind from the constant hum of the electric fence and satellite booby traps. The arsenal of weapons and technology nestled deep within these acres could provide the basis for a small start-up nation.

Despite its pastoral beauty, this compound is one of the most shielded sites in the country. Security is sound enough to keep unwanted humans out—but fortunately not the birds, frogs, and lizards, who screech and mutter at us as we head to the entrance of the main house. Marcus once told us that the surrounding acres are one of Israel's most densely populated refuges for nesting birds. A good justification for our existence!

Immense eucalyptus trees stand sentinel and shade the dusty plot surrounding the buildings. The eucalyptus trees are common all over Israel but are rarely so huge. These are almost as big as the redwoods that I fell in love with on the California's coast. Our grandparents' generation originally imported these trees from Australia to dry swamps. They were pioneers to the core, fighting mosquitoes and malaria, plowing difficult fields, and dealing with hostile neighbors. Their determination makes me feel like I am part of a do-nothing generation that just wants a better job three months down the road.

Marcus' office is on the second floor of the largest building. It is a small conference room, replete with an impressive Oriental oak table—a souvenir from the invasion of Lebanon, when many drug lords deserted their mansions and fled to their masters in Damascus. Several faded green chairs line the table and a few more are stacked in the back of the room. Marcus always gets the slightly elevated attorney's chair at the table's north end. The chair's leather is old and peeling, and grit has collected in the seams of the seat. When Marcus is not in the room, Harel and I fight to sit in it. Along the walls, stout steel shelves rise all the way to the ceiling, stuffed with bound files of god-knows-what. We've never bothered to look or ask. The whole room is covered in a layer of grime, a mixture of eucalyptus seed and salt blown in through the window by Mediterranean gusts. The sea is less than two miles from here and on quiet nights one can even hear it.

For all the wall space, however, only one large picture hangs in the room. It's a signed portrait of Sir Charles Otto Wingate wearing his official British Lieutenant General uniform. It's rarity, indeed, since Wingate usually wore only combat clothes.

My guess is that only Israelis know who this guy is, although his war exploits once made him a British hero almost a century ago. A devout Christian, Wingate took it upon himself to teach the Jews in their fledgling state how to wage war; one of his main disciples was Moshe Dayan, the father of the modern-day Israeli Army. When the British government found out what Wingate was teaching the ungrateful pilgrim Jews, it sent him on a certain-death mission. After he was killed, Churchill himself called him one of Britain's greatest sons. Helping Jews is always a risky business.

I mentioned Wingate once to an English colleague from the MI5, the British Secret Service, and he had never heard of him. But we haven't forgotten him. Many places in Israel bear his name, and his grandson, even today, gets the red carpet treatment. Harel's grandfather, now in his nineties, likes to tell this Wingate tale: Before he was booted out of Israel, the head of the Jewish Underground gave Wingate a bible. On it was written: "Don't forget the Promised Land, and don't forget to whom it was promised."

This is the kind of Zionist nostalgia that graces the walls of Marcus' office. Well, whatever works for him works for him. My generation doesn't shed tears over things like that. We're not sentimental people anymore. I'm not. At least I try not to be.

As we entered this room, there was Marcus, sitting in his best Einsteinan pose, hair curly and wild. He'd never stick his tongue out, though, as Einstein did for the famous photo. I know he's been mistaken for a professor before, but if you look closely into his eyes, you know he has seen too much. No dreams, no illusions in his gaze.

Ari Baram and Matthew Patterson were also there, leaning forward and murmuring to Marcus. The atmosphere was slightly tense. Only Matthew bothered to lift his head and greet us when we came in. He's American, so he couldn't quite repress a friendly hello. His watery blue eyes blinked as he gestured to a little table with water and food.

Something was strange. For one thing, nobody else was there. The room is usually packed with experts, ready to feed us information. Even Rafi, our technical wizard for electronic counter measures, communication, and computers, was absent.

I poured some mineral water, and watched a pigeon squatting on the windowsill of an open window. I watched it do its business until I needed a refill. Harel flashed a smile my way, slit a fig, and quietly stepped toward the window near the pigeon. The three at the head of the table stopped whispering to each other and stared at Harel, as if his movements were an incredible imposition.

Funny, they bring us in, all this way from the north, and then hardly have the courtesy to say hello. Marcus and Ari are aloof and full of themselves. Marcus is old, so with him it is a seniority issue. Ari's not always that reserved. He is overly personable one minute, incredibly volatile a moment later. Marcus and Ari—the quintessential European and Arab Jews, both native Israelis.

Ari's paternal grandparents are from Iraq. His mother's family is from Germany. It is from the former that he gets his Yeshiva-boy good looks—the dark and deep features

25

that make him appear wise, yet a little sensitive. At the same time, he likes to wear tight T-shirts to show off his well-developed biceps, for which he cares for as if they were two precious carrier pigeons. The body and head do not match. Ari is smart and he found a nice wife—a wildlife biologist—with whom he has five girls and a boy. Ari is pretty much second in command. Harel and I think he will take over as soon as Marcus decides to retire. I mean the old man is over seventy.

Harel closed in on the bird. He put the fig down softly, a few inches away from the creature and stepped back. His eyes were locked on the bird's red eyes. The pigeon finally nabbed the fruit, gave a thankful nod, and left the scene. Harel, who thinks he can communicate at "higher" levels with animals, smiled at me victoriously. I smiled back, knowing I had made the bird come in the first place.

"Okay, Tweedledee and Tweedledum, let's begin," Ari said, as he motioned to us, than patted the table like a stressed out broker. He leaned over and grabbed a few nuts out of Harel's hand, threw them in his mouth and asked, "So, how well do you know Rachel Levy?"

"Barely," I said after a moments pause.

Ari chewed and looked back and forth from me to Harel, nodding. Matthew and Marcus stared at the table. I winked at Matthew and said, "What did she do? Get a traffic ticket?"

"No," Matthew looked up at me ruefully. "She died two days ago."

"Well, Matthew, come on now," Ari cocked his head at Matthew for an instant, then turned to us with a stern look. "She was *killed*."

"She was murdered," Marcus sighed, and got up from the table.

Rachel was somewhat of a predecessor to me, because she had also been assigned to Germany and the West Coast in the States. Before her contract expired, we had on occasion trained together, ran some laps, and sparred a bit, that sort of thing. There was, of course, some unspoken camaraderie between us, since female operatives are still fairly rare in the Department.

"How?" Harel asked.

"She was run over by a truck in the States and died in the emergency room. Now you know pretty much everything we know." Ari glared and dropped his pen on the table.

"What, that is it?" Harel asked.

Marcus was standing at the window with his back to us, deep in his own world.

"We will know more when her body arrives. The plane from New York lands at midnight," Matthew said quietly. He leaned his tall, thin body back.

• The pigeon we had fed earlier suddenly landed on the windowsill near Marcus and cooed quietly. We all stared at Marcus as he watched it, in silence.

"So, are we sure it wasn't an accident?" I asked. I had the feeling Harel and I were going to be asked to play detective, so we might as well start asking the pertinent questions.

Marcus answered from his place by the window. "We know only a few details, but the American police told the embassy that she was alive when she arrived in the emergency room." He turned to face me and continued, "Even without the injuries from the truck accident, she had enough cocaine in her system to kill a small horse."

Nobody said a word, allowing that fact to sink in. Not many people do what we do, and when one of us is killed, death reminds us that the other world—the one I wander in sometimes—is just an illusion. The kibbutz, my parents, my sister, and the dogs become apparitions at moments like these.

Here's something loony. I barely knew the facts as I sat in that room, but I felt that this killing was on a different plane than the ones we usually encounter. I don't claim to predict the future, but I swear I can feel things other people can't. Call them premonitions if you will, but something was telling me Rachel's death was going to put me through a trying time.

Harel gave me a soft look and touched me lightly on the shoulder. I rarely feel vulnerable, but in those moments when I do, I am grateful that he is around. He is a tower of strength and reassurance. It sounds poetic but it is true. Maybe we did not lie to my sister after all.

The fact that Rachel had overdosed meant it was not an accident. Marcus and Ari are meticulous in selecting our people. I realize that we live in a society where most people below a certain age have experimented with drugs, at least on occasion. At least this is true in Germany and the United States. I can't recall even one student party in which I was not offered something to get me high.

But, being part of this organization means saying goodbye to all that, even to alcohol. This is true also when our service is over and we go back to civilian life. We carry too much sensitive information to risk loss of composure and control.

"Where did she die?" I was clinging to a straw of hope. Who knows, maybe the hospital was wrong. It happens a lot. A pathologist who works for the Department here once told us that more than thirty percent of deaths attributed to natural causes in American hospitals are falsely diagnosed.

Ari looked at some papers in front of him, squinting as if he were extremely near-sighted. I guess he had been briefed only shortly before.

"In Mizz-oo-lah," he said, and looked up with great disgust. "She was killed in a place called Mizz-oo-lah, and don't ask me if it is a town, a village, or what."

"Where the hell is it?"

"Missoula, Montana," Matthew broke in and smiled, while Ari started reading something in his notes. "It's in the Wild, Wild West, Yael."

"Like Marlboro Country?" I laughed.

"Over there, dear, over there, where men are still men and chew real tobacco." Matthew smiled.

"What was she doing there?" I questioned.

Harel looked at me with a dreamy grin and said, "Oh my god, touring the Rocky Mountains, running with moose, washing clothes in a hot spring. What else?" He sounded jealous.

"The militias live there, too. They are no friends of the children of Abraham," Marcus informed us. He always gets nervous when Israelis decide to live outside Israel.

"You can be one-hundred percent Gentile like me and they will shoot you anyway if you're from California or New York." Mathew is always happy to add something reassuring.

"Okay everyone shut up." Ari snatched up the papers and slapped them into a neat stack. "Rachel was there, wherever it is, and took classes at the local university."

"Studying what, the art of rodeo?" I made Harel grin.

This comment strained Ari, who always tries to be earnest and stoic around Marcus. He stared at Marcus and said, "From what we know so far, which is very little, it is a somewhat bizarre scenario."

"She was working towards a Master's degree in economics," Marcus' baritone broke in over our heads. He walked to his leather chair and seated himself. Even as an old man, he is graceful, like a cat. He lightly touched the purple vein on the side of his jaw, then dropped his hand and said, "I would like to stick to what we know. Rachel was a highly intelligent woman, verbal, straightforward, mentally stable, and—above all—very inquisitive. Maybe too inquisitive at times. As for her relationship to us, she has not worked in the Department for almost two years. Sometimes she would come and train with us when she was in Israel visiting her parents. So unless we are dealing with revenge of some sort, I must posit that her death might not be related to the Department."

He gave us one of his hard looks, although we were already silent and continued, "We will meet here Monday, after the funeral. By then, we will have something more concrete to talk about." He then turned to Ari and Matthew and stated, "I want to meet both of you tonight for a short preliminary report. But first, we are all going to do some work in the library."

7

The 'library' is three floors under the Department of Defense, which is only a thirty-minute drive from our headquarters. Harel and I took a separate car because Ari, Matthew, and Marcus wanted "to discuss things," a tiring act, since they would later tell us everything anyway. Harel took the wheel and followed Ari's speeding Toyota, and we made our way through the suburbs of Tel Aviv. It was a balmy summer afternoon, although spring had just begun. Israelis were watering their gardens, smoking cigarettes on their patios, and watching their kids play in the swimming pools. In poorer suburbs, they were hanging out on balconies talking, or sitting on the steps of their apartment buildings, following our Subaru with their eyes. Depending on the block, the air smelled of Arab food, cantaloupe, gasoline, or rancid dairy. After a few minutes, Harel got sick of keeping up with Ari's ridiculous pace, and slowed down. He glanced at me and smiled. We melted into the thicker traffic of Tel Aviv proper, and the Israelis we passed suddenly became too busy to notice us. Businessmen strode to work, and shopkeepers fiddled with mannequins in storefront windows, while taxis honked at whatever threatened to slow their passage. Driving through Tel Aviv is a trip through time. The ancient sector of Jaffa, a suburb, dates to pre-Roman times. In dramatic contrast is the sterile façade of Migdal Shalom, one of the very few skyscraper in the city and a testimonial to how unimaginative modern architecture can be.

"Stop," I yelled. Harel laughed and neatly swerved to the curb and parked the car in front of *Teomim's* (the twins)—our favorite falafel and ice cream kiosk. We opened the store door and a gust of cold air hit us in the face. Harel nodded at an old man sitting at a table in a yellow short-sleeved shirt, and the man nodded back and stared at me. I ignored him. Sometimes I get looks from men because I am in shape, or look comfortable, and I often resent their audacity—but not when they are old, like this guy. We ordered two falafels from the young owner behind the counter, and even though we had been in there a million times, he didn't greet us. Typical manners for a city boy.

"Mmmmm," Harel said, and scooped extra red pickled cabbage onto his sandwich.

"Mmmmm," I answered, and we carried the falafel outside and ate, leaning against a wall and watching the action from the street. "Come on," Harel nagged me. He started walking to the car. I ran up to him, gave him my last two bites, and we drove off quickly in the direction of the Kiria district.

The Department of Defense is located in a large building from the fifties. The outside is beige, with small windows that reflect on those viewing it. It's like being scrutinized by hundreds of secret agents, all wearing those annoying mirrored sunglasses. We pulled up to a high gate, where a cute Moroccan-looking soldier studied our blue Mossad ID. "Shalom," he said to me, and I smiled back. "Shalom," Harel mimicked him, as we pulled away toward the parking lot.

"You know, Harel, I always forget how gorgeous I am until I come to the city, because farmers like you have no eye for beauty like mine," I chided.

"Farmers like me," Harel said, "know that under all that tanned skin is a prickly wildcat they want nothing to do with." He parked the car.

We hurried through the corridors and three floors down to the archive. People in the hallway were earnest looking, most were in khakis and white shirts, except for a few female officers in uniform. Matthew was waiting at the desk.

"God, you two reek of garlic. Come on, or Ari will throw a tantrum." We flashed our ID's again, this time to a young woman behind glass, than followed Matthew through the heavy door that slid open for us.

"Ah, books. Yael, books are things with white pages and many, many little black letters. Maybe I could show you how to use one someday." Harel joked looking over his shoulder at me and ran his fingers along a row of bound journals. He is so full of himself.

Shelves ran in endless lines to our right and left, marked with obscure symbols best understood by library scientists. In the back, humming computers promised more information. This library would be any journalist's Disneyland. Monica Lewinsky was on file here before Hillary had a clue. Harel, Ari, Matthew, and I are among the very few in the country who have full access to this information, thanks in part to Marcus and to Harel's and my reputation for being the smart kids in the Department. We have learned to use the filing system, even though the staff is instructed to assist us, no questions asked.

When we first got complete clearance, Harel and I ran to our own files. We could not find anything super interesting, except a pair of identical remarks in both our files. According to someone, we were "slightly arrogant" and "sometimes childish." They had to say something negative. I think they have some prejudice against kibbutzniks.

We turned the corner and suddenly we were staring Ari in the face. "Did you at least bring me ice cream?" he asked, mocking us for our known propensity for health food. With crooked fingers, he motioned us to follow him. Matthew drew back, and we began following him through the labyrinth. "I've arranged for both of you to meet Rachel's ex-partner," Ari told us. "Six sharp this evening, in front of the new Hilton. Call when you're done."

He stopped, turned, and peered behind us. "Matthew, I'd like either you and me or Yael and Harel to be at the autopsy tomorrow morning."

"Yeah, definitely, although I'm not sure what her family knows, so getting permission to mess with the body could be difficult. Better tell the pathologist to perform the procedure with minimal damage."

We turned a corner and saw Marcus perusing a volume of something. For him, spending time in the library is recreation. Harel marched past Ari and tapped Marcus on his hunched shoulder. "Marcus, you said before that Rachel was almost too inquisitive, why?"

"Very attentive, son, very attentive," Marcus said as he smiled. He carefully laid the book on the shelf. "Any time you have someone experienced in international espionage, crime or intelligence, and this person has free time on her hands, things can get sticky. We have to realize that any one of us, once outside of the service, could easily make ourselves inconspicuous to others in the civilian world. We thus sometimes come to learn things that make us assets to people in all kinds of business. But we also possess knowledge that can make us liabilities to those same people. Keep this in mind. I want nothing and no one underestimated." And with that, he left us.

8

Only in books and movies do spies meet in restaurants or crowded, bustling streets. Of course, sometimes there is no alternative, but we much prefer parks, zoos, and river trails, where a bit of seclusion is possible. In Israel, we don't have any rivers worth talking about, other than the Jordan in the east. Forget about the Yarcon, the biggest river in the country. That is not water moving through there. Last year, a man fell in and died, but not from drowning. He made it to shore all right, but passed away a couple days later in the hospital from the effects of contamination. The Yarcon is the most heavily polluted, disgusting river in the Middle East. After the Nile, that is.

Sometimes I can't comprehend why the Arabs buy billions of dollars worth of weapons to kill off the few Jews that got away from the Germans. If I were an Arab, I'd make an immediate peace with the Jews. Then, while relaxing in the shade of my oil fields, or racing camels, or driving around in my Rolls, I would sit back and watch the Chosen People die from pollution. Or allow them to kill each other in their domestic religious wars. The religious minority likes to give us—the secular majority—hell. As if our Arab neighbors were not enough.

We met Rachel's ex-partner, Jakob, on the beach, in front of the new Hilton. The three of us took off our shoes and walked on the still warm sand, chatting over the sound of breaking waves. I pointed out to Harel the kind of sailboat I wanted, a blue and green one. It rocked among a brightly colored batch of boats dancing in deeper water.

Jakob told us his father was a rabbi and to the old man, Tel Aviv was Sodom and Gomorrah—so secular and free. Jakob had studied aeronautics at the Institute of Technology in Haifa, so to warm him up I asked him what he thought of one of the future planes of the American military. It's called the J.S.F., Joint Strategic Fighter. I've mentioned before that the West Coast was my area of responsibility in the States, Boeing, located in Seattle, was one of the companies lobbying for the contract to build the J.S.F. Its main competitor, Lockheed Martin, was developing its version in California. This meant a heated race for a $400 billion contract. Obviously, secrecy was at a premium.

"Well, let's face it," Jakob said. "Lockheed's version is technically far superior. It has stealth technology but it costs more. It would boil down to the best engineering, if anyone really cared about the actual lives involved. As it is, cost effectiveness will likely rein supreme."

"Well, let's give the Americans the benefit of the doubt. After Vietnam they are more sensitive to matters involving their soldier's lives," I said.

"They lost three hundred Marines in Beirut and around thirty civilians in Saudi Arabia, and although they know quite accurately who is responsible, I can't recall that they've done anything about it," Harel reminded me.

"Arab oil goes a long way," Jakob said. "The oil lobby is powerful, and I remember Marcus telling us that many retired American leaders of both parties, including American presidents, get high income jobs from Arab institutions."

So there we were, three young Israelis, sitting on the sandy Mediterranean shore, discussing the fate of an American jet fighter of which most Americans have never heard.

We couldn't put off what was really on our minds much longer. I broached it.

"After you and Rachel left the Department, how much contact did you still have?"

"Well, it depends on when you mean." He dug a hole in the sand with his foot.

"We had a lot of contact at first. She finished her degree in economics in Jerusalem—with honors I might add. She used to call me quite often. After she went to graduate school in Tel Aviv, I didn't hear from her much, but then she called and told me she had decided to take a semester at the Free University in Berlin. The University of Montana idea came later." Jakob added.

"Berlin I can see," Harel said. "But Montana? Graduating from Jerusalem with honors opens many doors, including Harvard. Why Montana, of all places?"

"I asked her the same question."

"And . . ." I became agitated. People in technical fields talk so slowly, pausing with every word, as if constructing a bridge, piece by piece.

"She said . . . she said that in a place like Montana you can do things that are impossible around Wall Street."

"What does that mean?"

"I can't tell you, because I didn't really ask. She was fixated with her research on *holding companies*. She kept telling me how she and her German classmate were on to something big."

"What are holding companies?" I asked.

"You got me. I can't give you a precise definition."

I grabbed the cellular phone and called Ari. Matthew answered.

"Is there anything in the library about a paper Rachel wrote in Germany?" I asked without any introduction.

"No, but she called from Germany around seven months ago and asked for a background check on a classmate."

"What was the person's name?"

"One minute." I could hear papers rustling in the background. "Barbara Skibbe. Typical European student: leftist, anti-Israeli, anti-American, middle class, harmless."

After thirty, Europeans seem to become more realistic. Some of them, that is. I turned to Jakob and repeated the name Matthew gave me.

"Exactly, that's the one."

Harel took my cellular, and asked Matthew, "Did she ever explain why she wanted the background check?"

He listened, and then popped the phone shut.

"They didn't pursue it further."

"It's beginning to come back a bit," Jakob said. "I remember that with everything she told me, the research paper in Germany seemed pretty unimportant. She was talking so much about investments and Wall Street that I asked her if she had inherited some money."

"Had she?" Harel asked.

"She said no. The subject just fascinated her, and she always liked to get into new projects. She was a woman of very diverse interests."

You mean she was inquisitive?" Harel asked.

"Yes, that is a good way of looking at it. She was a great partner, very professional, but she always had difficulty getting to the job itself."

"In what way," I asked.

"She would get into the theoretical or psychological implications of the mission and forget sometimes that we were, in fact, on a mission. She tended to ignore risks in favor of analysis. It sometimes put us in unnecessary jeopardy."

"Why didn't you report her?" Harel asked.

"Would you report your partner?" Jakob smiled sadly. "I had some problems, too, that she let slide and helped me to correct. I am assuming you both know how that works."

I was not sure we did, although we tried to sympathize. I'm sure Harel also considered for a moment the possible liability these two agents had posed.

"Are you coming to the funeral on Monday?' I broke an uncomfortable silence.

"Of course, I am very close to her family."

"One other thing, do you think it would be like her to experiment with drugs?"

"Out of the question," he fired back, as expected. "Don't read too much into what I have said before. She was a bit too theoretical at times, but she was very responsible and extremely accountable."

It was clear the meeting had not helped us much. Not unless the research paper and all this "investment" stuff had some relevance.

"So you guys are on this one?" Jakob stood up, tired.

"We don't know anything yet," Harel said.

"You two will be going. We all know Marcus." He gave us each a short glance. "When you get there, wherever it is, shoot the scum that did this. Do it for me. I wish I could go and do it myself." He said it very fast.

After that TV police comment, we all wanted the conversation to end.

The sunset painted everything in red. I couldn't tell where the water ended and the sky began. The lights of the ancient port of Jaffa were already beginning to twinkle in the south.

9

We were sitting in a local fish restaurant debating what movie to go to when Ari called. I told him about the discussion we had with Jakob, and he didn't sound surprised.

"We'll meet tomorrow or after the funeral on Monday. Tomorrow is a full-time training day for the both of you, beginning at seven. Matthew and I might join you part of the time. Any questions?"

"No, see you in the morning." I turned the phone off.

"Training at sunrise, eh?" Harel guessed.

We both knew what this meant. A mission was underway. When and where I couldn't say, but it was coming. I hoped the movie tonight would be light, fun, and have a happy ending. I once read that many movies have two endings. One is a happy version for American viewers, the other, a sad one for the rest of the world. Thank God that Israel likes the American way and imports the happy versions.

This is something that drives Eric, my little American intellectual, mad. He can't watch a movie with a happy ending and says I'm wasting my brain cells watching romantic crap. So whether or not his taste is good, if we watch one of "his" movies, I won't admit to liking it.

I don't want him in my thoughts right now. Happy thoughts before a mission are what I need. Simple movie, happy thoughts, pleasant dreams.

10

It is training day, but we do not mind. Harel and I both see it the same way—a good opportunity to show off while pretending it is a burden. We even groan about the numbskull rigor. I like these training days and the instructors are always good measuring sticks.

Training days have several objectives. The obvious one is to keep us in shape, making sure that we maintain our dexterity and speed. There's extensive proficiency training in various weapons. For us, the goal is not body building or developing stamina. These are a given. The goal is to respond as instinctively as the blink of an eye.

Ari and Matthew were there, too. They were supposed to monitor the autopsy, but I don't blame them for getting out of it. Autopsies are interesting if you don't know the person being cut open. The four of us training together meant we were all going abroad. Oddly enough, these training sessions relax me, despite their intensity. There is nothing like a feeling of total regeneration at the end of the day. I figure it's not a bad idea to be relaxed before you go and meet the unknown.

Two other guys were there, whom I didn't recognize. They were either very new or had received permission from the Mossad to train with us.

We began as always with a one-mile warm-up jog. The next two miles culminated in a sprint. No one can keep up with Matthew and his long legs. A five—minute break for water, then forty-five minutes of self-defense.

Harel and I have black belts in karate. Many thanks to our kibbutz, especially to Harel's father, since he hired a full-time karate teacher when we were still kids. They continue this training to this day, so for the children it's just a natural part of the school program. We've often said our grandparents should have called the place Sparta.

The brutality of the real world is a far cry from the realm in which the noble rules of karate apply. Unless you have the natural strength and toughness of Harel, you had better listen to the instructors. Many people skilled in martial arts could not use them in a practical, dirty street-fight. This transition from mat to street is what our instructors specialize in.

Harel is in another league. Even the instructors don't dare to demonstrate all their fancy techniques on him. As a matter of fact, they use him as a warning for us when they say, "Learn to avoid fighting unless there is no other way." Despite our education in self-defense, we need to know that there are other, unfriendly, Harels in the world.

When we were still in high school, a bunch of us kibbutzniks once drove to a movie in Nazareth. As always, without a driver's license, but the cops never caught us. We used to "borrow" a car from our kibbutz' greenhouse manager. She was old, and I think the Germans experimented on her in Auschwitz. Whatever the reason, she never noticed.

When we arrived at the theater, three soldiers pushed their way in front of us in line. Not only were they the muscular type, but they also proudly wore the famous red hats of the paratrooper elite, and obviously figured that soldiers don't have to wait in line. My sister, that no-nonsense broad, after having her shoulder bumped, told one of them that they could wait like the rest of the people.

So the three of us—Harel, myself, and another kibbutz boy—froze and cursed Naomi while waiting to see what would happen. The soldiers looked us over and grinned, assessing the situation and wrongly estimating the local balance of power. Then they focused their gaze on my feisty sister. One of them said something vile and touched her hair. Harel stepped forward and asked if they could help out a simple farm boy by apologizing to his girlfriend. They, of course, found this request humorous.

The rule, especially on our kibbutz, is never turn the other cheek more than once. The lop-sided fight that ensued was the start of the legend of Harel. Harel, the brute, broke one soldier's arm and nearly turned another into a eunuch with a precise kick. It all took less than ten seconds. The third soldier was spared so he could drive his friends to the hospital.

Delegates from the army came to our kibbutz the next day and we argued self-defense. We pointed out that it wouldn't have made sense for farm children to pick fights with soldiers. In the idyllic setting of our little commune, the conversation and accusations seemed ludicrous. Harel stood there with a bucket of goat feed and his little cousin Hannah on his arm. The army officials let it drop.

After self-defense practice, we normally get another five-minute water break before target shooting—my favorite. Hundreds of bullets are spent each session, on moving and static targets. Our session consisted of shooting while standing, as well as shooting on the run. All positions, different firearms, some with sights, some without.

Shooting is my domain, especially with semi-automatic hand guns. Beyond a certain point, it's just a question of natural talent. Harel is a slow but precise shot, good for seconding or back-up; he never panics and has extremely fine focus. Ari is only a fair shot or rather an inconsistent one, since his hits are either insanely perfect or completely chaotic. Ari's forte is his ability to react with extreme speed and intelligence, as when facing unexpected movement or having to distinguish so-called layers of targets—the good guys from the bad guys, the worse guys from the useful-if-alive guys, and all these from the guys hidden in the dark behind you. Matthew is definitely the closest to me in terms of talent and eye, with good speed and some useful tricks.

At the age of twelve, I was faster and more accurate than many of our training officers. At thirteen, I could put six bullets in six cans, forty feet away in less than three seconds. It's on my report, should you think I'm lying. No aiming, all instinct. As a matter of fact, already as a child I would bet the officers money that I could do it. I made a good amount of extra allowance until the kibbutz adults found out and forbade me to take money.

When we're finished with that aspect of the training, we move to the more cerebral side. Computers, communication, language acquisition, with emphasis on idioms, slang, and accent. In German, I'm close to total fluency. Harel and I learned German from our grandparents when we were young. My written English is top-notch, with the help of a thesaurus, but my accent needs some work. Harel speaks like a native. He spent a year in the States as a teen, at relatives in Connecticut.

My French sucks. I don't think I'll ever make it past the imperfect tense and Harel refuses to learn a word. So no missions to Paris for us, damn it. Then again, I am not crazy about the French. The Germans at least say they are sorry for killing the Jews; the French don't even say that. They sometimes reluctantly put the murderers on trial and always side with the Arabs against us. At least their government takes that position. Strangely enough, the French I've met hate anything even resembling an Arab. Matthew says their government hates Arabs too, but they need the oil.

Right in the middle of our training, Ari's phone rang. He listened, stood up and walked away. When he came back twenty minutes later, he didn't bother sitting down. He looked at the two Mossad boys.

"Sorry boys, we've enjoyed training with you, but the four of us need to go." We all shook hands, and Harel and I watched the two young men leave. I was sure they benefited from training with us. I know that it used to help us—way back when—to train with the pros.

We sat on the warm ground in the shade of a big eucalyptus tree, and Ari filled us in on the information he has just received. He told us that Rachel had a syringe full of cocaine or some related compound shoved directly into her neck. That was straight out of the pathology report. Marcus was right. She was murdered.

"We still can't be sure it wasn't just a domestic crime, can we?" I asked him.

"Your average crook wouldn't bother with the time or the expense, Yael," Matthew lectured. He has a tendency to pull that stunt with me. Perhaps it is because I'm a woman, or perhaps because I always nail him to the wall during religious arguments.

"And regardless," Ari began diplomatically, "would there be less motivation to solve the case if it were only a domestic case?"

"No," I admitted.

"How were they able to establish the cause of death?" Harel interjected, practical as ever. "You can't find a needle hole in the carotid artery—not on a seven-day-old corpse."

"Yeah," I said, knowing right where I was going. "After death, arteries collapse".

"Thanks, Doctor," Harel sighed.

♦ "It just might not have been clear to Matthew." I smiled to Matthew, whom I always tease for being a smaller-brained gentile.

"Yes," Harel said, "I always make the same mistake, giving too much credit to the people around me. Do I always have to state the obvious?" He looked at me. 'Besides, it's the veins that collapse after death, not the arteries.'

Ari, dismayed, looked at Matthew, who was grinning. "What am I supposed to do with these villagers?" Then he continued.

"If anyone has questions about the death, you can read the report yourself, then meet with the pathologist. Until then, you are to assume the conclusions are accurate. Clear?" We didn't answer, so he went on.

"Tomorrow, after the funeral, the four of us are meeting with Marcus. The doctor will be there and will be open for questions. Anything more?"

I was still bristling because of the villager comment—and was even more annoyed with Harel, who always patronizes us.

"Don't be so touchy, Ari. We all know Harel has a need to show off."

"But am I wrong?" Harel was smiling too, exactly like Matthew. "You want to argue, but you have nothing intelligent to say."

"How about this: They can dissect the artery and look through a microscope. The hole will appear bright and clear."

"No they can't, if she was alive when the shot was administered. Even if she died soon after the artery was punctured, the internal cells of the artery wall would have enough time to plug the hole. I thought you passed biology."

He meant business and didn't let go.

"Haven't you heard about the body's self-repair process? Are you aware that some cellular processes continue even after death?" Harel smiled like a Roman conqueror.

"Na, klar, Herr Doktor," I spit. "What I don't get is what my sister sees in you. That sounds like a self-despair process."

"Okay, okay," Ari put his arms around both of us and laughed. "Before you strangle each other, I want you to go to that damn kibbutz of yours and say goodbye to your sweethearts. Unless something new pops up in the next twenty-four hours, we're going to make a house call to Deutschland to meet this Barbara Skibbe.

"A helicopter will take you home and pick you up in the morning. Then straight to the funeral and, please, Harel and Yael, wear something appropriate."

We allowed that comment to slide, even though Ari knows I'm a bit self-conscious over this style issue. I was raised on a farm, and fashion magazines disgust me. I could change my appearance if I wanted to. It just doesn't interest me.

11

I love flying home and relaxing with my own thoughts, or trying to. Harel was next to me, holding a radio to his ear, listening to the news of a bloodbath in the streets of Jerusalem. Three Jews were killed, which is an example of why we try to avoid going there. There is always tension in the air. Jews and Arabs there make no pretenses about how much they hate each other. At least we try to coexist in our area. The first village in our valley is Arab. They are friendly. Still today, we play soccer together.

The helicopter glided gently over the Gilboa mountains, and I gazed down upon the rough yellow valleys and dry desert ridges. Naomi and Eric were already on the landing field, waiting for us with the dogs. Naomi wore a big maternity dress the color of blue flax, and Eric knelt beside her, grinning up at us while shading his eyes from the sun. We scrambled out, and the four of us hugged. The Ridgebacks wiggled their whole backs with joy and ran around nervously because of the roar from the helicopter. Harel and I got our knapsacks from the helicopter, and we walked home, past the fields of fig trees, where we waved to some kibbutz teens who shouted their greetings.

At home, I went into the kitchen with Eric and watched him prepare a dinner of filet of sole, some fresh purple potatoes from the garden, and a big salad with roasted red pepper, arugula, and avocado. "Come on, Eric, talk Hebrew with me," I teased him and he smiled bashfully. "Come on, tell me what you did this morning," I asked taking the knife from his hand and finished slivering some garlic. He began rambling in Hebrew, at first haltingly and then with such sudden fluency that I nearly cut my fingers off in surprise.

We had dinner with the parents—my dad, the math teacher; my mom, the veterinarian; Harel's mom, the former Russian ballerina and our kibbutz dance instructor, and of course, Harel's dad, our honorable kibbutz leader. My aunt stopped by with fresh halva, chuckled about some recent kibbutz gossip, and muttered about recent financial worries in the kibbutz. Harel reminded everyone that he and I had been gone only two days and, that well, thank God, not much had changed.

Harel, Naomi, Eric, and I took their two little children to the community garden and subjected ourselves to the pioneer parables of Harel's grandfather. His world was pre-Holocaust Russia and Poland, the ghettos, the monthly pogroms. As his grandfather tells it, on every holy day, especially on Christmas, Russians, Poles, or Ukrainians, in

40

their post-church drunken excitement, would rape Jewish women and slaughter their frail husbands. Harel bent over to put his hands over the ears of his children, Barak and Tamar.

I love this old man and I dream of being in that world, the same person I am right now, fully strapped in weaponry. I envision a massacre of those who dare approach me.

We walked back to our neighboring bungalows, Naomi carrying the sleeping Barak, and me holding Tamar's hand while she sang us a nursery song she had learned.

I'm thinking about sitting by a campfire tonight, preferably one built by Eric. I'd like to roast some onions, maybe speak a little Hebrew with him. I know he has been trying to finish a poem in Hebrew.

I figure there is nothing better than being with him, and maybe with Harel and Naomi and the dogs for an evening. It's funny, when Harel and Eric are around Naomi and me, they act like little boys, even babies. I am lucky to have those three around me

12

The entrance to the cemetery was crowded with people: Rachel's high school and army friends, cousins, and older family members. We didn't expect so many people to come. I spied Jakob talking with a pallid-faced couple in their sixties—her parents. Although they wore polite, slight smiles, their eyes were vacant, and they looked weary and confused. I noticed a lot of agents from the Mossad making sure no cameras were brought in. Marcus was there, too, with Ari, Matthew, and some other dignitaries from Mossad.

Except for the parents, the people carried themselves with their usual confidence and calmness, but I knew the group was stunned. Everyone wore black coats, and I suddenly felt stupid wearing only jeans and black T-shirts. If Rachel is watching us from up there, then I'm sure she knows we didn't mean any disrespect.

Matthew came to us. "Nice suits, you two," he said quietly. "The parents have been informed."

"What was he doing telling the parents?" I hissed.

He gave us a short hug and gracefully weaved his way back to the front of the crowd. I looked at Ari and Marcus, wondering what was up. The official policy is always to try to inform the family, but only as long as it doesn't risk the lives of agents involved in a mission in progress.

The body was brought out on a stretcher carried by four uniformed officers. Everyone moved closer to the grave, a bit mechanically, as they lowered Rachel into the open pit. Jewish burials are not as sterile as Christian ones. There is no coffin, and the body is covered only with a simple cotton blanket. Jewish funerals are more earthy and eerie at the same time.

Her brother, a red-haired teenager looking slightly white around the nose, his father, and Jakob said Kaddish while Ari and Matthew held the crying mother. Usually, only members of the family say this prayer. The fact that Jakob was allowed to join them told me how close he had been to their daughter. The rabbi talked a long time about her life and sudden death, but didn't mention her work for Mossad. There was no mention of foul play. Maybe Marcus hadn't lost his mind after all. We queued up to throw stones into the open grave. Don't ask what this tradition means. I haven't the slightest idea. I braced myself as Harel and I approached the parents.

Ari slid up to us. "Allow the others to go first. Be the last to say goodbye."

"Why did you tell them?" Harel asked Ari directly.

"Not now," Ari groaned. Harel's lower lip changed color, a sign of anger. Ari studied Harel's lip. Nobody shrugs off Harel.

"Okay. We needed the parents to do something for us. They would not do it if we didn't tell them what happened." He shot a glance at my face. "Please just bear with us. I know it isn't standard procedure."

Not many people were left, and soon the family would be alone. I found the mother focusing on me. She muttered something to Marcus, whose silk shirt was moving slightly in the breeze. He nodded and said something in reply. The mother took her husband's arm and approached me.

"Are you Yael?" She was small and thin. Rachel resembled her, only she had been a bit taller.

"Yes ma'am." I said as I removed my sunglasses.

"Mr. Marcus told me about you. I didn't realize you were so young."

I didn't know what to say, especially to that. Perhaps: "Yes, you are right. Tell Marcus to send me home." Or, "I'm young and innocent, but I can shoot an orange thirty feet away without aiming while lying on my back."

"And I was told you volunteered to go after my daughter's killers." She broke the silence with quiet words.

I could not say yes to that either. I'm not the volunteering type. Especially not for a situation that might end up killing me. I don't want my parents, Eric, and my friends staring at my open grave. Didn't her daughter know that she wasn't supposed to leave the country within the first three years after ending the service?

She began to sob, than embraced me. She recovered her voice.

"Mr. Marcus told me that you are the only other woman who does the work my daughter did. I want justice for Rachel, but I don't want anybody to die for it. I told Mr. Marcus not to put anybody at risk."

"I hope he listened to you," I was thinking. I still said nothing.

I noticed that several Mossad agents stood behind her, flanking us, making sure no one was privy to our conversation.

Rachel's mother looked up at me with wet eyes. She took my hand.

"I was hidden by a gentile Dutch farmer in the forties, who then adopted me. I was just a baby then. I never saw my parents or sisters because they were all murdered, and I thought when I came here that nothing would happen to my family again."

I didn't know how to handle her, so I just nodded politely. She began to sob again, then stopped.

"It's not that I don't want justice for my daughter, but please, go only if you think it may save other lives in the future. There is so much evil out there. Most Germans, Poles, and French who murdered or collaborated with the murderers of my family died peacefully in their beds. Nobody ever cared then and nobody cares now."

I thought she was a bit overwrought. There was definitely no evidence that Rachel's death had anything to do with anti-Semitism, but she had to blame something, so be it.

Magically, Harel appeared and took the woman in his arms.

"Let me be honest with you. We still don't know exactly what happened. We do know, however, what Rachel did for all of us when she was alive. She worked to ensure that the evils of the past would never fall on us again."

Good, I thought, "You found your tongue."

"It's not only about the murders," he continued. "It's exactly what you said: the fact that the slayers never were forced to pay any consequences. We can't let this happen again. We won't let the word forgiveness be cheapened."

I felt proud of him after those lines, especially the ending. Really, I did. It's not like him.

"We will go," he said, "because if we don't, nobody will."

Harel looked at me, smiling so slightly that only I could detect it. I'm not sure what he meant by that look. This eternal Jewish destiny thing gets to us both. Sometimes I wish I had not been born Jewish. Sometimes the burden is just too much. I mean, if we were just nice sweet gentiles from Seattle or Frankfurt, we wouldn't be standing here.

Then and there, the fate of Rachel's killers was sealed. I wanted to tell the mother, though I couldn't, that the killers would not be facing an inquisitive city girl next time around. They would have to deal with Harel and me. We, who never took being alive for granted, not even as children. Let's see how they deal with us, let's see how good they really are.

I gave the mother a very long hug, nudged Harel with my elbow. And we made our exit.

13

The cemetery is only a half-hour from our headquarters, but Harel and I decided to stop at the sea shore. With eyes closed, I felt the breeze gently touch my face and was calmed by the sound of the waves breaking on shore. A flock of seagulls were chasing each other, preying at intervals on the crabs that crowded the sandy shore. The hunted wandered between ridges of sand, naïve and unprotected, oblivious to the danger above. A phone call from Ari ended the interlude.

"Everyone is waiting for you!"

We told him we were stuck in a traffic jam. We needed time to cool off. Involving Rachel's family had compromised our safety and he'd better have a thorough explanation for it or we'd call it off. We don't mind taking risks if they are necessary, but involving civilians, especially when they are going through agony and grief, runs contrary to common sense.

14

They were already waiting for us as we strolled into the big room. We were at least an hour late. The group was assembled at the table—Marcus, Ari, Matthew, Rafi—our technical wiz, some staff, and a few distinguished-looking strangers—all had the unhappy look of people unaccustomed to be kept waiting. These are the guys who grill us when we come back from missions. Even Dr. Kleinkopf, the pathologist, was there.

Without overture, Marcus began the meeting, but not before flashing us an annoyed look. None of them were looking exactly cordial. We didn't really care. Let them go deal with the hairy-chested cavemen in Montana.

"A murder was committed, yet no one claimed responsibility," Marcus abruptly began his speech. "And somebody tried to cover up the murder with a car accident. Doesn't sound like personal revenge to me. I think you'll all agree."

No objections were offered.

"So we're left with several possibilities. It may be a civil case, which by itself raises several questions. Or maybe she was silenced because she discovered something of value to us. But there are infinite possible scenarios, and what I'm really saying is that we are in near total darkness."

"I don't agree," Harel interrupted. "I don't agree that we have no clues."

I smiled over at Harel as if I knew where he was going. Marcus faced him with quiet satisfaction.

"Good. Go ahead, Harel. Tell us what's on your mind."

"I still would like to know first what killed her and how," Harel nodded in the pathologist's direction. "From what we've heard so far, it seems that the murder was carried out with a high degree of sophistication. That alone has to partially identify the killers."

"It rules out some scenarios for sure," I added. "It is not a simple criminal case, because only professionals would kill that way." I looked at Marcus. I was upstaging him a bit, but he let it pass. He needed us and we knew it. *We are required to go only on missions that are clearly in the interest of national security.* This one certainly didn't qualify, and no intellectual mind games would change that. We knew it, Marcus knew it. He knew that we knew he knew it.

"Harel and Yael are right," Marcus said. "And had they listened carefully, they would have noticed that their boss said 'near total darkness'. Even the mob doesn't kill with such a high degree of *savoir-faire*. So we're in a position to make some intelligent assumptions."

Marcus always uses French or Latin to make up for his lack of formal education. His generation was too busy building the country to earn degrees. It's strange to compare their great brand of knowledge with that of some Ivy League graduates I've had the misfortune of knowing.

"Before we go any further, maybe our good doctor here can repeat for Harel and Yael what he's already told us." Marcus faced the doctor. "Try, please, to mention only the essentials. These two hate details and are not intending to go to medical school anytime soon." He smiled at us. "They like their present job too much."

Dr. Kleinkopf's bald dome reflected off Marcus's black portfolio, and it bounced when he stood up.

The doctor coughed, as if preparing for a lecture. I had heard him address people several times before. Sometimes for cases we've had, but also as a lecturer in classes we took from him as part of basic training.

This doctor is also a professor of medicine and the department chair of Forensic Pathology at the Hebrew University in Jerusalem. I know for a fact that he works for us on a voluntary basis. We have some good dutiful people in this country, even from Jerusalem.

Marcus gave Harel and me a long, very long, scrutinizing look, then spoke before the doctor could begin. Sometimes I think Marcus can read our minds.

"Before you begin, Doctor, I would like to take a break. All of you enjoy a nice walk in the sun and do some thinking. We have an unusual case here, and need some creative approaches. We will reconvene in thirty minutes.

"You and your three guys meet me downstairs in five minutes," he quietly said to Ari as everyone rose, motioning in our direction. I guess he was fed up with us, and I prepared myself for a verbal cold shower. Let's see how he will try to get us involved. No way, Jose.

On the floor below the conference room is a big space filled with technical equipment, mostly optical. Some of it deals with satellite photography, some with temperature sensing, but my personal favorite is the more unassuming 3D goggles, which not only allow you to view everything three-dimensionally but to differentiate between a poodle and a boxer from orbit—should the need arise. The concept isn't so mind blowing to your average first-world citizen these days, but to see the stuff in motion is at times overwhelming.

No pictures today. Marcus turned on us as soon as he stormed into the room.

"I understand that you might be upset. We involved the parents. Trust me; we had no choice, because we needed their cooperation."

"What cooperation?" I questioned.

"I don't want to repeat myself. We'll discuss it upstairs. I want you to know that nobody was acting carelessly, and her parents will not say a damn word to anyone. I give you my word."

I was thinking three months ahead. That is when our contract runs out and that's why I'm really so reluctant about going. If we made it so far alive, let's keep it that way. The truth is that I had accomplished missions before where the line between national security and personal revenge had been crossed.

Our skepticism apparently inspired Marcus to try a new angle.

"Despite the fact that the killers made some grave mistakes, I will be perfectly honest with you. I can't be sure that this case involves national security. If you want, you are off the hook. Go home. I won't hold it against you."

"Is this a dare?" Harel asked.

"No, he's just putting us on a motherly guilt trip," I said and snorted at Ari and Mattew, who were looking every which way but ours. Marcus never behaves like that, nor do we.

"Listen, both of you," Marcus said. "Rachel's mother was an officer in the army before you both were even born and before it was common for women to become officers. The father was an infantry sergeant before he became a high school geography teacher. They are not like you, prima donna agents with an overgrown opinion of themselves. They are decent people and deserve justice for their daughter. If you want to believe that I'm laying a guilt trip on you, go ahead. Believe it."

He looked at Harel and smiled. "Am I daring you? You know what, my boy, now that you've raised the issue, I will, in fact, introduce a little challenge. You two finish this case and you go home. Your four year contract is over."

"That's the challenge?" Harel asked carefully.

"Let me finish, damn-it. The challenge is that if you don't want to get involved you can go home now. Your contract is over. That doesn't mean that in a year I won't call again and try to convince you both to sign on. Go ahead. Eric and Naomi will be delighted if they have you at home tonight."

I got up smiling. "We can go home?"

"In twenty minutes the chopper will be here."

"Who will do the job, Matthew and Ari?" Harel asked, while still sitting.

"No," replied Marcus.

"Why not?"

"Because I don't want their wives to become widows."

"What?" I said. "What about the pining Penelopes Harel and I have waiting at home?"

Marcus looked at me square in the eyes.

"Matthew and Ari won't make it alone, but the four of you together will, assuming you and Harel take the job."

We were being manipulated like putty. I was beginning to hate the guy. Marcus went on.

"Let me explain something to you. I'll keep it short because they're waiting upstairs, and we don't have all day." Marcus sounded a touch emotional. This was also new for him.

"The fact is you two dazzled me from day one. I've trained generations of agents here—when we were part of the Mossad and afterwards and I've always had some ideal picture of the kind of people I needed. I want people that do things properly, and in this profession, that is not easy. The most important thing for me is not being put in a position where I have to talk to families, like I did today. It's a question of what could be avoided, or averted. The two of you do a job and it needs no follow-up. It is always a clean delivery."

We understood him beyond the obvious ego boost. So many reports of dead agents have 'human error' stamped on them.

"You both shoot and fight like no one else. If you made it alive to this day, it's because you combine all those talents with savage instincts that your brutish, eccentric upbringing didn't suppress. You are the only agents I've ever had, who, on arriving back from missions, are not reprimanded for making life-threatening mistakes. Besides . . . you are also the only two who could solve the triangle puzzle in less than a minute."

Ari had always refused to tell us if anybody had solved the puzzle faster than we had. Well, now we know. I'll get back to that one another time. It's a game to measure creative I.Q. Our Department takes for granted that an agent's conventional I.Q. must be at least 140.

He had us. It was not Marcus' sweet—talking that did the trick; let me be clear about that, but his little sermon on Rachel's family. We just didn't want Rachel's killers to get away without retribution. Her family didn't deserve it.

"Well, well, well, where does it leave us, sir?" Matthew laughed, putting his arm around Ari.

Marcus bent and muttered something in his ear and both of them laughed. Matthew was beaming. It was a day of ego massaging.

He turned to us. "In ten minutes we continue upstairs. You will either be there on time and get involved, or call the pilot and go home. The chopper should be here by now.'

Marcus left quickly with Ari and Matthew in tow.

49

15

Kleinkopf began his report without preliminaries as soon as we entered the room.

"The subject died from massive internal bleeding. The liver and spleen were ruptured as a result of the car accident. This was the hospital diagnosis, at least, and it was confirmed yesterday by our autopsy. We agree that she suffered heavy blood loss, but in our opinion, she died as a result of heart failure. She would have died from the bleeding, ultimately. Our chemical analysis found a very high concentration of cocaine, far above toxic levels. However, we also found a high concentration of chlorpromazine. She lived long enough for the hospital staff to try to counter the cocaine. Strangely enough, we didn't find any mention of counteractive drugs in the hospital report."

"What is chlorpro . . . good for?" Harel stumbled on the pronunciation.

"Chlor-pro-ma-zine. It is, so to speak, an antidote for cocaine."

"Was her heart failure due to the trauma of the accident?" Matthew asked.

"No, it came about because somebody gave her an I.V. full of highly potent cocaine straight into the vena cava superior. That's the main vein that enters the heart from the upper body."

"How did you establish that?" Harel didn't let go. "Could you actually see the needle holes in the vein?" He slyly looked at me, remembering our little argument.

Dr. Kleinkopf seemed competent. He wasn't intimated by the questions.

"Oh no, we usually can't see the holes, or, to be more precise, we don't look for them. There is normally no reason to administer the chemical analysis, though we did.

"What we do is take cross sections of different parts of the vein. Sorry, that is, of different sections of blood vessels. Under the microscope, one can see very clearly the necrosis which is typical and unique to cocaine poisoning. It's that simple."

"This is exactly what I told him," I interrupted. "Harel just doesn't get it."

Harel ignored me and continued to grill the doctor for more information. "O.k., you said she died from a heart attack and yet she was still alive when the accident occurred. How long does it take from the time of the injection until the point of death, assuming heart failure occurs?"

"Twenty minutes, twenty five at the most, considering the amount we found in her blood."

"Well, then we know that the place where she was injected was a ten minute drive at the most from the scene of the accident . . . crime . . . assuming the hospital is another ten minutes away."

Harel had a captive audience now.

Ari began barking commands at other people in the room, instructing them to find all relevant information about the time and location of the accident, including aerial photos of the town and whatever else they could find.

"So we can deduce some other things," Harel continued, oblivious to the buzz in the room. "If she had been killed in the accident, it is safe to assume that the local hospital would not have mentioned drugs. Then we might not have investigated further, assuming merely a tragic accident. But the person who ran over her had some connection to the killers. It was a premeditated "accident" . . . a killing. Whoever planned it—and whoever actually did the job—had less than twenty minutes during which to arrange the "accident.""

Again, Ari barked orders, this time about finding the identity of the driver. Two more people hurried out of the room.

"Any more questions for our pathologist?" Marcus asked.

"Yes," it was Harel again. "You said that the hospital didn't mention giving her the antidote, yet you found it in her body. Could that mean that the people who injected her with the drugs also injected her with the antidote?"

"Yes, this is possible, although I admit I didn't consider it. They could have done it in order to prolong the influence of the drug. They might have felt that she had not told them everything they wanted to hear."

There was a long silence. Everyone in the room was impressed. I was too, as much as I hate to admit it. Maybe Marcus had not been exaggerating with his praises before. But now I wondered if he meant me too.

Nobody had anything more to add, so Ari began to update everyone on other issues.

"Rachel used to call home and send e-mail regularly. We managed to retrieve a fair amount of the correspondence, and Matthew and I will go over some of the finer points."

"Matthew, please."

Matthew, tall and imposing, stood and delivered the information to us in solid Hebrew. Amazing, considering the fact that he learned to speak it only eight years ago.

Immediately after World War II, his grandfather put his career as a U.S. Senator in jeopardy in order to arrange a line of defense for newborn Israel. While the Arabs were drowning in weapons supplied to them by the British, Israel had nothing, and the Western weapons embargo to the Middle East didn't help.

With such a grandfather in his family, the Israeli military would not have turned him down. Matthew is not the only Gentile who's been allowed into the Israeli military; however, he's the only non-Jew in Marcus' Department. And he had to go through the same scrutiny the rest of us did. He's a top guy, great at the professional level and as a friend. I feel saddened that, when his contract is over, he and his wife Doris will go back home to Texas.

"Rachel definitely liked to write long e-mails and she did it quite often." Matthew uses fast, rough military slang, which, combined with his Texas-accented Hebrew, always sounds funny. "Two facts come up again and again: Her obsession with Wall Street investments and her deep connection to this German woman, Barbara Skibbe. We checked her bank accounts here, in Germany, and in the United States. Unless we missed something, she had nothing of real worth."

One of the men sitting at the table said, "We checked everywhere, but because it's the weekend, it will take two more days. Altogether she didn't have more than seven thousand U.S. dollars, and all of it was invested in simple savings accounts."

"So," Matthew continued, "we are still looking into her relationship with this Skibbe person. They met at the University of Berlin, and we haven't ruled out the possibility that they were romantically involved, despite the fact that there was nothing explicit in the correspondence."

"We are also checking Skibbe's history," Ari interrupted, "and, so far, we don't think she has anything to do with Rachel's death. She seems like a straight arrow. They both studied economics and as far as we know, they both planned to go to graduate school together." Ari nodded for Matthew to continue.

Matthew scanned the room. "Rachel had many opportunities to study anywhere she wanted. She had straight A's and top recommendations. In one of her e-mails, she told her father that Barbara was a top-notch student too, but that her grades didn't reflect it. She also said that she would go to the University of Montana a semester earlier, with the thought of somehow socially paving the way for Barbara.

"You might ask, 'Why Missoula?' The University there is not that prestigious, it prides itself more on its football team than academics. That, of course, means that a person with a sketchy undergraduate history could be accepted there. The two of them wrote about ways to be together inside and outside of school."

"Huge sacrifices to make for a friend," I said. "To give up Harvard or Columbia is . . . love."

"We are making assumptions here. She didn't say it outright," Ari interjected.

"Sure, besides, if you know the so-called 'right' people, one can get accepted into any place. For sure at Harvard or Yale. It's somewhat childish to assume that a friend's maneuverings are the way to acceptance. Or I may be wrong here," Matthew said.

"This talk gets us nowhere." Ari was becoming impatient.

Matthew went on, at the same speed ignoring Ari, "She never implied that she chose Missoula only because it was a place where her friend might be accepted. She might have chosen Missoula for reasons that have nothing to do with the University."

"Her partner quoted her as saying, 'One can do things in Montana that you can't do on Wall Street'," Harel said.

"Why didn't you mention this?" Ari abruptly questioned. He pounced on the stack of papers and started riffling through them. "She wrote the same thing to her parents in another e-mail. We solve this puzzle and we've unlocked half the mystery."

"Well, why don't we ask this German girl directly?" I asked. "After all, they were not only good friends, they wrote a research paper together. That reminds me. Has anyone read it?"

One of the cronies around Marcus answered. "Our preliminary investigation indicated that no paper was ever published, or even finished. The two women still had to hand in the paper to get credit for the course."

Sometimes it is really amazing what information our guys can collect on such short notice, I thought.

"What class was it, anyway?" I asked.

"Stock Analysis," Ari shrugged.

"Stock Analysis with emphasis on Graham and his student Buffett," Matthew added.

"Who?" I asked.

Graham was a Jewish economist who specialized in analyzing the real value of companies before investing in them. Buffett was his famous student."

"Who is Buffett?"

"The second-richest man in America. He is a buddy of Bill Gates and the primary owner of Berkshire, which is the holding company for some of the most famous American companies, like Coca-Cola or American Express." Matthew was prepared. I will give him that.

"Holding companies. Wasn't that the paper she wanted to publish with her friend?" Harel asked.

"Exactly, but they never did." Matthew answered.

Marcus suddenly spoke. "I don't want this meeting to go all night. Yael and Harel, you leave tomorrow on the 6 a.m. flight to Germany. You will meet Ari and Matthew in Berlin late tomorrow night. They will update you on what we'll be discussing here this evening. You'll then have one day to rest before you try to contact Barbara Skibbe."

"Get a good night's sleep." Ari felt obliged to say. "Rafi will take you to the airport tomorrow morning and update you if anything new pops up tonight. He'll give you all the routine instructions about where to get the guns, code words, escape routes, contact people in case of emergency, phone numbers, etc."

Marcus left his seat at the head of the table and came close to us like he always does before we leave for a mission. He put his hands on our shoulders. "I will be waiting for you."

We left silently. I was happy to be out of there.

Harel and I decided to catch an early movie in Tel Aviv before we went to sleep. We saw a nice easy comedy with Jim Carey and had ice cream for dessert.

I feel a lot of travel coming on.

16

We're on our way. As always when we fly El Al, we get the best seats in business class. We can steal glimpses of the pilots, who are all top notch, all veterans of the Israeli Air Force. At least this makes up for the lousy food.

The airplanes are the most guarded in the world. On international flights, at least five trained security guards are spread out among the passengers and equipped with small-caliber guns, usually Italian Berretta twenty-twos. The bullets are made out of soft grey lead, quick and smooth enough to pierce human flesh, but not hard enough to penetrate the airplane's thin aluminum walls. If you fear terrorists, this is the airline to fly.

We are not on duty, so we can sleep and relax. Nevertheless, the crew and the guards are informed about us, and, in case of trouble, we take over. Nobody complains. Most of them know us as guest instructors from their training. They are all ex-combat officers with one dream in common—to join Mossad one day. Romantics.

Harel and I are flying to Frankfurt. Ari and Matthew will go directly to Berlin, and we are supposed to meet them there—separate rooms, separate hotels. If something goes wrong, it will be infinitely more difficult for the local authorities to trace what happened.

Diplomacy also dictates that we can't take our guns off the plane. The German Border Police wouldn't appreciate that. We leave the guns with the crew for delivery back home. Usually, our replacements are delivered to us upon our arrival—a special gift, at times from the Embassy, at times from the local consulate. On other occasions local residents volunteer to deliver the necessary supplies. It happens a lot, especially in Germany. Guilt, religious fervor, ideology, drives them to help us. Whatever the reason, it is not the money. Purchasable services are an open invitation to betrayal. I'll take a Christian true believer as a volunteer any day.

We almost never demand help from our Diaspora Jewish kinsmen, even in the U.S., where they are numerous. It's simple: if they get caught, we don't want the media backlash to hit the rest of the Jewish community. This was a heavy issue with American Jews during World War II. They didn't want to be blamed for dual loyalty, so they didn't become as vocal about giving help to European Jewry. Unfortunately, that silence helped send my grandparents to Palestine instead of the United States, which is ultimately how I came to write a chronicle about an espionage mission instead of one documenting my spiritual growth.

I think I'm going to try to nap.

17

There was no bomb threat or hijacking. We landed safely and on time in Frankfurt. We finagled our way through the busy terminals and pale, grumpy droves of travelers to the rental car agency. Our mission was first, to find something to eat, because we had skipped the in-flight meal and Harel is impossible to deal with when he is hungry; and second, to pick up our guns in a small town called Soest.

Harel was feeling hungry as we showed the passports provided by our forgery department. It takes an hour or two to go through customs if you have a European passport instead of a Middle Eastern one. For that reason we had acquired shiny E.U./German papers. At the car rental desk, Harel nearly snapped a German girl's head off when she interrupted our query to chat on the phone with her boyfriend. He bent down over the counter and said in German, "I am hungry and my wife is pregnant. Get us the damn car, *bitteschön*."

We got the usual car, the Volkswagen VR6 Passat. I'm not a technical wiz or a car junkie either. This car is fast and ultimately understated—the first element being its speed on the Autobahn and the second for our line of work. This car can compete with any Porsche or BMW.

We drove into Frankfort Proper, a dull mixture of skyscrapers and neoclassic steeples, and found a little supermarket. I look forward to German food shops because they always have organic produce and remarkable whole wheat breads. We continued on a nice drive out of the city on speed-limitless Autobahn, until Harel got angry with me for dropping breadcrumbs on the leather seats. To calm him, I tried to stuff some bread in his mouth and then yelled at him to watch out for a BMW that cut in front of us.

I already feel the tension. It sets in from the moment we get off the plane in another country, and stays until we are back up in the sky on our way home. I wouldn't have it any other way. It reminds me that our lives depend on taking precautions.

We continued down the gray highway on a rainy mid-afternoon, past rows of energy-producing windmills and stretches of dense forest. I've been here so often in the last few years and yet every time I come back, I marvel at Germany's quiet, lovely countryside. The Germans keep in harmony with their surroundings. Even cutting a single tree requires written permission from the local government. And, of course, there is none of the horrible American-style billboards lining the road. I sometimes wonder, though, if their fanatical love of trees and parks keeps alive some exclusive, not-so-noble sentiments tied to rolling green woodlands and Siegfried the Great, along with a bevy of superior blond giants roaming the landscape.

18

We arrived in Soest after a few hours. The city is at least a thousand years old. Many of its odd-looking buildings were made out of peculiar green stones, which Harel thinks they get from quarries in the mountains which surround the town. I've never seen anything similar.

Harel and I had grudgingly parked on the outskirts of town, following one of Ari's European Rules. If we must make a fast getaway, the idea is to quickly jog to the car and leave, without having to deal with small-town traffic in the hideously narrow streets.

Like many other small, "unimportant" German cities, Soest had lived through the war without suffering Allied bomb attacks. It appeared to be a typical German hamlet, flanked on one side by a mountain and on the other by a lord's castle, now a museum. Its alleys are remnants of a feudal time, narrow with windows overhanging its cobblestone streets. Modern stores line the winding lanes, and on the corner, restaurant tables and chairs were getting soaked by the rain. That day, Soest was swarming with tourists in similar-looking rain gear. Postwar, uniformed invading forces. It was already close to four in the afternoon, and the narrow roadways were packed with the shiny cars of the smartly dressed people who were running under the eaves toward the concert hall to take in an early concert.

We were wandering around, getting wet, because the idiots back home made it sound like there was only one church in the center of town. In reality, there were four little town squares and dozen of churches scattered around them. Some tall, some not, but all built out of those peculiar green stones.

We took out our maps to check street names, and it took us forty five minutes to locate our pick-up spot. Harel and I stopped talking, out of frustration over our ineptitude. Finally, we came upon the church—a massive, green affair from the Renaissance with narrow, long windows and a huge brass door. We scanned the area outside the church as a routine measure. While checking the entrances and exits, we snapped photos of each other to avoid attention. You can do amazing things under the guise of shooting photos. A high school class walked by and one boy tried to jump in one of our pictures to make a face. With a smile I gazed at him through the custom-built lens, wondering what he would say if he knew I'd be able to see him in total darkness through this little camera.

We completed our check and entered the church. The walls were hung with tapestries bearing the portraits of saints and depicting biblical stories like Jesus' Ascension. Off to the side of the ornate altar, a life-size statue of Jesus bled under a stained-glass window. He was wooden and painted in simple muted colors, a simplicity I attributed to the Catholic austerity of those who had built the church. The blood running down the torso looked almost authentic.

Jesus and Mother Mary. What a distortion of decent Hebrew names. Her real name is not Mary or Maria, but Miriam. His real name is not Jesus, but Jeshua, meaning salvation. Most Christians never bother to learn Hebrew, therefore, denying themselves direct knowledge of the western world's most important text. The Messiah spoke Hebrew and Aramaic, a language akin to Hebrew, not German.

Harel figures they changed the names for the same reasons that the Romans, meaning the Italians, changed the name from Israel to Palestine after exiling the Jews from Israel. To cut any connection between the land and its original people, to cut the connection between their Christian Savior and his true identity: an Israeli Jew.

A white-haired pastor came from behind a corner as we opened one of the doors marked private. He looked friendly.

"Are you looking for the bathroom?"

"Oh, no," I answered, demonstrating use of my camera. "We thought the door led to a garden and we wanted to take some nice photos. It is so beautiful here, even romantic."

"I can show you where there is an exit to a nice inside garden is. It is actually private, but nobody will mind if you take some pictures."

"Bless you," I said.

"Where do you come from? Berlin?" he asked.

"Pardon me?" I paused for a second. It was the accent we used. "Yes, and this is my fiancé Axel. We're getting married soon."

"Berlin's a long way from here. I hope you enjoy yourselves."

"Oh, yes. It's a beautiful town and the people . . . they're so nice and friendly."

That really summarized our impression from what we had seen today. Most Germans I meet while on assignment are quite friendly. I still keep in touch with some old acquaintances. Doesn't that sound strange, after the holocaust and all?

I can only tell you that the Germans are no less friendly or humane than anybody else, and they certainly are less anti-Semitic than the French or the Eastern Europeans. In Eastern Europe, with this issue at least, even shame is difficult to find.

We stayed the garden for a while longer and then went to the main hall of the church. Our contact was painfully conspicuous with her vintage green, box-shaped hat and a red rose tucked in its brim. The rose was entirely unnecessary; we had seen her picture before we left Israel. Perhaps she had seen too many pickup scenes on television.

Harel approached her and they talked a bit before we left the church. Harel walked with her, holding her arm as if she were his grandmother. I followed them from a distance. My role was to ensure they were not being followed.

I had to smile when she hugged and kissed him while giving him the package. In Germany it is common for old people to ask younger ones for little favors like help in crossing the street or lifting a heavy basket at a grocery store. We always feel funny when those frail folks touch us. At least with this woman, I knew that whatever she had done, she was really sorry.

19

As Harel barreled down the Autobahn at some one-hundred twenty miles per hour, I opened the package for the first time. Everything was there. The usual stuff, nothing too fancy. The trusty two semi-automatic Smith and Wessons and the mandatory high-velocity hardened ammunition. Nothing is marked, neither guns, nor bullets.

There were also two toughened plastic daggers, small enough to slip between the leg and sock. The British Special Forces used this weapon well behind German lines in World War II. I've never used them on real people. We train on artificial dolls. The sharp blade pierces through ice or anything softer—easy penetration into the heart or other organs. When abroad we always carry these little toys, it is one of Marcus' craziest standing orders. The daggers, unlike guns, make it through metal detectors.

In the care package, there was also medication for emergencies. Wonder substances designed to alleviate pain, cause it, or make a person talk about anything. I've never been forced to use them, but since they're lightweight, there is no reason not to carry them. Laptop computers were a standby in earlier times, but now that they're so readily available, there is no use sending them. A waste of good machinery, in any case, since we incinerate everything at the end of a mission.

But what do I know about waste? Mossad salaries aren't that bad, but in our case, the damn kibbutz gets our paychecks—another socialist gimmick. A year ago, Harel and I asked the treasurer of our kibbutz—a 78-year-old true believer—for some extra travel money, and the woman refused. "The government covers expenses for you," she insisted. Each member in our Kibbutz—like in any other Kibbutz—gets the same budget, no matter what they do. No exceptions, not even for local heroes.

After two hours, we got off the main road and entered a city called Magdeburg. We know a nice restaurant there with great vegetarian food. It's a family business that has been there for generations. You can tell by the clientele that the owners have a lot of pride—a relationship between a small business and loyal customers that you don't see often in urban America.

No one seemed to recognize us as foreigners. I wonder if they would have been as nice had they known who we were. Harel, with his light eyes, broad face and massive shoulders, doesn't exactly look like Woody Allen. I had on my 'German outfit'—black leather jacket and short, cropped wet-styled hair, so I didn't look like their Jewish neighbor's daughter. We laughed about the clumsy experience in Soest while we had eggplant-tofu parmigiana, spinach gnocchi, and, for dessert, *streuselkuchen*, and strong shots of espresso.

I drove the last three hours of the trip and marveled over paying almost five dollars a gallon for fuel. We talked about our adventures with the Department, and then—unusual for us—we moved into more personal territory. I took some ribbing when I told Harel that, maybe I wanted to get pregnant sometime soon. That brought up some feelings about Eric, which I didn't and don't want to be dealing with right now. Despite everything, I think Eric and I will work things out.

We're now waiting to meet Ari and Matthew. I'm feeling slick and cool, armed to the teeth—and laughing as I try to sing some pop songs in Hebrew. I wonder how *Das Dritte Reich* would have handled two Jews like us.

20

(*Note: The following excerpt came from Matthew's journal. I will allow its relevance to Yael's story speak for itself—Ed.*)

Yael and Harel knocked on our door exactly at ten. I always have to smile when I see them.

It doesn't matter what they do. It can be in the middle of something that could end up killing us all or just taking a relaxing walk through the fields of the kibbutz. They always give you this reassuring smile and you know everything's going to end up okay. I remember when Ari told me to always follow their lead when times get rough. He said they play everything like a wild childhood game that has to end in their favor.

Yael came into the room without greeting us and stormed right to the television set. There was some rock-and roll program on. She grabbed her air guitar and acted like she was Eddie Van Halen . . . or Elvis, I couldn't decide who with her hips moving like that. She went up to Harel and did a Heil Hitler salute, "Ich bin jetzt ein Deutches Madel, und suche meinen Hans (I am now a German girl, and I am looking for my darling Hans)." It reminded me of *Cabaret*.

Harel looked at Ari and me for help but we let him handle her. He is a big boy. They went back and forth, and Ari and I exchanged smiles.

"We are not Nazis anymore," Harel told her, trying to master a Bavarian dialect. "At least most of us are not."

Yael stopped shaking her hips and mocked, "You're right, so right, mein Schatz, my treasure. We are all nice now. Politically correct and very, very kind. We protect the trees, love animals and all their poor dark descendents. We don't want *them here*, but my . . . they are so exotic.

"Leftists don't say dark people are like animals." Harel said.

"The way they patronize Third World people they might as well say it."

Yael was now all immersed in her act, "Let's rid our planet of the really awful things. All those polluting factories, all the fat Amis, the American Capitalists, and the Jews who control them from Hollywood.

"We are all true pacifists now; we have nothing to do with our Nazi parents." She was dancing slowly now to the music of some Bavarian Hee-Haw program that came back on. The music was quieter, and Yael started to break into a funny dialect.

"So now we can hate again diese Scheisse Israelit (these shit Israelis), the slayers of Arab babies. Finally free of past complexes. Hallelujah. No more Schuld, (no more guilt.)"

"Germans don't talk so anymore." Harel reminded her.

"Oh no?" Yael stopped dancing, "Didn't the Grüne (Green Party) leaders say, and on Israeli TV, that they 'understand' why Arabs kill Israelis?"

"Not all of them are like that" Harel stood his ground.

Yael smiled, "I know, but those who do drive me crazy, at least Germans should know better."

"You just have a love-hate relationship with the Germans." Ari interjected.

"So now you are a psychologist?" Yael didn't want to let go.

Ari smiled, "No, but my mom and her mother were once German Madels too, we will always carry that burden, whether we like it or not."

I know I'm going to miss those three when I go home, but I'm sure Doris and I will always keep in touch with them. When Doris, my wife, told Naomi that weeks ago, Naomi said she hoped it wasn't just polite American talk and that we would really keep in touch. I get sick of hearing that from Europeans or whomever. Everyone says Americans never mean what they say. I would not be here if I didn't mean what I say.

We haven't left yet and I already miss them.

21

(*Editors note: Yael's diary continues here.*)

"Skibbe is already under our surveillance, around the clock. You'll contact her tomorrow night." Those were the first words out of Ari's mouth.

"Anything new in the last twenty-four hours?" Harel asked.

Ari's eyes squinted as he gave us a wry smile and motioned to us as if he were going to tell us a good secret.

"In four hours, Rachel's mother, is going to call the president of the University of Montana and the Chairman of the Department of Economics to inform them that you'll be there in the next two weeks. You are going to enroll in some classes and are planning to focus on the same general topic that was of interest to Rachel."

"Me?" I asked.

"You will be Barbara, not Yael. It is still in the working stages, but after we talk with her, we'll have an idea whether or not it will work"

"Great, I love being bait." I rose and rummaged in my knapsack for a toothbrush.

"What if the University doesn't take her?" Harel asked.

"But they will." Matthew assured us. "It's America. If not, we'll orchestrate a little press leak about a bereaved mother, and her wish that the scholarly work of her only daughter will continue in the hands of her best friend and colleague . . . that type of schmaltz drives America."

"So why in four hours?" I directed the question to Ari.

"It will be twelve noon Montana time. If this is more than a local operation, they might try to silence Barbara. Their reaction time can give us some indication of whom we are dealing with."

"Besides," Matthew inserted, "once you go to Missoula they will have to go out of their way to make your death not look like an assassination. The second killing will have to be done in a very subtle way. Here in Germany, they can afford to be more obvious. It's a much easier task."

"When do you want to establish contact with her?" Harel asked.

"As I said," Ari has already turned to the screen of his laptop and was typing something. "We already have Mossad people around her. They sit near her, even in the classroom. But we can't go on with this indefinitely, and there is no use in prolonging the wait. If we are lucky, you will establish your first contact with her tomorrow night, outside her apartment."

"Are you going to be with us?" Harel asked.

"We'll see tomorrow, but I think Matthew and I will be around." There was little that Ari was definite about. "We will take over the surveillance from Mossad tomorrow around 6:00 p.m. From that point on, expect her life to be in danger. We want you both to be with her."

Everything was in motion. I hoped, for her sake, the girl would collaborate. I wondered how sinister our unknown enemies were, since in four hours, twelve noon Mountain time, our Fraulein would become a walking target.

22

Espionage in a city like Berlin, especially the surveillance aspect, is not an easy task. Most people don't use cars, because public transportation is so efficient. For students like Barbara, it's available for almost nothing—indulgences Germans love to complain about. Buses and subways follow the joint tenets of the Teutonic fatherland: efficiency and competency. It's difficult to shadow someone in these conditions.

Even the harsh-sounding orders of the blue-uniformed subway employees, directed toward the passenger herd, fit right in. The wagons are packed, but retain their cleanliness. The worst is the German national pastime—to stare and stare and stare at each other and mind everybody else's business. It interferes with the art of espionage when your subject is studying every mole on your face. There is an upside: You can set your watch by a U-bahn's arrival.

One downside to this city is its lack of crime. In American cities, messy operative work blends in beautifully with the plethora of random acts of violence waiting around every corner. While it's easier to get things done here, it's sometimes more difficult to clean up the mess or pin anything on anyone else. Damn the peaceful Germans.

Berlin is, or at least it seems, five times the size of Seattle, but the chance of being shot or stabbed in Seattle is hundreds of times greater. Two years ago in a cover-up operation, I had to work a fortnight as a nursing aid in a large Berlin hospital. One of the doctors told us that after one night of work at Harborview Emergency Room in Seattle, he saw more people with bullet wounds than in his entire twenty-year career in Berlin.

Harel says it's not fair to compare Berlin or even Israeli cities—except Jerusalem—with an American city, where the standards are truly barbaric. Every night, in Washington D.C., more people are murdered than in two weeks in the West Bank. That is sure not the impression I get watching the nightly news in the U.S.

23

Subject take-over from Mossad took place on schedule in a section of the city called Friedrichshain—a run-down, tattered area in former East Berlin. The building used to be an old bakery before the current occupants had transformed it into a hip little movie theater. Only avant-garde films play there—the right stuff for my Eric.

We went in two cars. Matthew and Ari stayed in theirs, and Harel and I crossed the street, casually checking parked cars for suspicious-looking passengers. We carried our cell phones so we could always contact the other two. One more walk around the block and it was time.

I inhaled a cloud of rank smoke as we walked inside. Germans love to chain-smoke, and I think we were the only ones in the building with healthy lungs. At a popcorn stand, which sold beer and espresso but no popcorn, I opted for a bar of organic chocolate. Might as well get some antioxidants with my second-hand smoke.

People were standing in line for a Cuban art film, and some joker had pasted huge posters of Che Guevara and Castro all over the place. I'm not so sure it was just for the movie. Those two are heroes around here. In the last city-wide election the Communist got the clear majority of the vote this side of the wall. I was glad that Harel and I looked like the rest of the crowd; we were both clad in black, and I wore a pair of obligatory black-framed schoolgirl glasses—which is what makes Germans look more intellectual than they really are. Americans, with their baseball caps, reflect the opposite. Harel looked the part of a German hipster-student, but I got the feeling he was not so comfortable in the gray nylon-blend pants I had bought him this morning. Germans like to dress up, and we had to fit in.

I pretended to study a particularly handsome poster of Che as Skibbe sipped her wine below it, deeply immersed in a discussion with some friends. Hi, I thought, and studied her form. She was quite pretty, although everything about her was pale—her skin, hair, eyes, and even clothes. She was one of those lanky, tall types, with the languid, graceful movements of a dancer.

Although her gaze was serious and sad-looking, I could see tiny lines of laughter around her eyes—a probable sign that she had seen better days and was, perhaps, the cheerful giggly type. Rachel's mother had told Skibbe of her friend's death in a "car accident" less than a week ago. After a minute or so, she peeled herself away from the group and strolled to the bathroom; she naturally moved like a gazelle, but carried her head low—a disarming mixture of beauty and impishness and, especially when she looked up, a bit demure.

This morning, we planned different approaches if she didn't cooperate. It would not be the first time we had kidnapped people and taken them all the way to Israel, but it's always cleaner if our party participates of her own free will.

She looked amenable enough to me. Here we were, several feet from an innocent woman who hadn't the slightest idea that somewhere far away, somebody who had never seen her may have ordered her demise. If Ari were correct, that is.

I decided to grab the chance and followed her. I didn't want to let her out of sight; bathrooms are textbook settings for assassinations. Luck was on my side. The bathroom had only two toilets, and only the two of us were there. I closed the outside door behind me and said, "Barbara?"

She turned around, surprised. "Kennen wir uns? Do we know each other?"

"I apologize for deciding to meet you here, but I have no time to explain." I kept my tone brisk and my speech tight. "I was a close friend of Rachel's, and it's important that we talk, outside, as soon as possible. If Rachel was as close to you as she was to me, you'll meet me outside. No more words."

"Rachel was my best friend . . ." Her voice trailed off. She was wasting precious time.

"Good, then we can take a little walk. I have some urgent information to give you about Rachel" I smiled what I hope was a reassuring smile. "I promise to answer any questions you might want to ask me. Meet me outside, and keep quiet." I quickly gave her some easy directions.

I left and walked straight without turning, out the main exit to the front of the building. Then I waited. Harel stood near the other students so he could control the girl's movements if she didn't follow my directions.

She came out, and Harel followed closely behind her. He gave me the o.k. sign. I was relieved. Perhaps my gut feeling that there would be trouble today was misplaced.

When she came out, I hugged her warmly. I tried without words and with an admittedly unorthodox technique to build some confidence in her. I was about to impart some heavy information.

The hour that followed, maybe longer, was one of stories, half-truths, and lies to calm her down and get her attention. I realized she was brighter than she looked and relaxed my bitchy tone. Barbara and I walked several miles, Harel always fifty yards or so behind us. Matthew and Ari walked along on the other side of the street. Lines of communication were also open with the local Mossad guys. Why shouldn't they, for once, do a little work for their pay?

We ended up in Mitte, a district that ironically is in the old Jewish Quarter. I glanced at my watch, and it occurred to me that none of us had eaten for a while. So I treated Barbara and myself to a nice falafel with tahini and some water in one of the many small Turkish restaurants while Harel hung around in a hungry sulk across the street at a bus stop. We both dripped the tahini on our clothes, and I was glad Barbara didn't get agitated. I like it when people are not so uptight about being too neat, it shows some free spirit.

I could see why Rachel liked her so much. She was very direct with her questions. She asked the right ones and wanted more than the stock answers.

I told her a couple of Israeli jokes to keep things comfortable but soon realized they weren't necessary. I could tell she knew more than most about Israel and that she cared about what was going on there. It always surprises me when somebody is *not* against us. I'm so used to that, even from some of my spoiled American relatives. Only very few people really bother to look at the historical facts in depth. Sure, superficially we look like the powerful ones who have nothing else to do but oppress our poor Arab neighbors. Well, I am ready any day to exchange our economical mess with their oil. The most difficult issue for us is this guilt driven need, Americans and Europeans have, to be politically correct with non whites. For example Westerners are unable to see that the modern Arab interpretation of Islam is virulently anti-Jewish. Nothing, absolutely nothing, we as Israelis can offer to them, except our total demise, could solve the conflict from the Arab perspective. Listen to what they say in Arabic, not in English.

Barbara was now under my protection, and whoever the Missoulites, Missoulers, or Missoulians might be, if they wanted to get her, they had have to go now through Harel and me. I just can't wait.

24

It finally occurred to Harel that he could cross the street and get a falafel to go without revealing himself to Barbara. Matthew and Ari took the two cars to her place while Barbara and I—Harel following from a distance—took public transportation, which offered us more time for chatting. I needed time to build some trust. After all, we entered her life out of the blue. By now I was sure nobody was following us but once we got to her place we would have to be on our toes again. We wanted somebody to try to get her and to protect her at the time. I know it sounds crazy, but it was not my idea.

Barbara led me to the S-Bahn stop, and we descended the stairs to catch the S1 train south toward the Lichterfelde West district in Berlin. She led me to the ticket machine and assumed a motherly air as she advised me which ticket to buy. We descended another set of stairs to the dark gray platform. It was already quite late, and the area was almost empty of people. I was glad that Harel stood there too. Barbara chatted about Berlin being a sea of construction cranes while I surreptitiously sized up the other few waiting passengers. Finally, our train rumbled in, we boarded, and sunk down across from each other on facing two-seaters, having the wagon all to ourselves. We barreled forward, under Berlin.

Barbara suddenly fell deathly still and made big eyes at something behind me. Harel slid in the seat next to me with his falafel wrapped in aluminum foil. He started to eat in big fast bites and Barbara simply stared at him. I guess she couldn't help it. She is German. "A good way to blow our cover," I muttered to him in Hebrew and laughed—a kibbutznik eating a smelly falafel. He grinned, wiping tahini from his face, and then looked at Barbara. "*Na, wie geht's? Ich bin der Harel*," he said, introducing himself and then returning his eyes to his meal.

Barbara gave him one of her impish looks. "I thought you were a starving Jean-Claude Van Damme, and was just going to ask you for your autograph."

"Ha," Harel laughed politely and continued eating. "I thought women didn't like him. I'm surprised a nice intellectual like you has even heard about a muscle-bound actor like him."

"My high school boyfriend was one of his fans."

"Sorry, Barbara," I said, "this guy is my partner, and he has been literally protecting our backs while we had our nice talk." I smiled at Harel and patted his knee proudly. "Besides, you are right, he rather does look like a Belgian. But he's ve-e-e-ery competent."

"Now listen, you two, this is Berlin," Barbara said with a patronizing laugh, "not the Middle East. I don't think I need a Mossad bodyguard."

"The Mossad," Harel chewed his food with a look of disgust. "We are a step up from those clowns. All the same, we are paranoid Jews like the rest of them."

Harel wiped his hands on his pants and got up to study a subway plan. Barbara and I turned to look out the window—the train had emerged at street level—when we were suddenly surprised by a commotion. Some young men, fresh from a night soccer match, stumbled by us and plopped down on some seats across the aisle. They sang loudly, with open mouths smelling of beer, then suddenly grew quiet and leered across at Barbara and me. They gave us those long, hard, dirty stares—a male specialty for lone women.

"Drunk drooling monkeys," Barbara muttered and stared out the window.

We were tense as it was, and a couple of lewd comments later, when Harel sat back down next to me with a loud sigh. I was amazed how quickly a legion of eyes suddenly left my face and went to the floor, skimming over Harel for a quick, fearful second. Fortunately for those young men, they didn't test things further.

25

Barbara lived on Kommandantenstrasse, the Street of the Commanders, a sleepy street lined with chestnuts trees in the boring suburb of Lichterfeldewest. The buildings were charming examples of old upper-middle-class understatement, with small manicured lawns tended by uptight hands; the only sound to fill the evening was the occasional purr of an Audi or a Beethoven piano sonata drifting out a window. Lichterfeldewest was the heart of the American sector in the days of East and West Berlin, and Barbara told us how tanks used to tear down the quiet cobblestone streets on the Fourth of July while the Germans watched in horror from their balconies.

"I live in that building." She pointed at a classic bourgeois mansion, which had been sliced up into fifteen or so apartments around the turn of the century. "Oh, look! My lights are on. Marian must be home. She's my new roommate."

"Huh?" I said dumbly. There was no Marian in the report. Goddamn Mossad. Hard to imagine how they maintain their super-cool reputation.

We had a problem. If our friends from Missoula were as incompetent as Mossad, they might confuse this roommate with Barbara.

Matthew and Ari were not there yet, perhaps, they are stuck in a traffic jam. We didn't wait for them.

Harel and I told Barbara to walk behind us as we drew the guns, cocked them, and slid them under our jackets, which we carried on our arms. If a nosy neighbor had opened the door, no problem, we looked like typical visitors.

When all three of us arrived in front of her door on the second floor, Harel and I changed positions. He covered our backs and watched.

"Are you sure all this is necessary?" Barbara asked for the second time that night. She looked a bit scared after seeing the guns.

I flashed a quick smile at her, and told her to stand behind us, and I knocked on the door.

"*Ich komme*," a German female said, and the door slid open. A voluptuous young woman with wild black curls smiled at our faces. When she saw the guns, her smile faded.

"What the hell?" she asked understandably startled.

Barbara angrily pushed by me into the apartment, apparently upset at our dramatic entrance. Ten minutes later, we were sitting in Barbara's kitchen and drinking an excellent cup of hot chocolate. She went overboard on the vanilla, but it was the perfect thing to loosen me up. I didn't tell her anything, other than how it tasted.

Marian went back to her room to arrange her stuff, freshly moved in from her car. Her sudden movement from the chair jerked me out of my relaxed state. It wasn't incredibly evident, although Barbara noticed.

"Wow, you guys are tense! This is Berlin, not New York."

The doorbell and my phone rang at the same time and Barbara raised herself from the chair to get the door.

"I'll go with you," Harel said, blocking her path and putting his back in front of her. "Are you expecting anybody?"

Before she could answer, Marian appeared from her room and ran directly to the door. I wanted to stop her, but she already had it partly open.

I threw myself on the ground behind the short bar-like counter separating the living room and the kitchen. Harel grabbed Barbara with one hand while drawing his gun, throwing himself down on the floor and on top of her. He somehow managed to push a thick wooden dinner table between them and the door while various dishes and glasses, piled up to be put away, were sent crashing to the floor.

The sickening all-too-familiar pop of a silencer was unmistakably clear and sharp. Then a much thicker, more brutal noise came. It was the sound of Marian's body being pierced, then tossed about the room by the impact of high-caliber bullets. It was an ugly scene, to say the least. The bullets were dum-dums. Nothing else could be so forceful.

Nobody moved. Barbara's scream disappeared into Harel's big left hand. There was no reason for me to shoot. I could hear people already running down the stairs. In the middle of apartment houses, I'd shoot only to kill and only after seeing a target. Shooting blind is senseless. We didn't follow them either, just in case somebody was waiting to ambush us. It was unlikely, since they most likely assumed the victim was Barbara.

My cell phone was still ringing, and I answered it. It was Matthew.

"Two people, a man and a woman, came running out of the building. They are now in a car with a driver and we will glue ourselves to them. Are you okay?"

"We're fine," I said. "The roommate is down. We will join you in a sec . . . leave our keys in the car. Keep the phone lines open. Did only two come in?"

"Yeah, it was a couple, a man and a woman. We're already on our way, hurry!"

Only in the movies can one car follow another without losing it. We were short on time, and we couldn't do anything more for Marian.

Barbara's face was ashen. We ushered her past Marian's crumpled, blood-soaked corpse and out the door. Harel touched me, and we sympathetically waited as Barbara stopped, took out her keys and, with shaking hands, locked the apartment door—an absurd, automatic action typical of someone in shock. She mutely turned to us, and we descended the stairs.

The Passat was parked across the street under the shadow of a chestnut tree, a black form in the dark-blue night air. Harel quickly dialed Matthew as he got behind the wheel, and I got in the back seat with Barbara. Harel started the car and began driving through winding streets in a manner worthy of cinematic chase scene, nevertheless following precisely the directions Matthew was giving. He glanced at me in the rear view mirror and said, "They're right on top of them." I nodded and looked at Barbara, who was silently crying and squeezing my hand. Her eyes wildly followed the traffic and moving scenery while her body was being rocked by the fast driving. I whispered to her to lay her head down on the seat.

I wanted to give Barbara one of the magic pills I had in my pocket. Sleep for her would have made things easier for us. If the Mossad hadn't completed a full background check, I would have forced her to take one. We didn't need someone we couldn't trust in the back. But I also trusted my feelings about her.

I climbed into the front seat next to Harel. Ari and Matthew were moving down a wide boulevard called Unter den Eichen, heading away from Berlin's center toward the green district of Zehlendorf. Fortunately, the traffic was light. We cut past many cars, and I could imagine the Germans cursing, "Du, scheiss Arshloch! You shit asshole!"

We zoomed through Zehlendorf and passed into Wannsee, the district which is home to Berlin's grandest lake, as well as the villa where Germans came up with "The Final Solution" to the "Jewish problem."

The trees became denser and the houses moved apart. Suddenly, we could see Matthew and Ari, also in a Passat, carefully following a white BMW. As soon as we saw them, we took over the chase from them, following the large BMW, which rumbled down the road ahead of us like a heavy fluorescent whale. It was a poor choice for a getaway car with its bright color and ostentatious model. Not very professional on their part, it was easy to follow them. No zigging or zagging, and apparently no checking to see if anybody was following them.

I guess the bad guys didn't have enough time to come personally from Missoula, and this was the best they could do on such short notice. Their stand-ins would soon be dead.

I constantly kept Matthew informed about our position. The BMW took a sharp turn onto the freeway, moving full-speed westward. The next big town was Potsdam. They increased their speed to one-hundred thirty miles per hour, and I was happy we had the Passat. It was noisy, but had no problems handling the speed.

I shot a look at the back seat and saw that Barbara was sitting up; she had regained control, although she looked extremely drawn. I wished we could bring her somewhere safe. I cursed the lack of preparation and foresight, but decided to deal with that later. Barbara returned my gaze and sadly shook her head, as if saying, I can't believe what happened. I gave her a smile and a pat, then turned my eyes back to the road.

We were very close to the BMW. I wonder now what Ari would have said if we had passed it and I had drilled the driver in the temple. It would have been more spy-like. But Ari and Matthew took over for us and we slowed down. Several minutes later, Matthew told us that they took the first exit into Potsdam and were heading in the direction of the old city.

We all had been here a thousand times, but tonight, danger made our visit precious and magical.

26

Old Potsdam is a fairy-tale town. I think every German emperor, king, or prince has had an urge to build a palace there. Not one of them was afraid of gaudiness.

The streets of Old Potsdam shuddered in the moonlight like old cold bones, and we tirelessly moved past the facades with the white BMW—our ghost heralded in its nightshirt. I saw Friedrich II, Napoleon, Churchill and Stalin on the doorsteps of the crumbling palace stairways, posing for pictures as numerous tourists do today, or simply measuring a doorjamb to complete their own architectural additions. We passed the monumental historic mansions and finally were zipping past Potsdam's gem—the Sans Souci palace gardens.

Sans Souci—without care—was the name Frederick the Great gave his residence and its vast French gardens. He was not only a musician, but also friendly to our kind, I hear. This is uncommon in Europe, even today. Surrounded by a high, regal fence, Sans Souci impressed visitors with hectares upon hectares of incredibly gaudy design. It appeared that the French had, at some point, convinced the Prussian kings to carve up their bushes to look like poodles, and to trim these green monstrosities for constant viewing.

That was the first sight that greeted you. If you ventured among the lanes of poodles, you saw that the Germans, in some desperate act of retaliation, had dragged in hideous, erotic statues and placed them among the bushes. In the 18th and 19th centuries, Baroque palaces had sprung up every few acres or so—a beauty farm for every queen and a tool-shed for every prince, and all the stately bungalows were named after a different country or fruit.

If you happened to venture into one of these royal playpens, you were blinded by gold radiating off the ceiling, banisters, and vases and you would be knocked senseless by the maelstrom of many color palettes. Even the toilets were gold plated.

Though I love to laugh at Sans Souci, I would thrash any tourist who snubbed it: after all, where else could you say that you breathed the same air of oppressive, wealthy tastelessness, as say, Voltaire once did.

Tonight, I couldn't find solace in the dark maples of the gardens, and the silly castles looked like savage, beastly fortresses. One of the palaces was illuminated from the outside with modernistic neon-blue projectors, leaving the rest dark. The German hang-up with saving on electric bills can get on my nerves. Not this time, though.

Not long after we passed the palace, the BMW started slowing down, and we crept forward at a slower and safer distance. "Hmmm," I said to Harel, "you think we'll have a night fight?"

"Maybe," he mused, "are you feeling up to that?" *Mais oui.* Harel and I were quite proud of our night combat capabilities, and not only because we owned the right technology for it. As children on the kibbutz, our regular weekend game, "night-fight," was a complex mixture of hide-and seek and capture-the-flag, played in the pitch-black fields and orchards. We kids honed our vision and movements until we could have danced the Swan Lake blindfolded, and learned to sense other objects, especially other children hiding, masterfully. Sometimes we use these bare animalistic instincts on our kibbutz dogs. Rarely did it work though. They were always so alert.

Once, Harel and I tried to convince Marcus to introduce a version of the game into training, but he had only smiled politely. His loss!

The BMW was parked, empty, in front of a big iron gate which led into the park. A single uniformed guard was talking with some women who were most likely prostitutes. It was amazing how lax security was, considering the treasures inside, but I always need to remind myself that this is not America.

We parked our cars two blocks away and began to prepare. That meant screwing small silencers on the barrels of our guns. There was no need to wake the locals with the sound of a .38 special. Germans are so grouchy when awakened after bedtime.

We also geared ourselves up with the typical secret service ear wear, essential for communicating without interference and keeping our hands free. Binoculars with built-in infrared were also part of the ensemble.

We walked separately toward the fenced-in park, staying within eye distance of each other. Only Barbara walked near me. We had tried briefly to persuade her to stay in the car, but she didn't want to stay alone, and we had enough confidence in her to allow her to follow along—and take orders. We tried to keep far away from the lighted gate and walked under the shade of the old trees.

The stone fence was almost eight feet high. Ari and Harel lifted me up first. Matthew came next, Harel pushing him from below and I help him from above. The rest followed the same way. All this action began only after I let my eyes get adjusted to the dark and after a quick search of the area with the binoculars. I didn't use the infrared lamps at first, hoping I could detect theirs if they had them. I expected none and I was right.

27

We saw them clearly without infrared. Give your eyes enough time to adjust to the darkness and you would be surprised how much you can see, especially when you're using binoculars, lying in the dark, and peering into a lighted room in the palace.

They didn't bother to close the curtains. The one man they had put outside was sitting on a bench smoking. They definitely were not expecting visitors; they assumed they had killed the right person in Barbara's apartment back in Berlin and that was the end of it.

It was a small, single-storied building—a storage-type place—with two spacious rooms.

We took another long look, this time with infrared. There were four people in the warm-looking room, and, as I mentioned, the guard outside, still smoking his cigarette. He looked like he was on the brink of sleep. The hit in Berlin had tired him out.

One of the four inside was a woman, and Matthew quickly ID'd her as the woman on the job at Barbara's. I was glad to see a woman on the work site, although she was playing for the wrong team.

Ari whispered a few words into the phone, then told us we had reinforcements on the way from the Mossad. Two men gently jogged up to us soon after. We hadn't asked for reinforcement, but I guess Mossad didn't want to be left out. They can't take a hint. We tried to tell them that all we needed was two simple long-range rifles, equipped with standard telescopic night lenses. Was this really too much for them to grasp? I don't know how Israel pulled the stunts it did before Harel and I arrived on the scene.

Our still unsuspecting targets were just hanging out inside. It was up to us to make the first move. How do our Arab neighbors from across the border say it? "When the mountain won't come to Mohammed, Mohammed must go to the mountain." We were on our own, and that was just fine.

Ari took command. He told the three other Mossad guys who were on their way to stay in their car and sit tight, in case of a possible quick exit. The two who had joined us were to stay here in the first position. Ari would take the back door of the building. Matthew, Harel, and I would do the actual attack. Barbara would stay between the two Mossad guys and enjoy the view.

The guns, the silencers, the agents, and the whispering Hebrew should be enough to scare Barbara, but she looked remarkably calm.

"Be careful," she whispered as we got ready to move.

I touched her softly in the darkness,

"I want at least one of them alive," Ari told us.

"What is this, Capture the Flag? Go and get them yourself." I thought, but kept silent.

I began the approach with Harel and Matthew angling toward the guard, who by now was sleeping. We moved in slow motion amidst the huge rose plants that grew everywhere. Kings love roses, I presume. They're beautiful, unless you have to creep through their thorns on dark nights. For the last stretch, we fell to our stomachs, stopping every so often to eye the guard through night glasses. We had to creep, cat-like, for the last stretch, closing the distance slowly. While two of us moved, the other kept an eye on the guard.

We hesitated as the guard suddenly woke, got up, and strolled a few meters to his right and sat down on another bench. He held a gun loosely in his hand. I exchanged looks with Harel and he nodded. I aimed my gun as Harel continued ahead without us, disappearing out of the corner of my eye to another bed of flowers. Matthew and I stopped forty feet from the guard and lay down on the wet grass to direct our weapons. If he moved before Harel reached him, we would have been ready to shoot. Was he one of the hit men at Barbara's? Was he the driver? It really did not matter. Committing a murder is not that much different from being accomplices to one, no matter what the moral folks in Europe tell you.

We could see the outline of Harel's stocky figure behind the unsuspecting man. As the guard tilted his head down to light another cigarette, Harel bent with him like a dancer, than lifted him like a straw doll. Not a sound, not even a slight one from the neck. It was a swift departure from life.

We moved a bit closer to the window. Close enough to see details inside, far enough to remain hidden. The four in the room were definitely not waiting for us. A shot through the glass would have roused half of Potsdam. The trick in sleepy towns is to avoid exposure. As I said before, Germans get mad when their night's sleep is interrupted. They are hard working people.

We decided to go through the door. Matthew and Harel would stay near the window. The plan was a bit tricky. If the door was unlocked, I could be in fast, finishing the job with no problem. But if it was locked, they would be warned and Matthew and Harel better move fast, noise or no noise.

I was poised at the door with my gun. And yes, I was a bit cautious . . . cautious, not tentative. Fighting in buildings is considered one of the most challenging forms of handgun combat. I had instructed people on this scenario since my army days, and it is a textbook, albeit dangerous, situation.

The door was unlocked. I was in. Harel said something over the earphones, but I could not take the time to listen. Once the door was open, the time for conversation was over.

It seemed so simple in a strange way, just me versus them. "Shoot for the center," my brain screamed, although my movements were fully automated. Even if they had protective vests, it would not help them much against our ammunition.

First the woman. She was the closest to her gun, and her hand moved towards it. Her eyes while leaving life met mine. The other two didn't even move as they remained frozen in their seats. It reminded me of the vipers' quarries I'd seen so many times in our mountains. They joined their female friend.

I could not see the fourth man, so I threw myself on the ground, shooting the two big overhead lights at the same time. I rolled several times on the floor with my gun constantly aimed in the door's direction, the door between this room and the next. My body hit the wall. Unless the other side had night vision, I was safe. I loaded another magazine. Click.

Harel was on the earphones again. "Are you okay?"

"Why didn't you tell me the fourth man left the room?" I hissed.

"I did, but you got too excited, as always. I'm coming in. I'll take it from here."

I checked my binoculars. They were still operational. (I'll give free advertising here to our tech guys. We always have durable equipment.)

"I'm going in." I told him.

"No, wait for me," he responded back.

"The other room is very large," I told him, remembering how it looked from the outside. "You and Matthew look in the windows and try to find the fourth guy."

I was on the move again, crawling slowly and quietly on the carpeted floor. While I advanced, I scanned the area through the glasses in my left hand. My gun was in my right.

Still sliding, I entered the room, a storage area for renovated antiques. In the dim green light of the infrared, I saw scattered statues of Minotaurs. The form of Pan held my gaze for a second.

It is a bit tricky to shoot a target while looking at it though the instrumentation, but I would have to handle it.

Matthew reassuring voice came through. "We see him. He is on the other side of the room. He seems to be eyeing the back door. Let him escape. Sit tight and let Ari get him when he comes out."

Then my binoculars failed, and to make things worse, I heard movement five or six yards in front of me. I shot twice in the direction and at the same time rolled as far away as I could. Bullet trails bounced near the spot I had just occupied.

It was pitch black. I can't stress this enough.

Again I heard Matthew. "Sorry about that. Now we've got full vision of the room and we see both of them. Yael, one is exactly on the other side of that dragon statue you're elbowing. If he comes out to get you, he'll expose himself and you can take him. My eyes won't leave him."

"Good, cuz' mine are not worth a damn right now. I can't see a thing!" I tried yelling in a whisper.

"Are you hurt?" he asked.

"No, Matthew, but there is zero light. You will need to lead the blind on this shot."

"Not as long as the other guy is still there. You'll be exposed."

Harel's voice came in. "Ari, are you on?"

"Yes, I've been listening to the three of you."

"Good."

Harel took command now because he was the closest to Ari, and yet he could see me, too. "Ari, I will let you know when the guy comes out, and you and I will concentrate on him. Matthew and Yael, deal with your target, but only after Ari and I have ours."

It took several minutes for anything to happen. It was so dark that my eyes couldn't make the adjustment. But my ears compensated, and the sound of my adversary's breathing was very close. I could smell him.

I carefully sat down, huddled against the statue's legs. If Matthew was wrong again, I would become the smallest target I could be.

28

(Editor's note: The following chapter was put together with the help of another excerpt from Matthew's journal from the same night.)

From my vantage point at the window I could see most of the room. I focused on Yael and the man who stood only a few feet away from her. The man on the other side of the room held Harel's full attention.

In the green light of the night vision, nothing looked real. The man near Yael twitched nervously. I could see he felt cornered, but didn't dare come out. His partner was moving very slowly toward the exit door, eyes open, groping his way in the dark. I had to remind myself that all three were virtually blind.

Yael sat as still as the statues. She was listening to us, trying to compensate with her ears for the total lack of vision.

Then Ari said, "If those men don't move in the next ten minutes, we are going in."

I agreed, because we couldn't stay here all night, and besides, we all knew that our infrared batteries wouldn't last more than thirty minutes. Yael knew it too, because hers had already gone out.

"The target is almost behind the door," Harel said. "Where are you, Ari?"

We couldn't afford a misunderstanding about positions now.

"Same place," Ari answered.

"Good. I want to be sure you don't shoot in Yael's direction. From where you are, it's fine. Get ready."

"I am." Ari sounded steady.

"Now—center." Harel's voice rang out clear, as if it were one of our training days.

Ari shot through the door three times and the man was thrown back upon a statue. He stayed there, bleeding, propped up by the figure.

"Target down," Harel reported.

The man near Yael became increasingly nervous, making me more nervous for her. She was still motionless, gun directed slightly upward in case he made his move.

"If you hear me Yael, move your head," I said.

She looked at me with blind eyes and nodded her head slightly. She knew I could observe her and she smiled. That's my girl.

"We have to finish it now," I told her. "I will be your eyes and tell you where to direct your gun."

Yael lifted herself slowly, but her move somehow alerted the anxious gunman. He stuck one hand out of cover and pointed the gun in the direction where he thought Yael would come out.

I immediately told Yael, and she exposed her own gun hand, low and out of his path. A flick of his hand and he could change direction. But I reminded myself again that he could not see anything.

I gave Yael fast instructions to correct her direction.

"Now," I said sharply.

She missed and he quickly withdrew. But Yael, without waiting for my instructions, came out fast and took advantage of the moment. She put her hand beyond the corner and emptied her magazine, twisting her wrist slightly to catch all possible angles. She was shooting blind.

It worked. After we stormed in and lit the area with our flashlights, we found the man dead.

Later she told me that he had screamed when she blasted the first shot and that she took advantage of him being dazed.

I'd rather forget the way the man's blood was painted on one of the statues. It made the stone seem . . . animated.

29

I took Barbara to show her roommate's dead killers. I figured the more she saw of reality, the more she could understand and help us. There would be no time to explain the Middle East realities that so many Americans and non-Israeli Jews prefer to ignore. Visuals were essential.

I remember my first year in the service, in a class about Americans and other outsiders and their perceptions of Israel and the Jews. We were asked by the teacher to peruse a mainstream American newspaper. On the front page was a large AP photo of an Israeli soldier and under it a headline: "Palestinian Killed in West Bank Clash." The text relayed the event, and then implied that the international community should restrain the belligerent Jewish state. The rest of the page covered domestic news.

"Now look at the last page, on the left column, at the bottom," he said. There was a brief article stating that the Syrian army killed the whole town of Hama, in less than 48 hours, almost thirty thousand Arab civilians of a religious minority. There were no photos or commentary. What ever happened to objective and fair press? Sometimes I find it hard to restrain myself. But even in the midst of this mayhem, I felt a great need to expose Barbara to the realities that have been part of my life since childhood.

I was getting very tired. Ari and Matthew took photographs of the dead, and then fingerprinted them. With gloves, they scraped the insides of their cheeks for a clear DNA picture. The documents found in their pockets would also be checked. We also recovered a suitcase packed with at least $300,000.

The Montana people might figure the killers didn't even try to assassinate Barbara after collecting the money. But at the time, I was too tired to concentrate on a thorough analysis of the situation.

We sat in a big Volvo with Harel and Matthew in the front, Ari in the back with both Barbara and me leaning on him. The Mossad had supplied the car. They like high-quality fancy cars, and tonight we needed something roomier than the Passat.

I heard Ari talking with the Mossad guys on the phone as I fell asleep. I guess the last several hours had drained me more than I cared to admit, even to myself. The last thing I heard was Ari saying that we would stay in Berlin for the next several days at Schlachtensee (lake of slaughter). It's a gorgeous lake, and the idea helped me drift off to sleep happily.

I don't know how I physically made it to bed last night. All I know is that I was carried upstairs and put into my bed. A soft wool blanket was over me, and when I reached under my pillow instinctively, I found my gun waiting.

The two of us were where we were supposed to be.

30

I woke up at noon and could have slept even longer. But the lake with its sparkling beauty, only thirty feet from the house, was too enticing.

Berlin, like the Berliners, is a city of extremes. When dreary and cloudy, it can be depressing and cheerless. But on a clear day like today, it's invigorating. It's such a green city. Through the beautiful parks, where wild boars and deer still reside, one can always find a path to a lake. Germans are known to be animal lovers. Even Hitler was a vegetarian, a lesser known fact. At the same time, one can still find all the culture and stimulation that a historical European metropolis should offer. By now, I think Berlin quite surpasses Paris in that regard.

We're staying at a safe house—an elegant old villa, supplied and owned by another German 'Friend of Israel.' As I walked into the large, richly decorated living room, Barbara was talking with Harel. Matthew was there too with an older man and woman I didn't recognize. Across the room, Ari spoke with a squat middle-aged man. Two more Mossad agents were sitting in another corner, talking on the phone, slurping their coffee. I can pick those Mossad agents out of a lineup any day.

When Ari saw me, he got up and approached with a smile. He looked relaxed and in control. Once we are abroad and he has command, Ari is in his element. God made him to be what he is.

"Good morning Yael," he spoke in German and gave me a fatherly hug. "Today you have a day off, but I still wanted to introduce you to some of our friends here. They were kind enough to make themselves available on very short notice."

He shot a glance at the older man beside him and added, "This, Yael, is Professor Shönberg from the Department of Economics in the University of München."

I shook hands with him, then looked at the other man and woman, who were introduced by Matthew as mathematics and business professors, respectively, from the local university.

Their curiosity about me was evident. They were all middle-aged Germans: the woman in tweed blazer and the two men in simple cotton sport jackets.

"We are preparing a crash course program for you," Ari said. "It will teach you the basics of economics. In the next four days, aside from some morning exercise, you will breathe, eat, and think only what these guys are going to teach you—they are going to turn you into a sort of Ph.D. candidate in economics."

Ari looked at the three older Germans, then addressed Barbara. "I realize it is impossible to teach Yael what you learned in over three years. But we're going to try. She will at least be able to talk intelligently about what you have learned."

He turned to me. "I explained to our friends here that you are sort of a wonder child."

I said nothing, who am I to deny an accurate claim, and flashed what I thought might be a humble smile. But seriously, take any university student and put him or her alone for several days with a hand-picked selection of top professors and one can be amazed by how much material can be covered and understood. The average beginning student sits in massive survey classes, more concerned with looking intelligent than learning intelligently.

Besides, as I already told you, in the first year in the Department, we were taught excellent fundamentals in many academic disciplines, including a very strong basis in mathematics.

"Two other teachers are coming this evening from Israel. They also speak German, so they can assist you if any terminology needs to be explained in Hebrew."

Metzuyan (excellent), we are alone with five professors. The next several days will be arduous and challenging. I like brainy challenges. In high school, Harel, Naomi and I represented our kibbutz in academic competitions against Tel Aviv and Jerusalem kids. Guess who almost always won? Although to be honest, we can mainly thank Naomi for the victories.

"Is Harel going to learn something too or just twiddle his thumbs?" I asked.

"Would you feel better if he does it with you?" Ari asked.

I looked at Harel. He stood there grinning.

"Would you feel better if I was there to hold your hand?" He drawled. The mocking bastard. He slithered into a chair at the table and flashed everyone in the room a big smile. "God, he thinks he's so cool." I knew he wanted to take the courses even more than I did.

"I will feel way better," I smiled to Ari. "Besides, his skull seems to be getting thicker these days. It needs conditioning."

"Good, then, you both have today free. But early to bed tonight, o.k.?" Ari suggested.

He took Harel and me by the arm to the other corner of the room. He spoke Hebrew quietly, almost conspiratorially. "Do well in the next four days and before you fly to Seattle and Missoula, I will guarantee a day at home for the both of you. Naomi and Eric would definitely appreciate it.

"Our people are already in Montana preparing everything for you there," he continued. "But we don't discuss it in the next several days, because I want you to concentrate only on what these folks have to feed your little villager brains."

Naomi and Eric seemed a great distance away. I miss them so much, it's almost painful. Naomi was right about calling only when we're on our way home. Hopefully it will be soon.

31

Matthew, Harel, and I got up at six to jog around the lake. I have no idea why it is named *Schlachtensee*. Perhaps, some pogrom of Jews took place here. Until the Americans stopped these games with World War II, the Europeans couldn't live without their yearly entertainment.

With all the morning mist, and my overactive imagination, I wouldn't have been surprised to see butchered corpses floating in the dark green water. Instead, I saw a lot of overfed ducks, peacocks, and swans pleading for food on the shore. Harel and I gave them some bread we brought for bird food. We raise those beggars at the kibbutz, and they can be aggressive if you're not forthcoming.

Matthew didn't have bread ready, and the biggest swan seemed ready to take him on. A girl in our kibbutz had to be taken by helicopter to the hospital suffering from a broken arm after a similar incident. The more you feed them, the less inhibited they become. Matthew is crème de la crème of the Israeli Secret Service, so I figured he could deal with those birds without our assistance. He is, after all, a professional.

After our usual health nut breakfast, we went to the room where our teaching team waited. Two more professors, from the University of Tel Aviv, had joined the party. They introduced themselves as Doctors Livnat and Blumfeld. I recognized them because they were among the teachers we had when we first joined the Department.

The five academics sat behind a large wooden table with a green blackboard as a backdrop. Barbara, Harel, and I sat on the other side facing them. Ari sat at the head of the table, flanked by Matthew. Textbooks were piled on the table, leaving space only for a bowl of nuts and berries and a few bottles of mineral water. There was also blank paper and sharpened pencils for notes.

Ari got up and asked for everyone's full attention. He loves this.

"Before we begin, I'd like to say a few short words and then I will leave you all alone for the next four days." He spoke only in German, and he focused mainly on the three professors.

"I would like to thank you again, in the name of the State of Israel, for the service you have done for us in the past . . . and that which you do for us now. I hope that one day, although that day might be in the distant future, we will be able to give you the whole picture of what we are doing. I mean the more juicy details of our project." He winked, and the five academics grinned and nodded.

Ari continued. "Just know that your help will have been essential in a valiant enterprise to ensure international justice and safety—not only for Jews, but for many people of the world."

I glanced at Harel. His face was stony, and I could tell he was barely winning the struggle to suppress a smile. Ari was in politician mode. He was on a roll.

Ari emphasized. "We are in your debt. Words cannot express our appreciation and gratitude."

His crisp voice was in accordance with the speech. Marcus shouldn't worry about a capable replacement. The three professors looked honored, but the honor was all ours.

Many people have helped us. I'm always amazed at how many professors from the United States and Germany like to come to Israel for a year to do research, and then become such good friends and staunch supporters of the country. Edward Taylor, one of the three main physicists who built the first hydrogen bomb for the United States, once said that one of the things he cherished most was the prize for his achievements he received from the Israeli Institute for Technology in Haifa.

Ari now directed his charm to Barbara. "Barbara, I'd like to take this opportunity to commend you for your courage and help. We'll need more of your cooperation as time passes. I've already talked with you about what we need in the coming weeks, but since I think you are under some risk at the moment, we are going to transfer you to Israel at the end of the week. When it is all over, you'll have a place in graduate school at the University of Tel Aviv—if you wish. School tuition and living expenses will be fully covered by us.

"You will, of course, learn Hebrew first." He grinned.

"Really?" Barbara looked quite surprised, but delighted.

"Think about all those sun-tanned Israeli students," I whispered in her ear. She looked already quite fond of Benny—one of our Mossad guys. I only complain about their job performance. I have nothing against their physiques or charm.

Israeli boys are fascinated by—or, one could say, suffer an affliction concerning—gentile women. On a friend's kibbutz near Jerusalem, I swear that half the guys were married to blonde Scandinavian and German girls who came for the sun and stayed for the Israeli boys who adored them.

Who am I to talk? I married a gentile, and I guess I sometimes show him off too. Besides, the offspring of such couples always look so cute, almost celestial. I hope that soon Eric and I will have one too.

Ari and Matthew left, but not before thanking the two Israeli professors and shaking hands with everyone. There is so much work for them to do before Harel and I leave. Once in Missoula, Harel and I will be on center stage, but a lot will depend on the preliminary groundwork. I feel better knowing that Matthew and Ari are taking care of it personally.

Barbara will have to be smuggled to Israel on falsified papers, a task that the Mossad guys, especially Benny, will handle with glee. Every detail will be checked and double-checked again by Ari and Matthew.

The female professor, the oldest of the group, began to talk.

"Before we begin, I would like to point out two essential points that Yael and you Harel need to bear in mind." She paused for a second. One could tell that she had spent some time in Israel. She pronounced my name correctly. Non-Israelis rarely do.

"All of us here look at this situation as a challenge to mold you into a graduate student within four days." She smiled to me and the rest of the staff.

"At least," one of the Israeli professors said, "she is very talented in math, and, I might add, has a decent knowledge of advanced calculus and basic linear algebra."

"That makes things much easier for us," she added.

"I should admit, however, that when I first heard about this idea, it sounded absurd—to teach, in a few short days, material which takes years to master, no matter how smart the student. Although, it makes a difference when you use a method where you focus on just two students and give your full attention."

Nobody said a word. Besides, I don't know why she thought I had a confidence issue about learning the material—especially when Harel was there to compete with me. We listened anyway, not saying anything, pretending we were just the average Israelis. Let them wonder!

I nodded and noisily opened up my notebook to a fresh page. Harel coughed and sat up straight, respectfully cocking his head. I grinned at her.

"Thank you for these encouraging words, I feel much better now."

She knew nothing about the virtual chess game Harel and I were playing. We made a bet this morning: Whichever of us convince the professors of our genius by the end of the last day would win. The loser would have to clean the dining room of the kibbutz for three months . . . poor Harel.

So the professors began with the theories of Adam Smith, the father of pure, all-out, sheer capitalism and free competition, kind of a creepy guy. Harel and I tried to appear interested as the professors read funny little excerpts of Smith's journal—boring, boring, boring. Then to Thomas Malthus and Ricardo, both were sure the human race was doomed through overpopulation and starvation. I wondered what the pair would have said if they could see things now, two hundred years later. More than half of the children in America are overweight.

Harel made his first move; he came up with some grand, philosophical question. The professors beamed and took turns answering Harel, each in reverent agreement with the preceding colleague.

Then they went on to Karl Marx—who wrote about the plight of the workers while sheltered in the British Museum, when perhaps his most personal experience with the proletariat was during a hot affair with a cleaning lady. He himself was poor, but he was lucky to marry a wealthy upper class woman.

We moved on to Alfred Marshall. With some precocious and presumptuous rhetoric, I spewed some outrageous opinions linking Marx to Marshall. The professors raised their eyebrows, then narrowed their eyes, and fought for the right to attack me. With heated words, they responded to my statement, but eventually turned on each other in the process. I sat back and let them ecstatically duke it out. After a good half-hour academic brawl, the five colleagues finally calmed down. Some wiped their faces with a handkerchief, and Frau Professor Klein's lip was quivering happily. Oh, they were practically trembling as they sat there, panting in the aftermath. I turned to Harel with a slow, victorious grin.

After a brief history discussion, the professors gave us a short introduction to economics, adding in basic notions when necessary. Information was given in both German and English. "Don't try to remember it," one of them told us. "Just try to understand the basic concepts. We summarized everything we teach you. Memorize it after the four days are over."

It seemed to me that the technical vocabulary, as in many social sciences, only serves to obscure things. The Law of Diminishing Return, for example, says that beyond a certain point, increasing input won't increase output. If you keep increasing the number of workers on a farm, at some point, you won't continue to increase production. For example, beyond a certain number, the workers might get on each other's nerves.

Some books waste so many pages, so many tables, and so many graphs, just to explain this one concept. One teacher told us that some books actually use differential equations to add a scholarly edge to the business. This reminds me of psychology. They don't have any scientific basis for most of their theories, as oppose to medicine, so they deal with their hang-ups by inventing a lot of daunting terminology.

Harel says that I sound too cynical when I say this. He believes every field develops specialized vocabulary as it expands.

After the basic concepts, they gave the tenets of micro and macroeconomics. Microeconomics: Specific cases of individual products of company's price changes. Macroeconomics: Same stuff, but on a national scale. John Maynard Keyes, the man who saved capitalism, introduced and developed many terms and concepts in these fields. As an aside, one of the professors mentioned that Keynes had strongly opposed the terms at Versailles that treated the Germans so harshly. Funny to think how life might have changed had the others listened to him. Without the humiliation of Germany, would Hitler have risen to power? And if there were no Hitler I'd have been now a German girl and Israel would not have existed. It is a shame no body listened to Keynes.

By the end of the day, they covered close to a hundred concepts and to be honest, I wasn't totally overwhelmed. I won't claim to have remembered everything, but the ideas were not difficult. The professors handed us pages of summaries and explanations of key terms.

Harel and I wanted Barbara to join us for a walk around the lake, but the Mossad boys had other ideas. They were still concerned for her safety.

We compromised, I gave her my clothes, and someone came up with a black wig. It looked funny, but given the situation, it was exciting for Barbara. Plus, one of the Mossad guys joined us for her "protection." It happened to be Benny.

We ended up taking two walks around the lake.

"God, guys, you're so down to earth," Barbara said. "It's fun being with all of you, which surprises me, all things considered. Maybe you remind me of Rachel and her sense of humor. Only two days ago, I had the most shocking experience of my life and now I'm in a world I never knew before and I feel content. I almost feel guilty, especially about Marian. Do you think it's normal?"

It was funny answering this question on the banks of Schlachtensee. Of course we said it was normal. I guess those fast transitions from one reality to the next have become a way of life for us, and we don't even reflect on it anymore.

Harel suggested that we go to a small coffee shop for a piece of German chocolate cake. After the last few days, we deserved it.

32

The next day was dedicated to econometrics, the mathematical analysis of economics.

Not to brag, but for the past 10 years our kibbutz out scored all high schools in the country in math. We were not born smarter; our private teachers just made sure that we didn't miss any key concepts in math. Home schooling has its advantages.

I remember now, last night I made a resolution—I decided to become humble. This might be the only way I can keep Eric. In America one can get away with murder, but you have to pretend to be humble. The problem is that this job makes a person self-assured to the extreme and definitely too assertive. A scene like two nights ago, for example, can be petrifying. But we can not afford to be paralyzed with fear. You must convince yourself that you can do anything—then convince everyone else.

If there is a mission that involves pure physical strength or supreme knowledge of computers, I would let Harel lead the way. If it comes to shooting or anything concerned with wit, I'd take the matter on myself. Specialization increases our chances of survival.

Harel or Matthew could have easily done what I did the other night. But imagine that there had been four and not three opponents. As a matter of fact, imagine there had been five people in the room, and at least one with a ready gun. In such a scenario, the only way to make it is to shoot on the run. Obviously, the targets move, too. I don't want to say that Harel or Matthew or Ari are incapable of such a feat, but my chances to survive, in such a scenario, are better. I could never forgive myself if one of them got hurt.

Anyway, today we took everything we learned yesterday by simple graphs and definitions and analyzed it all mathematically. We went through seven to nine examples, using differential calculus equations and linear algebra. In principle, if I commit the examples to memory, I should be able to handle almost any question thrown at me by a professor in Montana.

After each example, we were called to the board, presented with a problem and the basic graph, and asked to develop the theme mathematically. We were then allowed to look at the papers we received yesterday.

I can't help thinking it is a colossal waste of time. The analysis looks impressive, but it's useless. Even with all the math and statistics we know, economists still consistently fail to make correct predictions about economical developments.

But my focus is different. All I want is to look scholarly. Barbara went to the board first, and, as long as she didn't have to deal with integrals or complicated matrixes, she did quite well. The professors were gracious enough and helped her without causing embarrassment. Everyone learned, and I really began to appreciate our teachers.

Harel was next. He was given a more difficult problem. That creep was smooth, as smooth as smooth can be. An outsider would have thought he was a nerd whose only pleasure in life was to solve mathematical puzzles in economics. Our teachers couldn't hide the fact that they were very impressed. I found myself looking for flaws.

I smiled when they gave me my problem. I developed the model as deeply as I could, using a couple of integrations techniques Harel hadn't. It was not really necessary, but what the heck. We have a bet. After I finished, they all looked stunned. I think we sufficiently killed any stereotypes they might have had about military personnel, at least, our kind of military personnel.

33

Harel and I met in the kitchen during breakfast, and we leaned our heads in and rubbed our hands together with glee

"Ah, capital. How much do you and my pennywise, altruistic sister have, Harel?" I asked in the most avaricious tone. "Come on, we need some startup capital here. Where can we get our hands on some?"

"Come on, doesn't Eric come from old money? You have cash, I know it," He spouted back. We decided that the kibbutz had a stranglehold on all our money, and we would hassle it out of them. Then, to pay them back, we'd give them a generous percentage of the profit, like real stockbrokers.

Back in class, we looked at the same issues, but purely from the point of view of the investor or the shareholder. We listened to the touching American saga of Warren Buffett, his ideas and his investment strategy.

Barbara had briefed us beforehand on the subject from her point of view. This was, after all, the theme that fascinated Rachel and her, and it might have had some connection to her death. I think it's almost a given that it does. Otherwise, we are really shooting in the dark.

As for Buffett, his principles are remarkably simple. He used them to become the second richest man in the world. In contrast to all other tycoons, he made his fortune not by coming up with a new idea or concept like Gates or Ford, or by finding oil in his backyard. He just bought shares in companies which were cheap, or undervalued, and then kept them forever. The strangest thing: He used public information to make his investment decisions.

Most investors buy shares in order to make a fast buck. They're called day traders. Even the majority of people who buy mutual funds and keep them for many years, believing they are long-term investors like Buffett, really operate under an illusion. Most mutual fund managers don't keep the same shares for long, something the average fund investor doesn't realize. It's why Buffett-like success is rarely, if ever, reached by mutual fund investors.

The second point that most people overlook with Buffett is the fact that he doesn't believe in diversification. Diversification is exactly what all other mutual funds managers practice. By investing in only a few companies and selecting them solely based on their real value, he managed to create enormous wealth.

Buffett himself didn't buy those companies directly. He bought them through his company, Berkshire Hathaway. It's a holding company, meaning it holds a huge amount of the shares of any company he chooses to invest in. Actually, Buffett could have controlled the management of those companies and altered the way they ran. But since he buys only shares of well-managed companies, he rarely involves himself personally in those matters, although he does sit on some of their boards.

By the end of day, we had learned an enormous amount of information about stock market investments. It all boils down to the fact that a share is actually a small piece of a company rather than a piece of paper. If people remember this, they would not buy and sell their shares so fast.

Ironically, by being less greedy than most investors, Buffet and his partner Charlie Mongul outperformed the rest. It helped that they both have a broad interests in many other areas. One of the main traps when investing in the stock market is the fact that superficially it seems so easy.

I still had trouble connecting these facts to Rachel. In this regard, there was a long line of questions that Barbara and these professors couldn't answer for me.

34

Fourth and last day, thank God. It was a big one for me. I had to stand in front of the class and answer questions fired at me by the professors. Each asked me questions that they would, or could, ask their own graduate students. All of the teachers, including the Germans, posed their questions in English, although periodically they stopped and asked me for the German translations of terms.

I was allowed to use the handouts, and I proved that I had command of them. Still, I knew it wouldn't hurt to review them in Seattle. We'll have a week there to recoup from the jet lag.

Tonight, I feel so drained. I've never tried to pump so much, in such a short time, into my brain. Harel and I were too tired to argue afterward and decided our competition had ended in a draw.

The Mossad guys organized a very nice homemade dinner for all of us at the house. It was fun to joke with our professors and talk to them about subjects unrelated to economics. All of them had been in Israel several times, and one of them could even say some simple sentences in Hebrew. They all were born either after the war or were still children when it happened. So guilt was not what pushed them to help us. They were just kind humans who don't follow the herd, I guess.

Ari and Matthew were already in Israel. I can only hope that Harel and I, as well as the Mossad guys, hosted our new friends and colleagues in a way that really reflected our appreciation. From the way they laughed and hugged us before they left, I think we succeeded.

35

We returned to Israel after a direct flight from Berlin. Barbara, who got a new identification, was taken by car to Rome, a city known to be very lax on border control. From there, she and her escorts flew to Tel Aviv.

If the guys from Missoula try to track her down, they will find nothing. The body of her friend was disposed of properly, and the German government will be notified once the mission has been completed. As far as anyone knows, Barbara is on her way to the United States. That is what she wrote in a letter to her parents. It is also in a note left in her kitchen, addressed to the three students subletting the apartment next month.

In the next several days, Barbara will be questioned about every detail of her life. The plan is still for me to take her identity, which means I need to know every thing. Her parents are the hitch. The Skibbe family is quite close to their daughter; they like to talk to Barbara at least three times a week.

Their calls will be relayed via satellite to Israel from the phone in Montana, and Barbara can talk with them as much as her heart desires. The generous Israeli tax payers will foot the bill. Even if somebody were to tap the lines, they would not realize that Barbara is not talking from Montana. With a voice analyzer, of course, two voices could be heard coming from one person. That's a problem for Rafi to handle, though I doubt it will surface.

Each project is planned meticulously, but ultimately, when Harel and I arrive in the States—hopefully with Ari and Matthew—we will be on our own and unable to anticipate everything.

Harel's cover is to be my needy, jealous boyfriend from Hanover, a guy who can't leave me alone and whose possessive nature will get us out of a lot of pesky social obligations. We chose Hanover because that's where something similar to Harel's high-brow German accent is spoken. It doesn't matter, although we might encounter some native German speakers, we are unlikely to meet those able to distinguish a guy from Hanover from one from Stuttgart. I think we've got our bases covered.

36

We're back to the mountains today. We didn't tell Naomi and Eric that this is our last vacation and that next time we'll be home for good. We didn't tell them where we're headed, either. There are security considerations, and what's the purpose of making them worry? They have learned not to ask anyway.

In all the missions we've been in so far, we've been the ones to initiate things—even in cases of reprisal. We gain the advantages through surprise. The enemy doesn't know who we are until the last possible minute and until that point we try even to manipulate his own decisions.

This case, however, might be different. Once I enter the University and present myself to the registration office and to the head of the graduate program, somebody is going to take notice; somebody who likes to push needles in the necks of their enemies.

So we will adopt a wait-and-see approach. My gender is an advantage, since no one expects something truly deadly from a woman. Perhaps, the dead assassin in Germany is a sign of feminist emancipation, but for now, I can rely on underestimation from any opponent.

These thoughts invaded me at the dinner table, and they would not go away. We ate with my parents and Harel's father and grandfather. As the kids turned Harel and Grandpa into a jungle gym, Naomi blessed us with her new thoughts on the universe.

Harel and I exchanged equally dispassionate glances. We didn't tell Naomi that after the last several days in Berlin, we didn't want to hear anything more complicated than info about the new greenhouse Eric built for her organic vegetables and his roses. That or whether she had any extra cash stashed away for Harel's and my investment schemes. I don't understand why Harel and I never thought about the stock market before.

I also never thought the poet I found in Seattle would become so fond of gardening. He's even mixing several kinds of bushes in an attempt to develop a black rose. Grandpa claims it's impossible; he tried it himself for several years.

Naomi, still being hugged by Harel, looked at me, her eyes shining. "I have great news about teleportation."

"You have great news about what?" I questioned.

"Quantum teleportation."

"What is that?" I asked, hoping that one of her babies would scream for attention and save my day. No luck. They looked content with their great grandpa.

Eric hugged me and kissed my cheek. He said, "I will explain it all to you later, sweetie. It's not so complicated."

Even Harel's Grandpa was smiling knowingly. I guess Harel and I were the only ones at the table, maybe in the whole kibbutz who didn't know what it meant. Naomi had been subjecting the whole population to her great revelations.

"It is the concept of moving matter from one place to the next without using any transportation modes. Sort of like beaming you up . . . you know, as in Star Trek," Eric explained with obvious pride.

"And what does the word quantum have to do with it?' I asked.

"Simply, because they might succeed in doing it on a very small scale. That is, on the quantum level," Naomi clarified, stretching out the words to let us know it was a stupid question.

"I thought you said quantum physics is wrong and Einstein was right . . . I mean, right when he still objected to quantum physics," I tried to remind her.

"I thought it over. Einstein was wrong. He was wrong in the beginning, that is, when he objected to it." She made a grand gesture with her arms over her bulging, pregnant belly.

"What about that teleportation?" I asked, not caring to know. I was trying to avoid the lecture on how my brain had stagnated. I admire Harel's reserve with her at times.

"Well, they might actually do it soon. The scientists base their experiments on quantum mechanics. If they were to succeed on a molecular level, wouldn't it be exciting?"

"Oh yeah, I can't wait."

For the rest of the night I found myself wanting to talk about gunfire amidst statues, but the secrecy required in our line of work limits my storytelling possibilities.

37

In the morning, we all drove to Kinneret, the Sea of Galilee. We stopped at an Arab village in route and picked up some fresh bread from an old friend of ours—Kahra. It was delicious, but the cheese she gave us, courtesy of her sheep, was almost better. It's not really cheese; it's more like yogurt left overnight on cotton cloth to drain the water. It's called lebna, and she mixes it with homegrown green olives.

Their small village is located exactly between our kibbutz and the lake. The white stone houses are built on the mountainside spread along the eastern slopes that descend into the Jordan Valley. The face of the mountain has turned into a massive set of stairs, and it's on these that they grow their main plants: olives, wine grapes, and tobacco.

Kahra, who is a widow, began to work in our fig orchard after her husband died. Her male cousins don't like us too much, but they don't like Kahra much either—she is salty and has a sharp tongue, for a woman that is. They think our kibbutz has had a bad influence on her.

Today, she crouched on the porch while we ate, furtively dragging on a cigarette; now and then, her eyes, painted with blue shadow, would narrow, and she would hold the cigarette down. She finally threw the butt over the porch ledge and sat up, smoothing out her raw silk dress. "What, Kahra," I asked, "What would they do to you if they caught you smoking?"

"Nothing, Yael," she scoffed and hoarsely laughed, "Because they think I would cut off their most precious gems." A small, gold scabbard suddenly appeared in her hand, and she cackled. She put the knife back in the folds of her gown. "I just don't want the stress, the discussion, you know, Yael," she smiled.

Since we are friends, she always gives us everything free, including kisses and blessings. In order not to take advantage of this typical genuine Arab hospitality, we always bring some gifts. This time we brought some great new sprinklers from our kibbutz.

Her son wasn't there. He's an infantry officer, and his mother told us that he wouldn't come home this weekend. Unlike other Arabs, the Druze minority serves like the rest of us in the army. Their relations with the rest of the Arabs are even worse than ours, so they joined our side in the War of Independence. They saw it as an opportunity to become free of Muslim oppression.

The Druze have their own religion, around 1,000 years old, based on the teachings of the prophet al Hakim. Their lack of proselytizing makes their belief system similar to Judaism. They are fairly tolerant, at least by Arab standards.

We continued on the highway to Kinneret. We found it sparkling and rippling from a hot wind, which felt like it had blown all the way from the Sahara Desert. The Arabs call the wind the Hamseen, which refers to the fifty days during which it's likely to occur, and it induces tropical temperatures of close to 110° Farenheight. Even our water-shy dogs were splashing in the water.

I was amazed that Harel and Naomi's oldest daughter could already swim. She is barely three. I wonder what her world will be like when she joins the army. Everyone talks about peace, but I don't know a single case in history where a democracy had real, lasting peace with totalitarian regimes—and that's what we're surrounded by.

We came home early. Tomorrow morning we will return to base and I wanted some time alone with Eric. The four of us had supper together in our tiny kitchen, and Harel made his famous pancakes. He's the undisputed champion in this area.

It reminded me of the course we took about Americans. They tried to teach us everything about the culture, including, of course, the local cuisine. Harel and I refused to eat hamburgers because we are vegetarians and then we refused to eat the pancakes because of the preservatives in the maple syrup. I meant it when I said that Naomi, Harel and I fully intend to be the first people from Israel to reach the age of two hundred. Modern Israel, I should say. Some biblical guys excluded. Methusalah made it to nine hundred and something.

Harel and Naomi left around nine o'clock, and Eric and I stayed in the kitchen. He put a candle on the table and turned off the lights. There was a warm, romantic glow in the room, and I was glad it was dark outside. I had a strange combination of feelings, but I didn't say anything for what seemed like an hour.

"Eric, I don't know why I am telling you this, but this mission is the last one. When I come back, I'm staying for good."

He pondered this for a few moments.

"Why are you telling me this?" he asked. "It's out of character."

"Because I want you to know that . . . well, how should I say it," I smiled at him. "You'll be off the hook. Naomi won't kill you if you leave me."

"What about you?" he said. "Everyone tells me that you are tougher than Harel. Even your sister says so. I may be off the hook with her, but will you kill me if I want to go back to the United States?"

We both laughed. No one is tougher than Harel, even Harel.

"I kill only mean guys," I assured him. "You are the sweetest man I know, except for Duncan. I don't want you to go. God only knows how much I want you to stay, especially now, when my job is almost over." Duncan was lying on the floor in front of us, deep in his dreams.

"If I leave, what will happen to you?" he asked again.

"I'm a tough country girl. You know that, you just now said it yourself."

"Is it a dangerous mission, I mean the one right now?"

"Piece of cake," I assured him. If he wanted to skirt an issue, I could, too.

"What do you want me to say, Yael?" he asked quietly. "You know I hate your job."

"Yeah, well, I hope I don't die of boredom when I'm back here playing gardening wife," I lashed out, wanting to bite my tongue a second later.

Eric stared at me for a moment. "See. I don't even know you," he muttered. "Not at all, I sometimes think. Your reactions are like a stranger's to me. Your venom is foreign, like this country, and you know what, Yael, if gardening is the only thing here that gives you peace, so be it. Deal with it. I don't think that is asking too much, after you have asked that I wait here, alone for weeks on end, having to argue with little kibbutz grandmothers."

"Well, then, do you still love me?" I asked.

"Yes. Love is still what I feel for you right now. We will see if it's enough." He got up and walked out of the kitchen. I sat at the counter, playing with a piece of lemon peel, then jumped up and stormed after him with a growl.

"You know, Eric, I wonder how you would feel if I don't come back from this mission, and that is the last thing you will have said to me. That makes me feel quite estranged from you too," I fumed. "You don't know what I have to face for this job-you-love-to-hate, you don't even know how close you sometimes are to being rid of me once and for all, and then free to leave this godforsaken country. But you know what, fuck you, because I can't live in any other country and feel existentially safe, so I'm going to stay here and face death, and you know why . . . For a goddamn right to live in the first place."

Eric swung around with a look of disgust and barked, "Please, Yael, do not even try to feed me that Zionist line of crap. Come on, you know perfectly well that you could live easily in the United States, and no one would even notice or care that you're Jewish. Please."

"You disgust me," I was ice cold. "Your goddamn grandfathers, after biding their sweet time to join World War II, sent back boats and boats of Jews to Germany. And yet, your stupid generation still believes America went to war in Europe to save the Jews. Don't give me that Spielberg line." I grasped for a breath and kept on. "And I refuse to be treated as an intellectual dancing bear, and live in New York, and go to the synagogue, and be accused of money hoarding, and meet Jews who have changed their names from Goldstein to Gordon. Or meet Jews that are critical of Israel because unconsciously they want to prove to their gentile friends that they are 'good Jews'. Oh and furthermore, I refuse to leave Harel and Naomi to fight off crazy Syrians, crazy Lebanese, and crazy Jordanians, crazy Iranians, and crazy Iraqis on their own. And I refuse to hear of them getting bombed in the supermarket by some bloodthirsty Palestinian, and read about their deaths by a press which celebrates the valor of a fifteen-year-old, programmed terrorist."

"Listen to you," Eric interrupted sharply. "You sound like a crazy settler who likes to club Palestinian children to death just for throwing stones because they're sick and tired of living in refugee camps."

"Stones? Eric, stones?" I pleaded. "These children, as you call these little brainwashed automatons, are throwing Molotov cocktails, or have bombs strapped to their waists.

102

And let's say you have one really throwing stones, Eric, and let's say you ask this little Palestinian child, what is your political Christmas wish? Now, if you are the BBC or CNN reporter, the child will say, I want peace, I want freedom, I want a better school and no more mean Israeli soldiers. But you know what the child will say to you if you have no camera? He will say, I want every last fucking Jew dead, I want an end to their democratic presence, their Western stores, their loose women, and their godless lifestyle.

"Damn it, Eric, if I were killed, would you want the killers to pay?"

"I'm not sure I believe in revenge," he answered righteously.

'What about not getting away with murder?"

He took some time to answer. I know this kind of stuff is unfamiliar to him.

"Look, to be honest Yael, I don't really care," he finally answered. "I just want to see you back alive."

"Do you still love me?" I asked again.

"Trust me on that one," he said. "I love the 'you' I see. It's the 'you' I don't see who is difficult to love—because she's a complete stranger to me. How can I reconcile the playful, loving health food nut I sleep next to, compared with a woman of steel who, for all I know, is taking out foreign agents with an Uzi?"

He was getting into very painful territory. We needed to backtrack.

"Will you stay here, please, until I get back from this trip?" I asked quietly. "I swear things will be simpler then."

"Deal, if you tell your sister to shut up about quantum physics." He managed to laugh.

It was, perhaps, an unfair question to ask him. Of course he's not going to leave if I'm in danger of dying. No one wants to be seen in that way.

I regretted later bringing up the mission. What if this were the last time I'd see him? This man here, asleep next to me, is the only male companion I've had. He was my first. He may be the last. I hope so. I want him to stick around.

38

Back at base, preparations were in full swing, and not a thing was left to chance. Harel and I focused primarily on our new identities. I tried to learn everything about Barbara: childhood, upbringing, hobbies, friends, drug experiences, and love life. She was very cooperative, even telling us about her experimentation with homosexuality.

"I was attracted to Rachel," she said. "She might have been attracted to me too. But neither one of us had the confidence, or the experience, I guess, to bring it up. It was probably better that way."

She was, essentially, the German student next door. No unexpected revelations or startling disclosures. Perhaps, she is a bit more open-minded and wild than most Germans. Depends, I guess, where you are coming from.

She smoked marijuana at parties. That's common enough. She didn't drink a drop, though, partially because of childhood issues with her mother, a recovering alcoholic. She tried LSD twice, and once, before an examination, she sniffed cocaine with her classmates to "keep my mind sharp"—also not so uncommon among students.

She gave more details than we needed, but we thanked her for her honesty. Most people try to hide or revise their own history. She seemed comfortable with hers.

Meanwhile, under the name of a California straw man, we bought a secluded house with several acres of land just outside of Missoula. This particular house was selected because of its elevated location, seclusion, and adjoining guesthouse. The place would be rented to Matthew under the alias of Mike Jones.

It is not so uncommon to buy property, because it assures more privacy than renting. No landlords hovering around, waiting to ask awkward questions. When things cool off, the property is sold, sometimes for a nice profit.

A lot of equipment would be installed prior to our arrival. If anyone paid us a visit, we would be forewarned, day or night. Of course, we have no idea how they will eventually try to get me. How do Americans like to say it? That is the $64 thousand dollar question.

Ari and Matthew have already left to begin preparations. They are going to rent another house in the University area, and it will be occupied by one of our former agents, Solomon. He's now doing his Ph.D. in economics at the University of Be'er Sheva, but we recalled him to do my homework for me. He might come in handy if I have to take a test.

Rafi, our techie, will be joining Ari and Matthew shortly to finish up the electronic installation at the new place. The Mossad offered us one of their Seattle men, but we kindly declined. As added support, perhaps we'd use them later. But we will take care of the basics first.

I couldn't imagine being without Rafi, anyway. I love the guy, but Rafi has a love-hate relationship with himself. He is one of the finest computer and technical nerds in Israel but would rather be an agent. So he walks around in a leather jacket and Ray—Bans. Thanks to hours of obsessive weight lifting and calorie shakes, he does look like a Mr. Universe—albeit a short and hairy one. Moreover, he proudly carries a custom-made automatic pistol, but couldn't hit someone from twenty yards away. Rafi would rather be a tough guy than a nerd. It's just not in the cards.

We call him Sylvester Stallone to keep him happy, and it works most of the time. But one day last year, he came to the base, shoulders drooping, and his head down. This transformation from Israeli to New York Jew was staggering, but given the story, it was understandable.

His younger brother, Alexander, married an Iraqi woman. Jewish, but nonetheless, Iraqi. Jews reflect their homeland culture. Rafi's old naïve senile German father was no match for his new daughter-in-law, and she began to coax him into signing documents that would rob Rafi of his part of the future inheritance.

Our hero is a good family man with three sweet children and a dedicated wife and mother. But Marcus has his reason for not allowing Rafi do what we do. First, Rafi has his family, and second, Rafi's lack of street smarts, being the tender city boy that he is. Fortunately for him, Rafi asked Harel and me for advice about his sister-in-law predicament.

We told him not to worry, and that we'd handle things for him from then on. He was skeptical, but we assured him everything would be all right. We had dealt with more diabolical creatures than his sister-in-law. It turned into sort of a private project, and we got Matthew and Ari involved, too.

Ultimately, we had to call upon Danny, Rafi's older brother, an agent emeritus. He'd been a very good agent. The two brothers have nothing in common except their close brotherly bond. At the time this situation arose, Danny was studying Medicine in Germany. When he comes home to visit on semester breaks, he still trains with us.

So we called him in Germany, and he confirmed what Rafi told us. He personally didn't care about the money. Like all of us here he confronted life and death to the point that he had separated himself from the money rat race. He also made a fortune before returning to school, but that's a story in itself.

Danny, unlike his emotional brother, maintained a decent relationship with his father and a polite one with his youngest brother and his lovely wife. So we arranged some documents stating that buildings had been found in East Berlin which had been confiscated by the Nazis from Jewish families. Nothing strange here, a lot of property was never given back to the Holocaust survivors. But this block of buildings was being returned to the owners, and the father of Danny, Rafi, and Alexander was a primary owner.

Danny, as the only German speaking son, would be sole representative, since the elderly father was in no condition to deal with financial matters. Danny was after all also the one who "discovered" the lost treasure. Authentic looking 'certificates' were prepared by some experts in our Department which indicated that the worth of the buildings was at least twenty-five million Deutschmarks, at the time equivalent to more than fifteen million dollars. With greedy people the best lies are the big lies. I think Hitler said that too.

With the promise of fortune, peace and harmony came back to the family. All it took was a quick signing over of the other parts of the inheritance to Danny—just to make the entire three-way split, including new and old money, easier. No one suspected anything treacherous. Danny had always been his father's hero.

By the time the Iraqi sister-in-law began to suspect something was fishy, the father passed away. Needless to say, Rafi got his due share—as did the rascal Alexander, thanks to Danny's benevolence.

So why do I recount this story in my journal? For a bit of comic relief, and I suppose, as supporting evidence for my acutely cynical view of fellow humans.

39

We had our last talk with Marcus. Solomon, our other man in Missoula, and Rachel's mother was there, too. Marcus was being tender which is atypical of him. I didn't know if that was because of the presence of Rachel's mother or because he thought he might be sending us to our death.

"Rachel's mother wanted to say goodbye to you both," Marcus told us after we sat down. "While looking through Rachel's stuff yesterday, she found some more interesting papers." He pointed at a bunch of papers which Solomon was reading.

"Basically," Solomon said, "they deal with holding companies and the idea that by buying relatively few shares of a big company, one can exert a lot of influence on very big corporations."

"How?" Harel asked.

"She explains it here, and she uses Buffett as an example. He bought less than eight percent of Coca-Cola's shares and, by doing so, he could significantly influence who ran the company and how. Not to mention, that he was then in a position to know first-hand inside information."

"Inside information?" I asked.

"Yes, the information that heads of the company know before Wall Street does. It's like having the one up on the market, allowing someone to buy and sell stock before anyone sees the reason.

"But that is not the way Buffett made his fortune, is it?" Harel said.

"No, remarkably. She mentions that after Buffett buys a piece of the company he barely interferes with the management. As a matter of fact, one of his main criteria for buying a company is to buy companies which are well managed, so he will not have to become too involved."

Solomon looked at the papers again. "Yes here's something relating to that. She says that Buffett has an elevated sense of integrity—an exception to the Wall Street rule."

"So what's the point?" I asked. 'Do you think the paper tells us anything new?"

Our wise Solomon took his time before he spoke, "Well, she was clearly fascinated by the possibility of controlling a multi-million company with relatively small amounts of money. Still many millions, mind you. The investing hysteria in the U.S. also piqued her interest, especially the fact that so many people hold shares in companies but that as owners they still have no say in running the companies."

"The owners being the shareholders, you mean?" I said.

"Precisely. Your training sunk in, it seems. Yes it is an overlooked fact."

The training hadn't totally sunk in. It took me a second to come up with this point. The stuff was still not in my active memory.

Harel jumped in. "On one hand, you say that because of the huge number of shareholders, one can, with relatively few shares, control a company. On the other hand, if I understood you correctly, you said that shareholders lost control to management?"

"One doesn't contradict the other," Solomon explained patiently. "The fact that the shareholders are such a huge and diverse group allows the management to be elected by a very small interest group. As long as the majority doesn't become united and focused enough to vote out the directors."

"Is this always the situation in corporate America?" Marcus asked.

"In most cases this is the situation, but not always. Not too long ago, a big U.S. company, Pfizer wanted to acquire a smaller company. That would have meant that the shareholders of the small company would make big gains because Pfizer was ready to buy each share for more money than it was worth at the time of the offer. Yet, the management of the smaller company tried to stop it because they cared more about their own jobs and special benefits than the interest of their shareholders."

"What was the end result?" asked Harel.

"The shareholders won, in that case, because Pfizer helped organize them with a huge and expensive campaign. But this, too, was an exception, not the rule."

Harel is always considerate; he cut off the discussion and included Rachel's mother into the conversation by changing the subject. "When we come back I hope to see you."

I wondered what he has in mind but didn't say anything.

"I more than hope so," she said. "And again, I'm grateful for what both of you are doing."

She looked in my direction. "Mr. Marcus told me not to attempt to convince you not to go. He said that he himself tried to talk you out of it."

"Yes, I was adamant about it," I told her with a straight face. 'Rachel would have done it for me. We have our own internal ethics here."

"You're a bunch of sweet liars, but you all have my blessing." She left the room after hugging each of us.

• His mission accomplished, Harel wasted no time resuming the conversation. "Do you know what struck me before, when you told us about the newly discovered papers?" Nobody answered, so he continued. "It struck me that Rachel had not said or 'discovered' anything that is already not public knowledge. Public, I mean, to anyone who is involved in the investment world."

"What are you saying?" Marcus snapped.

"I just stated a fact. I don't know what it means."

I left it alone. Harel had an idea up his sleeve, but didn't care to share it right then. I wasn't too concerned about it. As soon as we were alone, we would discuss what he had in mind.

It was like our childhood, when Harel and I played combat games against the other kids. Even when we were fighting on one team together with others, we were always a team in ourselves. He and I against the world, and I can't see any reason for us to change our ways.

40

We didn't fly directly to the U.S. First we flew to Frankfurt under different names. While there, we had a driver take us into the city where we could buy some last-minute "German" items and Harel could get a haircut. Short hair and an unshaven face—'two days' beard—were his orders for appearance. My hair was dyed to a light brown.

In Frankfurt, we again received new papers. I became Barbara Skibbe. Harel was now Martin Hainz, my wealthy, jealous, good-for-nothing boyfriend. From this moment on we would speak strictly German with each other, unless we knew for a fact we weren't under surveillance.

We took a plane to Amsterdam a day later and then continued on to Minneapolis. The Amsterdam-Minneapolis passage must be the most boring flight known to man. Maybe, if the weather is clear, Greenland will offer five minutes of entertainment. I like ice, but no such luck on this flight.

The Immigration Office in Minnesota didn't give us any hassle. We were carrying German passports. These days, Germans are well liked everywhere.

With all the flight delays it took us nine more hours to get to SeaTac airport in Washington State. In our jet-lagged state—rumpled and genuinely grumpy—we were happy to find a Mossad agent waiting at the predetermined location, an old gray Volvo station wagon parked on the seventh floor of the parking garage.

For the next five days we got temporary new identities—we would be naturalized Americans. We even received Social Security numbers, local driver's licenses, and several credit cards—the key to happiness and fulfillment in today's world.

We don't know who our opponents are, and we won't take any chances. If somebody can arrange, on such short notice, contract killers in Berlin, they could easily track us down if we kept the same names from our flight.

I always get almost sick after long flights, a fact that still boggles me since I pay so much attention to my health. We're going to take it easy for a couple of days in hopes of avoiding illness.

On Thursday, four days from now, we will get down to business. Be the people we were sent here to be.

41

Marcus must assume we are going to die. They have spoiled us with an unlimited budget. We got a two-room suite, downtown Seattle, with the entire luxuries one could imagine. We were not even sure how to use all the gadgets in the bathroom. Marcus was blowing Israeli tax money like desert sand. I guess that when Bill Gates, who lives not far from here, fights with his wife, here is where he comes to cool off.

The place has everything except food we can eat. We didn't want to sample the disgusting room service food. First thing in the morning, Harel and I went to the market between Pike and Pine Street, down at the port, and found real fresh-baked whole wheat bread, sardines, organic yogurt, vegetables, and fruits. We put everything in one of our bags and smuggled it into our rooms, as if it were not allowed there. I'm sure that up until now, these walls have witnessed nothing but caviar and aperitifs.

After the big breakfast, we called the local Mossad people and informed them, in a no-nonsense tone of voice, we would not meet them at noon, as planned, but we had to take care of other important business that just presented itself. We would try our best to liaison in the late afternoon.

So we did what we always do in a big city first: visit the local zoo. We had been to the one in Seattle many times before, and had always liked that it was small, but modern. They take good care of the animals. I glanced at Harel, who looked funny with crumbs flying all over his Ralph Lauren sweater. He was staring at a bear in one corner of the area.

"They have those things in Montana?" I asked Harel.

"Montana is full of them." He muttered as bread flew out of his mouth. "Not necessarily everywhere, but sure close enough to where we're going. Several years ago, three students from New York stayed overnight in the northern part of the state, by a glacier or something, and awoke to a grizzly chewing up their tent. One was lucky and climbed up a tree, high enough to get a good view of the bear mauling her friends."

"Get outta here."

"I swear."

"No way."

"Yeah way."

"And they were from New York?"

"Yes, and that's why nobody really cared. They don't like outsiders in Montana. Anyway there is a book about this particular event."

"How do you know so much about it? You're just trying to scare me, creep." But I wasn't sure.

"While you studied economics, I took the time to read about Montana on the Internet."

"Were they Jewish?"

"Who?"

"Well, not the bears obviously . . . the three students. Or, at least, the two who were eaten."

'I don't know, the article didn't say anything about it. Do you think they'd taste different?" We both laughed. The idea of a Jew being gobbled by a grizzly bear has its humorous side. A gentile as bear food sounds more believable. Jews are city people and rarely go into the woods.

"Do you think there are bears where we are going to stay?" I asked again.

"Well from what they told us, we'll be staying in a house in the forest. I guess we will see some bears, probably black bears, because they are more common."

"I hope we won't have to shoot them. I would hate it."

"Most of the bears are really shy and would attack you only if they see you near their cubs."

"Good, I hate hunters."

"Don't say that too loud. After Alaska, Montana is the Mecca for hunters." Harel advised.

"Maybe we should let the hunters hunt us. We would be fairer game. They kill those innocent animals and think they're real heroes."

"I would prefer not to end up as hunted game," Harel said.

42

In the evening we met our three men in the city. We usually have more than three in a place like Seattle, but we figured three would be enough. They're all registered in local universities as full-time students, and, if things don't get too hectic, they might go home in two or three years. Some even manage to graduate with a degree.

We met at their rental house. It was great to tell jokes and shoot the breeze in Hebrew again. They didn't know exactly why we were here, but they had everything we needed. It's not difficult in this country. One of the things I love about America is the easy access to weapons. There is no bureaucratic rigmarole for licensing and no need to involve the embassy. It takes one quick trip downtown, especially First and Second Avenue in the old part of town, to find everything we need, almost everything. We still needed the Mossad guys to supply our favorite brand of ammunition and some other little toys. The rest of the equipment we needed had already been picked up by Matthew, Ari, and Rafi.

They also arranged a crew cab pick-up truck for us—a ten-cylinder, four-wheel drive monster—enough to make any rancher envious. They even managed to install armored glass instead of the normal windows. In America, anyone can make that nifty adjustment for less than ten grant. Every metropolis has several shops which specialize in that kind of thing.

I found a small used Berretta .25 with a nine-bullet cartridge, so small that if I have to go somewhere in shorts, I can still hide it. It's what people refer to as a "woman's" gun—although not after they are shot in the throat with it. It cost less than fifty bucks. No questioned asked. They even let us shoot several bullets in a special shooting area in the back of the shop.

43

We slept until late in the day, allowing our jet lag to melt away into the heavy Seattle air. Our bodies were almost used to the new time zone. We've often experienced the dreary, rainy environment, and it is easier to adjust here because of the lack of intense sunlight. A beautiful place really, and it's amazing to me that a second city like Vancouver, British Colombia—equally as gorgeous—could exist right across the Canadian border.

It's also nice to know that Mount Rainer is only an hour away. It is, as far as I know, the highest mountain in the world. Not in absolute terms, of course. Mount Everest is twice as big. I'm talking about relative height to immediate surroundings. A friend of mine who visited Everest couldn't hide her disappointment that Everest wasn't more impressive. When you stand at its feet, you're already at a very high altitude.

Mount Rainier just shoots out of the ground, and I'm sure that if the ancient Greeks had seen it, they would have chosen it over Olympus. That thought entered my mind when we were there today. The forest areas are deep, dark green, and the abundance of yellow flowers creates a golden glow against the dark foliage. Despite our proximity to Seattle, we seldom encountered people. Ever-present signs warned of black bears, and I felt better that we were carrying our guns.

It was already dark on the way back. We took the wrong exit and found ourselves in the southern part of the city. It wasn't the Seattle you see in the movies or on postcards. These were slums—American style—very poor and very black. Despite myself, I was happy that our gas tank was full. This is the Americana most Americans never see, an oppressive, other worldly scene, where garbage cans are overturned and children wail behind screen doors, where teenagers join gangs and old grandmothers stare dejectedly ahead, as if they are walking down the plank instead of their street.

* In other parts of Seattle, if a person is shot, the police investigate. In this neighborhood, a shooting is shrugged off as an internal social problem. Here, drugs, violence, and poverty run rampant like very few places in the western world. Every large American city is home to whole blocks of refugee-like camps, and American leftists dare call *us* cruel.

I guess we were still tired, because we also missed the entrance to our hotel's private parking place. Instead of moving ahead to the next one-way street, turning around the block and returning, we entered the parking garage a block away from our hotel.

It was a long walk after working hours, and we found ourselves alone in the lot. The obvious dangers didn't occur to us at the time. As we started to get out of the car, we noticed five young black men standing near the exit door. It was a dumb idea to put ourselves in a potential street fight situation. On the other hand, if we couldn't handle ourselves on the street, how could we handle ourselves with the real pros in the Wild West?

We drew our guns, cocked them, and instinctively put our jackets over our arms. I also grabbed some cash out of my billfold before stepping down from the truck. As we approached them, we saw one leave the group and walk behind another parked car.

"You cover them and I'll cover the guy behind," Harel said under his breath.

They could not have known our guns were already pointed at them. It was safe to assume they didn't realize we were super heroes from Israel either. I just did not want to get hurt, and for sure I didn't want to hurt them. They were not the ones who killed Rachel.

One of them blocked the door as I walked to it.

"Can I borrow a buck?" He spoke in Ebonics, a sort of Black English that my Israeli ears could barely understand.

"Not only one, but five," I said as I flicked the five-dollar bill at one of them.

He was still blocking the door when both of us heard the quiet pop from Harel's gun followed by a scream from the corner where the other guy stood. I threw myself on the pavement, but didn't shoot. I know it looks stupid to throw yourself down every time there is a little misunderstanding, but it increases the rate of survival. The group of guys laughed at me until they saw my gun in full view.

The guy Harel shot was only very slightly wounded. We're not at war with these guys. Anyway, they didn't look so imposing now, and after catching their eyes, I could see that two of them were drunk or high. Their movements seemed too jittery for drunkenness.

"We don't want to kill you," I assured them. "Would you mind letting us just go through the door? That is all we want."

He moved, still not knowing what to think.

They were all quite impressed. Harel had shot the guy's gun out of his hand from thirty feet away. That's quite a stunt to see, even with a numbed mind.

We took from them two guns and a knife, but gave them $200 on top of the five I had already dished out. We didn't figure that expense into the budget.

I wish I could have heard their conversation after we left.

44

It was our last day in Seattle, so we toured the University District. This is where I met Eric for the first time—in the University Bookstore. It is a funny mixture of people in this area—students, sharply dressed business people and street people, who create a sharp contrast to the mainstream majority. Every time we visit Seattle I notice more and more of them, despite the booming local economy. They sit with their dogs as a bid for sympathy. In Berlin, I would see homeless foreigners sitting with three or four children. Often, the children are crippled or disfigured, and you can count on the parents to highlight any disability.

If Eric left me, would he really want to return to that? But I guess that home is home. Look how many German Jews remained in Germany even after the *Reich's Kristallnacht* pogrom.

On a happier note, we bought a puppy for twenty dollars today from one of the street people. He's a husky and malamute mix, a little grey fur ball. We called him Alaska, and with his big white feet, we figure he will be a big boy—a good northern comrade for Duncan and Fiona.

45

We left Seattle, Harel behind the wheel, Alaska sleeping in my arms. Harel couldn't stop talking about the superiority of the truck. Boys stay boys.

It was raining hard as we crossed the long floating bridge marking the city's Eastern limits. An hour later, we hit the glorious summits of the Cascade Mountains. Those sharp, Alpine-contoured peaks extend all the way to Canada. Fortunately, ski season is over, and the road wasn't crowded. It isn't so bad on these mountainous passes when there is less traffic. Every so often a 18-wheel semi, hauling goods from coast to coast, mars our view of the landscape's beauty.

The flat land of Eastern Washington brought us sun, as if the Cascades had blocked entry of rain clouds. A hundred miles further east, the deep and roaring Columbia River greeted us, as did the realization that we were entering the vast emptiness of the Northwest Territory. At times, Harel and I found ourselves alone on the interstate, winding and ascending along with the river. The Columbia River makes the Jordan look like a small stream.

We stopped for the night in Spokane rather than go the short distance to Coeur d' Alene. The reason for this would be obvious to someone from around the area. Just a few miles north of Coeur d' Alene, there's a place called Hayden lake, where some self-proclaimed neo-Nazis, the Arian Nation, have a compound. Fortunately, their bullying behavior finally passed the legal limit, and they lost their property by losing a legal suit brought against them. Nevertheless, their stomping grounds are not a place I would choose to sleep on.

We pulled over in Spokane and set up camp for the night in a Best Western motel, sneaking Alaska, wrapped in a sweater, into our cozy quarters.

46

We left Spokane by early morning, and, for the first time since arriving in the U.S., I felt as sharp as I needed to be. That despite the fact that Harel and I had to take turns taking Alaska into the dark motel parking lot, shivering in the cold night while the puppy took its good time before getting down to business. We crossed the border to Idaho only a half-hour into our trip and zoomed through Coeur d'Alene. The highway curves along the large lake, which bears the same name. Upper-class ritzy houses litter the shoreline.

Many boats were at the docks and despite the early hour we could see people already water skiing, or riding their polluting and noisy jet-skies. We saw other people playing softball, but none of them looked like Nazis to me. It was hard to tell while going seventy mph.

We were soon traversing the Rockies, climbing the highway pass that wound itself through crisp alpine woodlands. An hour of ponderosas, lodgepoles, and fir trees later, we crossed the border into Big Sky country. A big sign greeted us: Welcome to Montana.

It looked a lot like Idaho—cold, green, empty, and big. We passed yellow deer-crossing signs once in awhile, and I strained to see an elk. I finally saw one, dead, off the side of the road; it lay torn and crumpled, with its stomach falling out where a car had hit it. "God," I muttered, and held Alaska close, while his little nose quivered with the smell of the carcass. I forgot the sight when we reached the Clark Fork River—a smaller, more wiry and devilish cousin of the Columbia. It would guide us all the way to Missoula.

From the perspective of a desert person, Montana seemed incredibly wealthy with water; I stared at the river and the different shades of green, like a poor person would stare at a parking lot full of Mercedes.

"No way, Harel," I muttered when we got pulled over twenty minutes outside of Missoula.

"What?" he protested, "I had it on cruise control, and this guy must be crazy."

The highway patrolman approached Harel's window slowly—maybe because he was a cautious cop, or maybe because he was a bit on the heavy side. He greeted us and we smiled expectantly. As Harel handed him his international license, issued in Hanover, the policeman made a friendly exclamation and welcomed us to Montana. It turned out that our license plates were unreadable—they were caked over with Washington State

118

mud. Relieved, Harel and I thanked him, and, as he drove off, we splashed some of our mineral water on our plates.

"Look, it's literally high noon," Harel pointed out, grinning at the car clock as we climbed back in.

Harel and I looked at each other and smiled.

"Here we are at the dragon's mouth," His eyes narrowed, but he was laughing.

"Here we are, and here we go," I said.

47

We took Missoula's third Highway exit, Van Buren Street, and drove around aimlessly for awhile. I was amazed by how warm and dry it was. I'm not complaining—after the constant wetness of Seattle, I was pleasantly surprised—considering the fact that we're so far north at high elevation. I just didn't expect it.

Missoula is a little simple ski-town, with a charming old core and then, a few miles out, the ugly commercial strip. It is nestled in a valley too small for its population of seventy thousand, which is slowly starting to spread into new developments. Harel and I were not going to meet Ari and Matthew or Solomon and Rafi, for that matter, until evening, so after we parked the car in the old downtown, we strolled around.

Casual restaurants, gift stores, and offices lined the street, and hippie kids sat and sunned themselves at a few outside cafés. I happily felt overdressed—a prissy German in Montana for the first time. We continued on, passing a few bad boutiques and an old, turn-of-the-century movie theater and hotel.

I turned to Harel and said, "*Hör zu,* listen, you want to hear my first impression after twenty minutes?"

"Not really."

"OK, but let me tell you what I think anyway. I think Missoula is not as cute as a little Oregon town, but also not as silly."

Harel absently said uh huh, and I went on. "Yeah, you see, I see more ranchers on the street, more hicks, but also some city types, and hippies, but not as many hippies as Eugene, Oregon. A few streets back, I would even say—a teeny slice of Portland. Maybe because of those pseudo-intellectual punks I saw. At the same time, there are lot of baseball cap types, rich and poor, fraternity and trailer."

We crossed one of the many bridges in town that run over the Clark Fork River and from which we had a nice view. Missoula is flanked by two small mountains, one marked with a big "M" and another one with an "L", looking like college symbols from the fifties. Tough westerners like big letters. We made our way through the quiet streets and past the sumptuous homes of the University District.

"See," I continued, "this is all bourgeois, but I bet you that three miles from here, there are rusty cars in the front yards."

Harel turned and looked at me.

"Yael, you're talking a brunch of crap. Just enjoy the scenery, o.k.?"

I shut up and obediently took in the surrounding mountains and vast blue sky. Harel is so unreflective.

He read aloud from his tour book. Apparently, we were strolling something like 3,000 feet above sea level, and Missoula had once been a lake—Glacial Lake Missoula—formed by enormous glaciers and ice dams and repeatedly broke and reformed, intermittently refilling the lake for about a thousand years. The change had exerted pressure on the mountains and caused them to rise from different layers; some of these layers were then suitable for trees, some were not. I looked around and noticed that some mountain faces were thick with hairy green trees, and some dry like a lunar surface. A strange intermingling.

In the middle of our respectful, scholarly tour, we came upon the campus of the University of Montana—a large, ten thousand student affair. To go into the campus itself we had to cross a footbridge over the Clark Fork. People underneath were floating on inner tubes, enjoying the warm spring weather. One group had several tubes attached, and a pair of dogs—a Golden Retriever and a black Lab—followed them on their float. My mind skipped to the day Alaska would enjoy that privilege on the River Jordan, which is not half as cold. I noticed that the people in the river wore wet suits.

We walked through the shady campus, relatively empty because the school was still on a break. A few professors came in and out of an array of buildings, some from the 19th century and some from the 1970's. A classic, ivy-colored building towered over all the others. Its tower, with clocks facing in each direction, presided over a vast grassy lawn, aptly named the Oval. We found an immense bronze statue of a grizzly bear at the far end of this lawn, its frozen eyes staring out toward the University's front entrance. A welcome only a Montanan could appreciate, I presume.

While Harel and the puppy waited for me under the grove of trees, I had some graduate student things to do, beginning with the Registrar's office. Friendly big women in jeans and T-shirts asked me to please get an okay from the Dean of the Economics Department, after which they would love to sign me up. Welcome to bureaucracy. I didn't expect anything different. We hadn't received an official reply saying I was accepted, so there was no room for complaint.

I left the bureaucrats and collected Harel, and we walked across campus to a little brown building with a plaque that included the Department of Economics. Inside, the chairman's gray-haired secretary informed me that my papers had been transferred to the Graduate Department at the Business School.

I already left the building when I decided to turn back and ask her why they were transferred to the other department.

"Oh, Professor Cromwell asked us to do it. Your thesis fits their program better."

"Professor Cromwell?"

"Professor Cromwell—the Dean of the Business School."

The secretary leaned closer to me and whispered, "He's a very important guy around here, and you know . . . some say he's in the running for President next year."

"President?" I whispered back and leaned toward her. "Of this country?"

"No, no," She sputtered and giggled, "Of the University, I mean."

I thanked her and wondered if this was business as usual around here. This should prove interesting. Rachel was in the Economics department, not the Business School.

"Let's go," I muttered to Harel when I walked out of the building. He picked up Alaska, who was getting tired.

We marched over the lawns of the campus yet again, till we arrived in front of the School of Business. We stopped and took a minute to gaze up the walls. It is definitely impressive with its massive windows, tasteless exterior, and cowboy statues in front of the main entrance. While the rest of the campus is simple and dignified, even slightly shoddy, this hall screamed of money and affluence—without the slightest apology.

"Oh god," Harel moaned, "I bet the liberal arts students really don't appreciate this."

"You both wait for me here." I told him.

The inside was impressive, in its own way. Tacky and pricey. I guess money was really no object, which struck me as strange, since I read the state was one of the poorest in the country. I made my way to Professor Cromwell's reception room. Out the gigantic window, there was a spectacular view of the dominant mountain. I was informed of its name, Mount Sentinel.

A tall blonde woman asked in a shrill voice if she could help me. She was thirty-five at the most, but her voice sounded pre-pubescent.

"I don't know if I'm at the right place, but I was sent here from the Economics Department," I said.

"Your name, please?" she asked.

"Oh, I'm sorry; my name is Barbara, Barbara Skibbee. I'm a foreign student."

"Oh yes, the German girl, we thought you were arriving a week ago."

I smiled and asked myself who would still call women "girls" these days. Maybe Montana had not yet caught up.

"You need to speak to Professor Cromwell," she continued. "But I'm sorry. Miss Skibbee, he is already out for the day. Are you available tomorrow?"

"Sure, I'd be happy to meet him. Will he be my mentor or thesis advisor, I think that what they're called?"

She looked a bit overwhelmed. "Boy, I can't tell you that." She flashed me a sugary smile. She must have been hired for her politeness or something else, for sure not for her secretarial prowess.

I set up an appointment for the next day, and before I left, I asked about apartments and places to eat. She glanced at my Hermes scarf and latte-colored blazer, and recommended an expensive hotel for the night.

I chatted with her a bit more, remembering the intensive crash course of information collection we took in our first year with the Organization. Rule No.1: Speak to the peons. I'd already found out that Cromwell, whoever he was, had intervened personally in my transfer.

But what really struck me was the comment the secretary made regarding the fact that they had expected me a week before. The semester would not begin for another five days, and there was no way she could have known that I landed in the United States a week ago. It was certainly no secret, but it still isn't easy to find this kind of information. The computer list where names of foreigners are registered when they enter the country is not normally open to the public. Even the Immigration and Naturalization Service might find it hard to have that information so close at hand.

Harel and I walked to the car and gently tucked Alaska in a basket on the back seat. We checked our James Bond watches—nothing too fancy—just miniature bug detectors. We found nothing but dog hair, but still, we spoke only German.

We stayed at the Four Seasons Hotel along the river, the one the secretary recommended. If somebody had been listening to us on our telephone line, they would have heard us make some calls to the "Missoulian," the local newspaper, regarding apartment rentals.

We made several appointments with different landlords before answering one particular advertisement. Matthew answered the phone. After introducing myself and telling him I was looking for a place to rent for my boyfriend and me, he described the area as quite secluded. Matthew lived in a big house with a friend, and his smaller house, the so called "mother-in-law-house," was for rent. He agreed to accept dogs if we kept things clean. I'm sure Matthew was smiling on the other end. I asked him if we could come tomorrow, but he said that it might be taken by then. He waited too long for a responsible renter, and he wanted the deal done tonight if possible.

He gave us directions to the house, and I drove as Harel directed me through a neighborhood called the Rattlesnake. We were gaining in elevation, and I caught a glimpse of nice large homes neatly tucked against the mountainside. I assumed that professors either lived in the University District or, if they wanted more room, privacy, or a few horses, they moved here.

When we reached the house we were quite high up, surrounded by acres of woods, thick brush, and fields of alfalfa and blue flax. Ari and Matthew happily waited at the heavy front door.

"Oh no," Ari wailed when Alaska stuck his head out the window at him.

Once we were in, Rafi and Solomon showed us around the seven-bedroom house. I noticed the nice, high ceilings and was happy to find the bathrooms clean and roomy. The kitchen was enormous, with generous, sturdy counters and a brand-new blender. Ari had bought some plants and a few simple pieces of furniture.

"Look," Harel squealed, "three fireplaces." He was in heaven, probably trying to figure out where to hang his killer whale calendar.

I unpacked and, while I sat in the bathtub for an hour, read again the summaries the professors had prepared for me back in Berlin. I had better come prepared for the meeting tomorrow.

48

"Here I go. Wish me luck," I said the next morning, waving at Ari, Matthew, and Harel, who mumbled their good-byes from the kitchen table. Rafi and Solomon had spent the night in their U-district apartment.

"Remember," Ari said to me, barely looking over the newspaper, "no sweat."

"Yeah, yeah," I thought as I got into the truck. Let *him* try playing a nerdy graduate student. Some days I can't remember why I like this guy.

Missoula was sunny and dry as a bone despite the early hour. As I approached the University, I glanced at the river and spied a fly fisherman below letting his line dance across the water. Ten minutes later, I had parked and was on the steps of the Business School.

I made my way to Cromwell's office, and found the blond secretary from yesterday, smiling at me. We chatted about nothing for a few minutes—Americans are the masters of small talk—before she finally rose to usher me into the lion's den.

Dean James Cromwell stood up from behind his grand mahogany desk and approached me with one hand extended. He exuded wealth. His blue eyes glanced at the azure face of his Schaffhausen watch. The British parliament gave Churchill such a toy as retirement gift; a present from a thankful nation. Those details are what I like about our check up reports from Mossad.

He was tan, in his late fifties, and had the good looks of a man with a facelift—just the type who would drive a $150,000 Mercedes Gelaendewagon and have a wife who drives a cherry-red BMW. All described in the Mossad report. The man loved quality. I will give him that. I hadn't expected his height—even taller than Matthew. Big, but not fat, maybe a basketball player in college, I thought.

"Hi there, Barbara," his eyes twinkled under a full head of white hair. "And hey, welcome to America! You know, I went to Germany once after college. Oh, I loved Munich, especially, all the good beer and that decadent pastry. My god! I'm afraid we can't offer you any of that, but we have scenery that almost beats Bavaria. You'll see!"

I guess polished manners go along with being the head of the Business School. These guys make deals; they bring in the bucks from corporate America to support the education of even more businessmen and businesswomen.

He had one of those small Irish noses. Giving him the benefit of the doubt, I decided his nose was an original. Perhaps, people of my ethnic background are too quick to question the authenticity of this particular feature. He was loud, but not annoying, with a voice higher pitched than I expected. I also decided he wasn't as dumb as his first few comments would have led me to believe. I smiled and sat down in the chair he offered.

He barreled on, "But I think you brought the summer, Barbara. Why, just last week we had a snowstorm. Can you believe it?" he grinned at me and blinked.

"Yes, I've heard the horror stories," I said with a cool smile, knowing his game. He wanted me to know three things: that he was an extrovert and, probably popular, that he would always dominate our relationship, and that he was confident enough to be inane—a dangerous sign of power.

"You know what they say about Montana though?" Cromwell leaned back in his chair, still grinning. His eyes were slit narrowly, like a cat's. "They say that people come here in the winter to ski and stay for the rest of their lives because of the breathtaking summers."

I smiled. "I guess if the winters are so rough here, one can appreciate the warm weather even more. Not take it for granted."

It was getting a bit thick.

"Like being alive," I wanted to say, but didn't. Instead, I smiled politely to show him he'd broadened my philosophical horizons. "What can I say, I'm looking forward to it. It is quite a change from Berlin."

"Anyway," he became serious. "Before we get down to business, I wanted you to know that we fully understand the unusual circumstances you're under. We are here to help you any way we can. We all loved Rachel very much."

He looked at me. "I was deeply saddened by her death."

Unless he was a very good actor, this last sentence sounded authentic.

"I really appreciate you saying that. It's especially because of those circumstances that I want to do a good job here. I've never really taken my studies so seriously but all will change right now . . . radically."

'That's just great," he said. "So let's move on to some other issues."

"Issues?" I echoed.

"Well, not issues. It's just that my secretary told me you asked for help finding a place to rent. We might be able to help you with a nice place right near the University."

I looked up to him and hesitated. Let him squirm.

"In fact," he continued after a few seconds, "at this point in time, it's free, because you would be house-sitting for my friends Jim and Ciel. They're in South America for a year, and you would really only start paying rent in a few months if you decided to stay in the house."

I wondered if he knew we already found a place. He seemed very eager to help. Was I being overly suspicious? Nice cars and watches don't make or identify murderers.

"Oh," I hoped to sound disappointed. "I wish I had known yesterday. I called everywhere and finally found a place. Unfortunately, I have already signed the lease."

"Great, I am happy for you. That's a real coup. Students are coming to me all the time because it's so difficult to find a decent place here. Where is it? Not too far away, I hope?" he sounded moderately concerned.

"In the Upper Rattlesnake. It's very beautiful and secluded."

I was already sick of using and hearing the word '*secluded*'.

"Good, you will be able to concentrate up there. There are some nice trails in the Rattlesnake, too. You'll have to hike them and see for yourself. I can recommend some."

"Do you live there, too?" I asked, turning the focus back to him.

"I live in Pattee Canyon, also very secluded. As a matter of fact, this Friday my wife and I are throwing a party for all the new graduate students and staff. Hope you can make it."

"Yes, I'd love to come." I rose to my feet and jumped slightly. He looked at me carefully as if taking inventory.

Then I remembered, "By the way, what was the other problem or issue you mentioned?"

"Well, this is a delicate situation, and I think it's a blessing that the head of the Economics Department asked me if we can fit you in our program. You see, we can be a bit more flexible." He lowered his voice a bit: "Since we are better funded than any other department, the University Administration tends to be a bit more flexible with us."

I smiled at him and lowered my voice to playfully get in on the secret.

"But what is the problem?"

"Oh, it's nothing really, but we are required by the Graduate School to accept only the students who have taken the GRE." "The what?" I asked, feigning ignorance. "I am German, not American."

"The Graduate Record Exam. Graduate students must take one before being officially accepted." He sighed apologetically.

He must assume by now, unless he knows I'm an Israeli spy, that I'm the most unprepared student to ever enter an American university. "Oh. In Germany we do not have such a test."

"Yes, yes, I know. You see, here in the U.S.A., we have thousands of universities all over the country. The GRE is a standardized exam, which has become a basic requirement.

"We can grant you a provisional status because of special hardship or some other reasons until you take the test. I don't like bending the rules, but in your case, we just had to make an exception."

"That's very sweet of you. When can I take it? And does it have a lot of questions in economics?" I was the worried student.

"Not at all, not at all. It has really only two main parts, including Mathematical Logic, which is similar to an IQ test, although it is not," he was quick to assure me, "and a vocabulary section. On that, we don't expect foreign students to score too high anyway."

"Okay," I said, "When can I take it?"

"Well, theoretically if you want, we can do it on the computer and get the results immediately. It is really up to you."

"So can I take it now and we get this thing out of the way?"

"You know what? That might be a good idea, and I'm sure we can work something out. And again, don't be worried about the results. Whatever your score is, we can arrange something. But why rush things? Most students like to prepare themselves for several months. Some even take special classes."

What could I tell him? That I'm from the Gilboa Mountains and, that if I got one of the highest scores in the Israeli Army special IQ test, I could for sure handle whatever is expected from graduate students here? Besides, even in English I trust our teachers to be the cream of the crop. They were hand picked by Marcus and Ari, like anybody else in our Department.

I told him I'd like to take it within the hour if possible, and forty-five minutes later I was being escorted into an empty room with several computers. He asked me if I wanted to go to the bathroom or have a cup of coffee because the test would take several hours. I said no, and after some final words of wisdom and encouragement, he left me alone with the exam.

The math part was straightforward. I think any Israeli or European who graduated from high school would have done fine. In Israel and in Germany, unlike the U.S., high school is not mandatory. Unlike here, there are no students to slow down those who really want to learn something. The English part was a bit more demanding, but as I said, our language instructors are top notch. As a child I also gobbled up books and books, almost like Naomi. I finished the exam at least 30 minutes ahead of schedule and went to inform the secretary.

He was still there and invited me into his office.

"Whatever the results, don't worry about it, you can repeat the test as many times as you want and we always figure out something." He assured me.

The secretary came in and handed him a slip of computer paper with my results.

I looked at him and couldn't help but give him one of my brazen smiles. His expression tensed, and I relaxed.

He was clearly amazed. "Your score certainly doesn't reflect the grades you received in Germany! In fact, young lady, it puts you in the top one percentile of the nation."

So . . . I'm in?"

He gave me a long curious look. "Glad to have you aboard."

I realized afterwards that I should have dumbed myself down a bit. That was an arrogant oversight on my part. I'll have to correct that somehow. But then again, any less than almost a perfect score, and Harel would have given me a bad time.

49

That night, Ari returned from doing some shopping with Matthew, and I told him what had happened. He was mad as hell about the discrepancy between Barbara's performance and mine. But I distracted him with platitudes on the great European-Germanic education system. Anyway, after considering that nothing could be changed, Ari decided there was a positive side to my mistake, although he didn't say specifically what it was.

We were all there, including Rafi and Solomon. The curtains were closed, so no one could look inside. There was no danger of that—ten acres of private forest surrounds us. This used to be a Forest Ranger outpost. In fact, those ten acres are connected to thousands more that are part of a State Park—established to protect the elk when they come down in the winter to find grass. The whole damn thing is bigger than Israel. Montana alone has several forests that are bigger than our whole country. Of course, we couldn't have the whole area wired. However, Rafi and Matthew did a good job, of setting up an early-warning system.

Because of the many big animals around here at night, Rafi also arranged some cameras so we could watch from monitors inside. Thermal cameras utilize body heat to detect things; they are more accurate and informative than other kinds of conventional cameras. Rafi also programmed them in such a way that only the register of human heat sounds the alarm in our monitor room. The fact that humans don't run naked in the cold made his job much more difficult.

As I already said, officially the house was bought by a wealthy Californian, also an old Israel supporter, I think he is a born again Christian or something of that sort. He rented the place to Matthew's alias. Our Matthew is what Americans call "independently wealthy," and he is another aspiring writer lost in beautiful Missoula.

* The town is the center for many writers. There is no place in the country with so many published writers, or at least that's what the locals would have you believe. The romantic and gritty feel of the surroundings, half-empty, or deserted mining towns in the middle of raw nature, seemingly endless forest and mountains, is the mix writers apparently feel they need.

Ari is Matthew's poet friend from Kuwait. Ari has a dark complexion, and with half of his family from Arab Jewish extraction, he speaks fluent Arabic and also some sub-local dialects. He speaks even Turkish-for cover in places like Berlin. People might think they are lovers. That's all the better for us, fewer questions asked.

Rafi and Solomon are representatives of a high-tech company from Europe which is considering expansion to this part of the Northwest. We won't have any contact with them in public. They don't come here with their car. They drive with Matthew, always by night.

The file on Cromwell was meanwhile getting thick as updates arrived. Aside from his official position at the UM, (University of Montana), he also sits on the board of directors for several companies. According to Solomon, these positions are usually, although not always, only symbolic, but very lucrative. Such directors are legally empowered to vote the company's president in or out and vote on the main decisions concerning the company. It is a given that the people who hold these positions are to represent in good faith the best interests of the shareholders.

In America however, according to Solomon, this is not always the case. Usually they are there only because the law requires it, and they just give a blank check to the CEO to run the company as he or she sees fit. Many times, the people who sit on the boards are nothing more than respected public figures who know nothing about the business of the company.

It often happens that certain people are on the boards of many different companies, like belonging to several exclusive yacht clubs. In Seattle, for instance, the head of the local big timber company also sits on Boeing's board. Is there any connection between aerospace and wood? I don't think so. Generally, these highly paid people, who receive very fat stock options, are nominated by either the CEOs themselves or by big stockholders, but as long as the stock prices go up, few complain.

"But, if those members of the board and the CEOs get their benefits in the form of stocks of the company, don't they tie their own well-being to that of the shareholders?" Harel asked.

"Well, yeah, that was the original idea in America, where this payment method was first established. But things got out of hand." Solomon answered, "To begin with, many of those people get, besides a huge amount of the company's stock, outrageously high salaries and retirement benefits. But even if we only look at the stock options, whose value can easily reach in the millions, many of those options can be cashed in the near future. In other words, the directors who get those options are interested only in the short-term gains and not what will happen to the company several years in the future.

"They might, for example, support a decision to sell some very valuable company assets because in the interim it will look good on the balance sheet. This in turn will have a positive short-term effect on stock prices. But the average shareholder who keeps his shares as a long-term investment gets hurt."

"Any remedy?" I asked. "Most Americans today count on the stock market for their retirement."

"There's one simple solution," Solomon was happy to explain, "requiring that the stock options given to the executives be cashed only ten years after they were issued. That way, management would have the long-term well-being of the company in mind. Also, they should have a law prohibiting an individual from being on the board of more than one company, unless he or she owns a big personal investment in that company."

At least now we understood how Cromwell could finance all those cars. It's pretty moronic to be living that conspicuously in a place like Missoula. His lifestyle would be less extravagant if he were only a University employee.

"I wonder how he got all these positions." Harel wondered aloud.

That was a question that the Mossad files couldn't answer. With all due respect to his academic status, we didn't think that alone was enough for Cromwell to have acquired all this clout.

50

Late in the afternoon I walked Alaska around the property, climbing uphill a bit on the mountain's slope. I knelt down and gazed over carpets of wildflowers, the sharp scent of pine in my nose, and my eyes rested on the Bitterroot Valley far below. Patiently, I waited for Missoula's daily pre-dusk show. Finally, it started. The sky seemed made for us: the clouds and their colors fighting for our benefit, playing a child's game of shapes and contours, and the sky enveloped by thick swathes of purple and orange. I tried to memorize the section of dove-gray and blue, so beautiful I gasped, and its swirls of crimson and yellow. Green clouds appeared from behind the mountain range. They exhibited more colors and arrays than the clear rainbows that attempted to follow the storm. Right before the rain started, the face of the "M" mountain-Mount Sentinel—appeared poured in gold.

Harel jogged up to me just as I felt raindrops on my cheeks. I called Alaska over to us and we all hunched low. The puppy trembled against me as we watched the sky, scared of the occasional lighting streak and booming rumble of thunder. Even Germany's Black Forest doesn't come close to the beauty of this place. And Europe's famous painters missed for sure their opportunity for sublime beauty if they didn't visit here.

We're located in the most northeastern part of Missoula, and, as I said before, the property borders on a thick forest, dark even in the daytime—an ideal place from which to wage an assault. But we all agreed that whatever our adversaries might try, they would do it in the most subtle way possible. Even with Rachel it was supposed to look like a freak accident.

We found it remarkable that nothing had been leaked to the local newspaper. Everyone took things at face value—a tragic accident, nothing more. But we couldn't rely on whomever was against us to share our logic—that it would be fatal to attack us here outright—so Rafi's gadgets give us some peace of mind.

We also had debated whether I should go to the party with or without Harel. If I went alone, I'd look more vulnerable. On the other hand, there's no sense hiding Harel, because whoever ultimately might be after me will know about him. Trying to hide him would look very suspicious. One of the nice things about Harel, or, if I may say, useful things about Harel, is the fact that his appearance gives no indication of how bright he is. He appears a bit like a Neanderthal with all those muscles and hard tough eyes.

Also, any attempt on my life would require preparation. It doesn't matter who the object is, those things take planning, a lot of planning. So it is better to be up front about Harel. The fast assassination attempt in Berlin against Barbara was an exception to the way these operations are usually planned and executed.

We also do not want to raise suspicion about my identity. They might not try anything if they know. It is one thing to kill an innocent student. Nobody cares. It's entirely another ball game to kill an agent with the backing of a country, even a country other than Israel. That's why we also don't think the killers ever suspected who Rachel really was.

True enough, missions like this one must be based on national security, not personal vengeance. But when Germany released the murderers of the Israeli Olympic athletes in Munich, even though their guilt had been established, Golda Meir ordered the Department to ensure that justice was done. In the next seven years, one after the other, all were killed. Tragically, an innocent Arab was killed by mistake in Oslo. Although, many would argue against such extrajudicial killings, I would argue that German justice failed and once again let killers of Jews go unpunished.

51

Matthew helped us find some suitable party clothes. That meant jeans, slightly wider in the legs for our guns. Pendleton flannel shirts and tweed jackets. Cool, smart, yet not uptight. This dress wouldn't work in many places, but it was definitely Montana chic.

A lot of cars were already parked by the sprawling, ranch-style house in Pattee Canyon, which blinked at us like a Christmas tree under a night sky. We rang the doorbell of a heavy oak door, and in the next second we stood face to face with Patty Cromwell. She wore a green silk dress, deep red lipstick, and, before we even introduced ourselves, she exuberantly extended her hands and lips. Patty was already quite tipsy. Immediately mesmerized by Harel, she attempted to corral him, but when the doorbell rang anew, we slipped away down a peach and mauve-colored hallway. We found a large crowd, standing or in comfortable chairs, lounging in the lavish sitting room and adjoining dining area. The floor was covered in Persian rugs—some signed by the artist—and a smattering of ornate antiques stood among the party guests. Most of the people, a diverse lot anywhere from twenty to sixty years old, were finely dressed and carefully made-up. And as we were in Montana now, I only saw white people.

A classic academic scene. Just from the way they talked and behaved I could see who was a tenured professor, who was still vying for a spot, who had given up on the prospects, and who was living contract to contract. Then there were the graduate students, some eager, some cool, but few with any idea about what they were getting involved in. You can deduce a lot by observing how the people look at the people with whom they talk. And the way they avoid looking.

I held Harel's arm, and we snaked through the crowd and out the large terrace doors. On the patio we found the second half of the party ensconced upon lawn furniture, eating and laughing, dropping crumbs on the marble tiles. I spied Cromwell and lightly motioned his way. He stood by a buffet, holding a martini and laughing with his head thrown back while a naive-looking brunette giggled next to him. As we were about to approach them, a young waiter in khakis offered us a tray of drinks. We took the glasses. Unlike in Israel, if you are among Americans, you always take the offered glass. You don't have to drink it, but you take it. Otherwise, they will think you are a recovering alcoholic or a weirdo.

Cromwell suddenly had his hand on my shoulder, grinning ear to ear. I introduced Harel as Martin, and for a moment, I saw Cromwell eyes pan across Harel's handsome face. As they shook hands, Cromwell leaned in and asked Harel what he thought of my unbelievable GRE score.

"Well," Harel said in a slight German tilt, "she is the smartest woman I know," Harel gave me a loving hug.

Cromwell exploded in laughter, wagging his finger at me. He then complimented Harel on his English, wondering why, like mine, it was almost accent free; I dutifully recounted a story of student exchange years and study-abroad programs. I pretty much used our real stories here, and, in any case, this seemed to satisfy Cromwell.

"Are you from Berlin, too?" Cromwell asked.

"Well, I wasn't born there. I'm really from Hanover, but I've spent a lot of time in Berlin since high school."

When we were trained in working undercover, one of the first things we learned was how to answer direct questions about our identity. The rule is, always answer simple questions with a complex answer rather than yes or no.

"I have a friend from Germany who is visiting professor here. When he comes, I would like to introduce him to both of you."

This didn't pose a threat. Our cover stories were waterproof, and our German spotless.

"Your English is simply marvelous, wow," he exclaimed, "oh, you know what, I absolutely have to introduce you to Professor McFarlane. He will work with you on your thesis project, since he was the one who worked with your friend Rachel." He lowered the tone of his voice before speaking her name. "Where is he, I was just talking to him, oh—Dennis!"

I would not have pegged Professor McFarlane for an academic, perhaps, because he was rugged and good-looking—a smaller, a bit older version of Harel. Well, not exactly. His eyes were wiser. He was a medium-sized man, and seemed to be at the most thirty-five. He must be very talented, I thought, if he was already a full professor.

The man didn't ignore Harel. He even tried to say some sentences in broken German. He then introduced the dark-haired woman with him. Her name was Michelle Levine, another graduate student. I did not have to be a genius to guess she was Jewish. With such a name you can be either a German or a Jew, and since she didn't look like a blond farm girl from Iowa, the answer was clear.

"It's nice to meet you," she said. Her voice was very soft. "I was very close to Rachel, and she talked a lot about you."

• "Yes, we were very close friends although we only met less than two years ago," I said. "Her death is still quite painful for me."

I quickly glanced at McFarlane, and then lowered my eyes when Rachel's name was mentioned. Harel put a comforting hand on my shoulder. Cromwell looked at me sadly, but then a newly arrived guest pulled him away and into a cheerful embrace.

"We were all shocked by the accident. It more than saddened me," McFarlane said, "and I am overjoyed to hear that you will carry on her work."

I nodded and studied his gray eyes, trying to gauge his expression. "I put on hold everything else I was doing back home, so I could come here, if not for her, then at least for her family's sake. I don't mean to sound too forward, Professor McFarlane, but is there a way for me to see what she had written before her death?" I was a bit concerned about the direct leap I took into practical matters.

"It will be the first thing we will do Monday morning," He answered.

No harm was done, I guess.

"I will go through the material with you, and then it's up to you to decide how you want to pursue it from there. We are quite lax here in Montana. Far more than you people in the Old World." He smiled and winked to me with far more than the obligatory smile Americans always give to each other.

"Old World, eh?" I smiled. "I like the way you put that. Where in the 'New World' do you come from?"

"I like the straightforwardness of your girlfriend, Martin." He looked at Harel, maybe looking for a hint of jealously. There was none, to his disappointment, I think.

He looked back at me. "A purebred Montana boy my dear, you couldn't find purer. I'm from Libby, Montana, a bit to the north, near the Canadian border."

A big, hard-faced man with red hair stuck his head into our midst. He laughed too loudly. He wasn't yet drunk, but he had been trying. He reached for Michelle and she shrieked. Then she slid into his arms happily, and they kissed.

"Barbara, Martin, this is my friend Dale." Michelle said over their embrace.

"Dale's one of our football stars here at UM," Professor McFarlane said as he gave Dale a hard, friendly slap on the back.

Dale turned, grinning over Michelle's head, and his eyes rested on me.

"Hi there," he drawled and raised his half-empty bottle of beer.

I turned around to see where Harel was, but he had slipped away to the other side of the room. He was already in deep conversation with somebody.

"I'm going fishing tomorrow morning. Are you up for it, Dale?" McFarlane asked.

Michelle answered instead. "Tomorrow, we are invited to my parents for the Passover meal."

It's supposed to be on Monday, not tomorrow I thought. Oh well, convenience over tradition for our American cousins. Germans normally don't know Jewish traditions I reminded myself, so I asked, "What is a Passover?"

"Oh, you don't know?" Michelle looked at me, happy to instruct. "It's the Seder, the celebration of the Jews' escape from Egypt—the beginning of the journey to the Promised Land." She giggled when she said that.

"Oh, I'm sorry, I really didn't know."

"It is okay, how could you know? Would you like to join us?"

"Of course, I'd love to. Are you sure it will be okay with your parents?"

"My parents would love it. Besides, my grandmother is staying with us for the holiday, and she speaks a bit of German, too."

"May I bring Martin with me? I don't want to leave him home alone."

"Of course, my parents like to meet new people."

I could see that Professor McFarlane was watching the discussion with interest; my part, in particular.

"So what about fishing on Sunday then, Barbara? You are more than welcome to join us. You can't live in Montana and not go fishing at least once."

"I've only been here a few days."

"It is always best to get an early start on a good thing."

"I'll check with Martin, but I don't think I have plans. What do I need to bring?"

"Just yourself," he grinned. "Oh, and maybe a gun. There might be a lot of bears near the river."

"I don't like guns, and I would never shoot an animal. I wouldn't even know how to use a gun," I answered with a hint of concern.

His laugh seemed a bit forced. "Don't worry. I was kidding. Bears are real shy."

Professor Cromwell waved his hand to me from the other side of the room, and I acknowledged him with a smile, thinking again how friendly Americans are. They have this above the Germans and Israelis. If you go to a party in Israel or Germany and no one knows you, you will be totally ignored. At least in Berlin, Germans in the South are friendlier.

"Your boat or mine?" Dale asked McFarlane.

"Mine. It's bigger, and we want to make Barbara comfortable."

"That is nice of you. I'm not the greatest swimmer, either." I hoped that I wasn't overplaying the helpless female role.

52

We left the party at close to midnight, Harel feigning a stomach ache and a bad mood. On the way home, it started to rain again, and we crept through the shiny dark town. Harel slowed down as we wound up the mountain in the rattlesnake, and we completely stopped when seven or eight deer crossed our path. All of them seemed hypnotized by the oversized headlights. A few minutes later, we pulled into our driveway. A figure came toward us from the house. It was Ari.

He swaggered toward us, holding a big wine bottle. "Hey guys, how was your party?" He spoke English, which meant we were under observation.

"We had a good time," Harel told him.

"Would you care to come and drink with us? Let's put a dent in this jug of vino, neighbors."

We followed him into his house, while he chatted away, apparently very tipsy.

"Since you taste it now, let me show you where this great wine came from," Ari said. "We have one hell of a wine cellar."

We closed the door behind us and followed him to the storeroom downstairs. The room had no windows. Solomon sat there, watching the monitors.

"We detected two people on the screen, not far from here in the forest. They left after almost an hour." Ari now spoke quickly in Hebrew. "Rafi and Matthew went to check the area with the detection equipment. They should be back any minute."

"Once we detected them, Rafi and I came here to this room so they wouldn't see us," Solomon informed us.

"When they left," Ari added, "Rafi could see that they left some instruments for taking pictures or something. No voice detection, however, but it is best to take precautions."

"Rachel didn't have a chance against those guys. We're here for only two days, and they come down on us with all this heavy equipment," I said.

We heard steps above us, and Rafi and Matthew came down, legs muddy and soaking wet.

"Only visual," Rafi confirmed. "No sound recording or listening equipment, but they use very advanced camera gear. Money is not an issue for these guys."

"You're sure, Sylvester? There's absolutely no sound?" Harel asked.

"Yes. But I knew that when we were still inside. Our equipment would have detected it. We only went to make sure. We can all relax."

"Did you touch anything? Could it detect you at all?" I asked.

"No, we hit it from the back, and the cameras are directed at the house," Matthew said. "Of course, we didn't touch anything, Yael." He gave me a patronizing smile.

It was a stupid question. All of us were feeling the heat rising, and maybe the initial excitement was causing some tension. We want our enemies to think they're successful voyeurs. They'll see what we want them to see.

"Why do you think they're not using sound detection equipment?" Harel asked.

"Too easy to detect," Rafi answered, "but mainly because from that distance, with all that snow and wind, the equipment would have to be super elaborate."

"They're coming down on us strong." Solomon started as if he smelled a battle. Rafi seemed right there with him.

"Let's slow down," Ari said. "If I were the killer or killers, maybe I'd just want a picture of the new girl in town filling in for the one I murdered. I don't think they have grounds for heavy suspicion yet. They could be paranoid, but I don't think they've arrived at anything close to the truth. Not this early."

"I agree," Harel said.

I did too. They would have provoked into something only if we had some real leads. We had nothing at this point.

"Maybe your GRE score worried them." Ari said, just hammer home an earlier point about pride ruining missions. "The average graduate student doesn't even come close to getting such a score."

"Well, at Seder tomorrow I might get something out of Michelle." I changed the subject. "She said she knew Rachel. On Sunday, I'm going fishing with the professor who helped Rachel, and I meet him again on Monday to discuss the nitty-gritty of her work. This reminds me. I may have to come up with some ideas of my own."

"I'll prepare something for you," Solomon said.

One thing was clear. We found worthwhile adversaries. Things might roll faster than we thought, and I would be the last to complain about that.

53

Seder, the Jewish Passover, is the only religious event we ever celebrated in our Kibbutz. Normally, I don't like anything that has to do with tradition, because tradition is wound up in history and thinking about history, especially Jewish history, is not something I find cheering. On the other hand, I have found that in the years when I couldn't attend a Seder, I really missed it.

We don't restrict our celebration to the short version, like most American Jews. We go all out—read the whole *Haggada*—the Passover book, start to finish, the full three hours—any rabbi would blush with envy at our zeal.

We do the real thing—we sing every last song, recite every last poem.

Exactly, so I hear, like our Jewish ancestors did more than two thousand years ago. It always surprises me when people who call themselves Christians have never heard about it. Jesus, after all, celebrated the Seder. It was his last meal before the Italians; I mean the "Romans" crucified him.

I think I like this holiday because the message is something that even non-religious Jews like me can grasp—freedom from oppression. Moses, after all, freed a bunch of slaves from Egypt, and those lucky guys were my forefathers.

There is, however, this tricky sentence predicting that God would take revenge on the Gentiles. In Eric's first Passover with us he got a bit uptight, and I assured him that if one reads the Hebrew carefully, one can see that God meant only those Gentiles who are, or were, nasty to the Jews. The Arabs and the Europeans—both still not always so nice to us, are definitely in hot water, at least from God's perspective, is my educated guess. Fortunately, Matthew and Doris were there too, and as objective Hebrew-speaking Gentiles, they confirmed what I said. Eric warily accepted that.

The real Seder should take place on Monday, and we already decided to celebrate it in the room downstairs. We six ex-combat officers of the Israeli Army are celebrating Passover while hiding in a basement in Missoula, Montana. As if we are in old Europe again. Isn't it something?

When Rafi was preparing his equipment to be delivered here, he even put some *Matzah*—Jewish Passover bread, in the package so we could have a real Seder. But today we're going to Michelle's parents' Seder and for us, it is part of the job. It's strange, because here we are as Germans going to a Jewish Seder. I hope there won't be too many awkward moments.

She said her grandmother spoke some German. What should I say if she gives us hell for the Holocaust? Should we tell her that we were not born when it happened, which is the standard answer the Germans like to give? For some reason, the same Germans attack us for what happened to the Palestinians. Well, guess what. I was not born when that occurred either.

54

Michelle's parents lived in Target Range in western Missoula—a flat, spacious suburb with characterless, tract housing. The muddy pastures we frequently passed didn't look as if they'd offer much nourishment, but the horses grazing there looked healthy enough. One white stallion was so striking we stopped to take a closer look. His owner came out of the house to chat, explaining that the mustang herd, from which the horse came, was rare and under federal protection in Wyoming. Before Harel could get into a discussion about protecting other animals, I pulled him back to the car. The horse was beautiful, but I prefer llamas. They seem to have a better sense of humor.

We have a few horses in our kibbutz too; they are older ones that we saved from being slaughtered for meat. I can't believe how people that "love horses" sell them when they are no more suitable for riding. We don't ride ours; we just admire their beauty and gentleness. Our horses are very affectionate.

Michelle greeted us at the gate of the modest, well-built house. Elegant columbines and moss roses lined the path to the front door. "I'm so happy you both could make it," she said as we walked in. "We even made a vegetarian dish just for you."

The house was simply tastefully furnished. Her father and mother were warm, bright people—they were English professors from the East. For a quick and painful second, I wished Eric could be here. Michelle's grandmother, visiting from Boston, immediately took liking to Harel. I asked Michelle where Dale was, and she quietly mumbled something about a late football practice.

As we sat down, I found myself sitting across from a fifteen-year-old boy with freckles; Michelle's teen-age brother Jake had reluctantly torn himself away from his computer for the meal.

"Hi," I grinned.

Uncomfortable with the influx of strangers, he blushed a dangerous shade of crimson. Pretty soon, Harel captivated Jake, like all teenage males. Even as the nondescript Martin Heinz, Harel exuded a captivating scent to all pimply boys. His appeal to young boys and older women continues to be one of life's mysteries.

The Seder was quick, the shortest I've witnessed. Harel and I pretended to be awestruck. Less than 20 minutes later we were eating a delicious meal of lamb, wild rice, and squash and tofu for Harel and me. The whole procedure was non-religious, but very Jewish in other ways. Michelle's grandmother told us the story of her family's flight from Germany in 1935, when she was only seven. The others presented us with a battery of questions about our German background.

Have you ever met Jews before? As young Germans, what do you feel about the Holocaust? Do you feel guilty about what happened?

"Rachel was really the only Israeli I have met," I told them. "And I guess she is the only Jewish person I know, unless I knew a Jew and they didn't tell me, right Martin?"

"I can always tell if somebody is Jewish or not," the grandmother said.

"Really, how is that?" Harel smiled at her curiously.

"It's just a quality . . . a sixth sense, I have," she said.

"Oh mother," Michelle's father sighed. He wanted to change the subject.

"Were you close to Rachel? We absolutely adored her. She was extremely smart, articulate, and kind."

"And she had a hot temper," Jake blurted out grinning at Harel.

His mother gasped angrily. "Oh no, that's o.k.—she was feisty at times, that's all."

"What would you do to make her mad, Jake?" Harel asked.

Jake looked at his father and said, "Well, when you and her talked about Israel or something."

"Oh yes, we'd have marvelous hour-long arguments," Michelle's father said, looking down sadly. "She hated it when I said Israel is too aggressive."

I smiled to him, nodding, good for you Levine, I thought, wondering if that would have been his opinion if his parents had ended up in Israel—had not been one of the lucky few taken by America.

So many times in Jewish history, well-established Jewish communities haven't helped the more unfortunate ones when they needed it. German Jews did nothing to help the Jews from Russia and Poland in the 1920's, and I still wonder why American Jews didn't help the Holocaust Jews more. And I feel saddened how even today so many young American Jews don't have the guts to stand up for us, even if it is out of fashion. Do they really only love us when we are the victims?

"Well, as a German, I don't think I have the right to voice my opinion," I said demurely. I hoped I'd managed to hide my annoyance.

Luckily, Harel changed the subject. "Michelle, are you in the same field as Rachel was?"

"Well, Dennis was responsible for her thesis, and I worked with him on mine, but our fields of interest were different." She answered, also happy to change the subject.

"What is your specialized field?" I butted in, feeling that familiar urge to take the lead.

"Mutual funds," she answered.

"Shouldn't that be part of the Economics Department, instead of the Business School?" Harel asked. If the question was stupid, I preferred he asked it.

"Well, it is kind of a gray area," she said.

"Anyway, if Professor Cromwell says it belongs to the Business School, then it belongs to the Business School," she smiled. "As a matter of fact, Rachel began her thesis in the Economics Department and moved to us unofficially only two months before the accident. The University's so small, a transition like that is easy."

After that, I understood the discrepancy in the Mossad report that said Rachel was in the Economics Department. Again, I wondered why a guy like Cromwell really cared where a graduate student did her thesis.

Before we left, Harel asked her what had happened to her arm.

She looked down from him to her arm, a bit shocked that he'd noticed. "Oh, I didn't think it was so obvious. I was playing tennis this morning and fell while diving for the ball."

I made a mental note that she was a bad liar.

After a little small talk, we hugged the Levines and left, promising to stay in touch.

"I'll call," Michelle promised.

"But I'll see you when we go fishing tomorrow." I said

"No, I'm not coming," she said quickly. "I urgently need to do some reading."

Yeah, right, I thought to myself.

As soon as Harel and I were alone, I asked him if he thought she was holding something back.

"She was lying through her teeth," he said.

"Exactly. She seemed scared of something, although she tried to hide it. This was totally different from the party."

"Scared, you think?"

"I think you scared her when you asked her how she hurt her arm and about the fishing trip." I touched the steel strapped to my leg. Missoula was proving to be an interesting place.

55

Missoula's 70,000 people take up an inordinate amount of room—the metropolitan area is bigger than Seattle in square miles! This excessive consumption of land is due to that except for the student population and some modestly endowed homeowners in the city's core, people live on spacious lots. Our dwelling, for example, sits on ten acres. Cromwell's home is surrounded by sixty, and he owns another 2,000 somewhere near a town called Bozeman, southeast of here. He's in good company there. Mel Gibson and Jane Fonda and other big names, own big ranches there too.

Celebrities like it here. The scenery, of course, is spectacular. And where else could they go to the supermarket without being bothered? People here mind their own business. That's why the Unabomber chose this state. This is the last best place, where rugged individuals still rule supreme—they proudly display rifles in their beat-up pickups.

Professor McFarlane fits right in. He's not as well off as Cromwell, but he isn't exactly poor either. He owns a big country house on forty acres of waterfront—the confluence of the Bitterroot River and the Clark Fork. If you like fishing, you couldn't find a better place.

His house is fully paid for, no mortgage. Having no mortgage is not common in this country—Americans like to believe they are a nation of homeowners when their houses actually belong to the banks.

Most of Montana is very poor, and there are only a few jobs, so a lot of young-native born people are forced to leave. At the same time rich outsiders come for the quality of life, eating up property like candy. Prices have rocketed so high that locals cannot afford to live here. It takes only a couple days here to know how Montanans feel about out-of-staters. Californians are sometimes referred to as "Californicators." Economics have drastically polarized this place between the haves and the have-nots.

*   *   *

In the end, I went alone on the fishing excursion. We had decided that dragging Harel everywhere would look suspicious and might make McFarlane and his pals clam up. As I parked the truck, McFarlane came out with Dale. Both already had full gear on, big wading boots and chest waders.

"Good morning, Barbara," McFarlane greeted me with a smashing smile on his broad, tan face. "Despite the rain last night, it's a beautiful day again today—perfect for fishing. Have you done it before?"

"No, and I'm telling you now that I won't look when you kill the poor fish."

"I don't believe you," he laughed. "Let's go to the garage and try to find some boots for you."

The garage could have been a shop for hunting equipment; guns of all sorts, camouflage clothing, infrared projectors, boots and knives.

"Have you ever hunted?" Dale asked me, noticing that I was watching the guns.

"I don't like guns. I've seen '*Bambi*'."

"Don't say that out loud in Montana," McFarlane laughed. "This is hunters' country."

"Maybe some other time we'll go and shoot at cans," Dale suggested. His chestnut-red hair fell around his eyes, and he smiled mischievously. "I've taught lots of girls to shoot. Michelle's a good shot, now."

"Well, I'm just a bit too European that way. Guns and even more, hunting, are simply barbaric to me. Sorry, but thanks anyway." I was proud of my little lecture; although—or so I thought—the point was lost on them.

McFarlane looked at me with narrow eyes, but his mouth still kept a very faint smile and his gray eyes flashed. "Well, that's not very diplomatic stance, Barbara. You might do better to leave the European preaching behind. Let's not forget that Europeans have participated in their fair share of barbarism, including straight-out genocide."

Blushing isn't part of my repertoire, but I came close. I was coming on a little heavy. I like him for calling me on it, but I need to let on. I hoped I wouldn't have to kill him in the coming weeks. I raised my nose in the air and snapped, "You got me, Professor. No more European pseudo-intellectual babble." It was the first spontaneous answer I'd given since coming here. I kept going, "I spoke for myself. I still can't imagine killing a living being who isn't threatening me. Let's see you hunt for a tiger with a knife," I smiled at him, "or another guy with a gun. At least it would be fair and square then."

"I see your point," McFarlane said. "It's a crying shame men can't kill each other in hands on combat. It would provide some relieve for overpopulated areas. In fact, Montanans would gladly take some suburban runoff from California or New York. Give them a gun, a direction and ten minutes to run. Besides, I killed a bear with a bow in Alaska, last year. Is that more like what you're talking about?"

"I was born a hunter." The conversation had apparently grown tiresome to Dale. "And I am sure I can kill any man with a gun in the forest."

"What Dale's trying to say is that hunting is an ancient art," McFarlane winked at me. "An unfair art that tastes good."

"Yuck," I said to him with a smile," I'm a vegetarian."

"Christ, little lady," McFarlane aped a cowboy. "You'd had better stay around me; around these parts, saying words like ve-ge-te-rian might get you killed"

"Even before being Communists and Jews?" I asked smiling.

"Vegetarians," Dale piped from his back, "are just lousy hunters."

145

We all laughed. Dale, whom I figure resented me for the last conversation, found some old waders and wading boots that were at least two sizes too big for me. I didn't mind. I needed the space for my gun.

Besides being armed, I was also wired for sound. Through the microphone attached to my leg, Harel and Matthew should have been picking up voice and location. Not that they could help if things got really serious. I wondered if Ari was listening too—or playing on the Internet. I asked Dale where we were exactly heading to, feigning mere curiosity. Got that, Ari?

Ari had stayed home with Rafi and Solomon. The poor guys were confined to the rooms downstairs because they didn't want to be seen. It was driving them crazy, but if somebody tried to get into the house by force, then Ari wouldn't be alone. My solo venture today was a rare exception to our policy of working at least in pairs.

The wooden drift boat was already on the trailer behind the Landcruiser. Everything was ready. I went to my car to pick up my jacket. I grabbed a bottle of mineral water and pushed two high-energy chocolate bars into my pocket. Even as kids wandering the mountains, we always carried concentrated food and water. Before I closed the zipper of my bag, I fished out a miniature bottle of olive oil and started rubbing some on my neck and hands.

"What are you doing?" Dale was suddenly peering in the window of the car.

"We have ticks in Germany too, you know, and olive oil is even good for your skin." I smiled and wiped my hands on a tissue.

"I've never heard of that trick." He scratched his head.

Another guy came from the house, and I wondered how many Montanans were going on this trip. He greeted me politely but wasn't overly friendly. I almost prefer that to people like Cromwell, who are more dangerous because they numb you with their superficial friendliness.

McFarlane drove. I sat in the front, and the other guy, who was introduced to me as Bill, sat with Dale in the back. I didn't like the seating arrangement, but I really didn't have a choice. We drove almost an hour to a quiet remote area along the Clark Fork. I barely remember what we talked about, or the view for that matter, because I was focusing my attention on Dale—quite a performance. It gave me an excuse to be half-turned around. Had anything happened, my first reaction would have been to throw myself at McFarlane's legs push the accelerator and pray that I would survive. That was the worst-case scenario.

When we arrived, I was quick to get out. Not that it made me feel much safer. I was still with three guys in a very remote area. Also, with the waders, there was no way I could reach my gun. I guess I had seen too much in the last few years. Maybe everything is an overreaction.

Another group of people stood there taking their boat down into the water. At a little landing area, we slid the boat into the river. Dale actually drove the trailer until it was half-submerged, and then released the drift.

"Bill will drive the car downriver and leave it there," McFarlane explained to me, his friend will pick him up. These boys will do anything for a 12-pack of beer."

146

"How long will it take us to go downstream?" I asked.

"Four to six hours. It depends on whether we let the river carry us or use the oars." He looked at the river. "The heat from the past few days has messed with the snow up there." He pointed to the mountains. "The water's higher and faster than usual, not to mention cold as hell."

"Is that good or bad for fishing?" I asked.

"Makes it a bit more difficult, but don't worry. We'll turn into sleuths; find the spots where the buggers are hiding."

Dale helped me on the raft, boosting me up easily, and we got on our way. McFarlane sat at the rear, I sat in front and Dale in the middle, coaching and controlling the boat. The water was white and fast, we moved swiftly, cutting into the middle of the river. I noticed some big rocks slide under the raft but Dale and McFarlane were laughing and joking as if we were picnicking on a rowboat on a city lake.

It was a warm day, but the water made things colder and I was glad that I'd worn my jacket—a German-brand Gore-Tex shell that sparked infinite interest from McFarlane, a connoisseur of outdoor wear. The Mossad is fastidious about these details.

McFarlane was playing with the fishing rod.

"I've never seen a fly rod," I told him.

"Oh, then you don't know how lucky you are to see this one," he laughed. This is a Winston graphite rod, considered the best there is.

"The Jaguar of rods, eh?"

"The Bentley, my dear, the Bentley."

"Where is it made?"

"Believe it or not," Dale said, while lifting the two lines out of the water, "they make it in Twin Bridges."

"Where?"

"Less than fifty miles from here, it's a tiny place."

"What are you going to do with the fish you catch?" I asked. "Can you eat all of them?"

McFarlane turned to me with an amused look. "After we catch them," McFarlane explained to me, as if I had a learning deficiency, "we release them gently back into the river. Why do you think we have more fish in our rivers than in any other state, except Alaska?"

The thought really hadn't crossed my mind. For once, I gave him a genuine smile. "You don't fail to surprise me, Professor McFarlane. Very pleasantly, I might add."

I wasn't trying to sound interested, but I think it came out a little that way. I'm sure he thought I had a crush on him anyway.

"Dennis is my name, and unless you're presenting a paper in front of the class, I will only respond to Dennis. That is, unless you want me to begin calling you Fraulein Skibbe."

"No, Dennis and Barbara are fine, Professor."

Our eyes locked together for a moment too long. Dale seemed a long way away, although he was still sitting between us.

Then Dale broke the magic. "We'll eat fish only if we stay overnight, and then we'll only take as much as we need."

Montanans have a certain charm—this attachment to their land, and the rest of it. It's a deep connection that an outsider like me would fail to see, or at least it will take a long time. I assume that this is also what the outsiders can't see about Israelis and our connection to the land of our forefathers. Personally, I don't care about the issue. For me, there's only one reason why we have the right to our land. It's the long damn history the Gentiles made us live through.

We were moving now in a more forested area where the only thing that we could see were the trees, water, and birds, tons of them, many of which I hadn't seen before.

I think McFarlane was following my eyes.

"That big one is a bald eagle, our national symbol. That other bird, an osprey, is also a fishing raptor. If we're lucky, you might see it dive and come up with a fish." He looked at the eagle through a small pair of binoculars, and quietly told Dale to row to the shore and stop. "Don't lose the eagle." He told me. "It might be your lucky day. It looks as if our guy is hungry."

We sat motionless in the boat, following the big-winged predator with our eyes as he circled at least a hundred feet in the air. We sat there for at least one hour, I began slowly to grasp why these guys were good hunters. Still, they should shoot with video cameras, not guns.

The eagle kept circling, gliding effortlessly, or so it seemed. Our world had stopped. Everything was focused on this bird. If the river had stopped, too, I wouldn't have been surprised. The bird was not circling; the world was circling around the bird.

And then, without warning, the eagle came down like a rock. I don't know how. Redistribution of weight or something to do with the wings, but the speed was enormous. There was a big splash of water, a flicker of white, and then, a quick ascent. In the eagle's claws was a fish, still twitching, and perhaps a quarter his size.

"Whoa, that was a badass Cutthroat!" Dale screamed

It was a Rainbow, damn it!" McFarlane countered.

I don't know what was more engrossing, the magnificent drama of predator-prey interaction, or the transformation of these men into 13-year-old boys.

"Those are kinds of fish, trout to be specific," McFarlane explained without me asking.

After we left the place, we continued further, and by then I was amazed how many kinds of greens the trees exhibited. The flowers along the banks were beginning to bloom and among them I could spot beavers playing hide and seek.

"In an hour we will reach the slough and do some fishing," McFarlane told me.

"Slough?" I asked.

"This is not exactly a slough. That's what we call it here when part of the river takes a parallel track and the water on the side runs slower. As a matter of fact, it's where fish spawn."

As we approached the opening to the slough, the water became faster.

Despite Dale's efforts, he couldn't shift us to the slow side. McFarlane and I had to get out of the boat and help put it into the calm. We were close to the shore and the water was shallow, but it started to seep into my boots.

"I'm wet, damn it." I cursed.

"No big deal," Dale assured me. "The water is trapped there and in several minutes it'll warm up and you won't feel any discomfort."

I couldn't tell him that I knew the principal of wet suits. We had recently been subjected to intensive diving courses. What bothered me was the fact that the microphone Rafi had installed was now saturated beyond use. I had to reevaluate my vulnerability. My gun would work also when wet but was out of reach. I could've gotten though to my plastic dagger, under my arm. That was my only defense, knowing we were three and they could witness anything for each other if they needed to. I needed to interrupt that way of thinking. So far, I was no threat to them, and if they wanted to kill me after what already happened to Rachel, they would need to make it look natural. Even if everyone in town believed she died by accident, the death of her close friend soon after her own would be too coincidental.

McFarlane snapped me out of my analysis.

"Let's drag the boat to that small shore and walk downstream. I'll show you the magic of fishing."

"How do you know there are a lot of fish here?" I was trying not to sound suspicious, but I was finding it difficult to stick with the logical analysis I'd just worked through. Under the circumstances, walking alone with two guys in the bushes is asking for an "accident."

"Here, wear these polarized glasses and look at the rings that are caused by the fish," Dale said. "It's so crowded there."

"Okay, but I need to pluck some flowers first," I said.

"Pluck flowers?" They both looked at me.

"That's the way a nice German girl says she has to go to the bathroom on a field trip."

"Cute," Dale smiled.

I wanted to be alone so I could take off my left boot and put my gun somewhere else, more reachable. Fighting against two men, even with a dagger, can be a messy affair. Harel could handle three with no problems and without a dagger. I'm not Harel, I had to admit reluctantly.

We were approaching a grove of huge bushes when I heard something crashing through the undergrowth. It sounded massive, very massive, and I swear the ground trembled. I ran straight for the water without thinking. Whatever it was, as a barehanded human being, I felt helpless. McFarlane and Dale were startled, too, but they didn't move. I guess they figured that if it were a grizzly or a mountain lion, shallow water wouldn't save the day.

Good thinking. There are some things it's hard to prepare Israeli agents for. Angry bears weren't part of the curriculum. I turned around, already with my feet in the water, and was relieved to see no hungry forest beast heading for me.

"What was that, a mountain lion?" I yelled, in what I like to think was a controlled loud voice. Israeli Secret Agents don't scream on duty, and I was here on duty.

"It was close, very close," McFarlane said.

"Yeah, what was close?" I asked again.

"It wasn't a mountain lion," Dale explained. "You never hear them when they move."

"It was either a bear, a very big and heavy bear—given all the broken branches—or a moose," McFarlane said

"Moose?" I asked in disbelief. "Like Bullwinkle? They're not dangerous, are they?"

"They can be far more dangerous than a bear if they decide to charge you. They can roll over a medium-size car with ease."

"I give-up, guys, you know everything."

I learned how to cast a fly rod. I won't bore you with the details. Let's just say again, for now it looks like McFarlane won't be a necessary casualty. And I even think Dale, thick as he is, isn't capable of diabolic behavior. I hope I'm right.

56

All six of us sat at the fireplace downstairs this evening—no camera can peek at us there. On the agenda is my next encounter with McFarlane. Tomorrow I meet him to discuss my thesis.

Matthew and Harel went to collect wood, plentiful everywhere around here. Matthew held a big bottle of wine the whole time. Anybody watching the house would see us having a little party with our generous half-drunk landlords. Rafi and Ari built a cozy fire. Ari took command of vegetable soup, and before we really relaxed, Rafi checked all his smart equipment again. We didn't want any unexpected visitors.

"I find it extremely remarkable that we've never found or seen Rachel's thesis," Matthew said.

"The fact that we haven't, reinforces the assumption that there is or was something in that thesis that pushed somebody to eliminate her," Rafi stated the obvious.

"I'm not sure about that," Harel offered. "Graduate students submit their suggestions for theses the first few weeks after school starts, and it took several months until somebody took her out."

"What are you saying? That the thesis has nothing to do with her death?" Rafi asked, sounding worried.

"No, I think that writing the suggestion for her thesis didn't threaten anybody. There was something that came afterwards, something that no one expected her to uncover."

"So what suggestion should Yael present tomorrow for her thesis?" Rafi inquired. "We don't know what sounds threatening to them."

"We can take our time, Sly," I said, "and I hope that in the next six months we will find something. In that time, your brother's wife will have all your father's money back again."

"Oh, god," Rafi drifted off, back to his inadvertent impression of Woody Allen.

"Well, the best approach would be to go to the meeting with no particular suggestion," Harel advised. "Just tell the professor that since holding companies are such a broad subject, perhaps he could offer you some guidelines on how to get about it."

"Exactly," said Solomon. "By looking at what he suggests, we could see what he tries to avoid and that would be what Yael could offer as a thesis."

"How long would it take you to write a proposal for Yael?" Ari asked him.

"Those proposals are not so difficult to write once we agree on what we want to say. I could finish the job in two, three days max."

"Do we have current detailed reports about our two professors and Dale?" I asked.

"Mossad said tomorrow at the latest," Rafi assured us. "I'll have it printed as soon as possible."

"Okay then," Ari said, "tomorrow, after the meeting with him, we'll have a very short discussion, then have our Seder, and on Tuesday morning, we'll discuss Yael's proposal for the thesis after all of us have a night to sleep on it."

He gave us that serious stare again. "I don't want to be melodramatic, but if we aren't able to provoke them with our proposal, then I don't know how in the world we can. Time isn't on our side, and we can't afford to let them decide when to make a move."

"I know we're on to something," I decided to reassure everyone. "Something is strange about the wealth those guys accumulated."

"The real question is: Are we ready to stay here until we find out the answers?" Ari asked. "Or better put, how long will Marcus let us stay here?" He sounded mysterious.

"I don't think it will take so long," I said

"That's not what I asked you."

"I'll stay as long as I feel that we're on the right track," I said defiantly.

"I'm with Yael, but I guess we all understand that," Harel said.

"What is this, a revolt for no reason? Matthew said with a smile to Ari.

"How do you feel about hanging out in Missoula, Montana, Matthew?"

"I'm not leaving anyone behind."

"Me neither," Solomon said. Rafi had regained his Stallone-like posture. "My sister-in-law can go to hell, and if she and my retarded little brother steal my money again. Well, if she does . . . I'm moving to a kibbutz. That's the perfect place for my family anyway. What do you say, Yael? Will your kibbutz accept my family?" He was grinning too.

"Absolutely, Harel and I will put in a good word for you. We always wanted a real muscle man in our area." I winked at him.

Ari sat there, wondering, I guess, what the goal of the conversation had been. I think he knew we were just trying to rally each other. We all had feelings about Rachel—more than we cared to admit. Not the best basis for a mission, but we didn't want to come back to her parents empty handed.

"Let's try to solve it fast," Ari wrapped up. "Otherwise, I'll be submitting a resignation to Marcus and joining you on the damn kibbutz."

• There was going to be action, even if we had to force it. I hoped again that not all of my new Missoula acquaintances would turn out to be guilty of murder.

57

At eleven o'clock Monday morning, I knocked on the door of McFarlane's office. At this point, I was getting used to the Business School and its ridiculous, carpeted hallways, its pots of ferns, its bad Mondrian prints, and the mahogany glimmer of Cromwell's reception room. McFarlane's office was in a more subdued end of the building, as would befit a more subdued kind of guy.

He was sitting behind a simple oak desk, feet on the windowsill, with his glasses pushed down on his tan nose. Bookshelves lined the walls, and his parka was thrown on a small stool in front of the desk. A second chair held Michelle, who turned and greeted me cheerfully enough, but her eyes were troubled. I smiled in greeting to them both, and turned to shut the door. A National Geographic calendar was pinned to it; a picture of a saber-toothed tiger bobbed up and down as the door fell shut.

He was discussing with or lecturing Michelle about turnover in mutual funds. People entrust their retirement money to funds, believing they are safe, long-run investments, he said. But they don't understand that, by putting their money in those funds, they unknowingly turn into day-traders. The average mutual fund in America and Europe buys and sells each of their holdings many times a year.

Michelle was asking if she could divide the funds, not according to their kind of holding in value or growth companies, but according to the amount of turnover. She wondered what the correlation would be between investment style and consumer profit.

Before she left, she gave me her shy smile, "The University arranged for us to share a room for our on-campus studies. When you finish here, come on down and we'll get some lunch." She looked sad.

"Sure, I'd like to. And maybe you could give me some tips about how to write the thesis proposal."

"I'd love to. I did mine last year."

"And it was a very good one," McFarlane complimented her as she left. He got up and closed the door. "Well, Barbara, did you enjoy our little fishing expedition yesterday?"

"I admit that I didn't expect to have so much fun, Dennis."

"Well, how about giving hunting a try? One never knows . . ."

"Hmmm, I'd still feel too sorry for the animals and it's unfair, anyway. Let's see how those great macho hunters could perform against something more equally fitted."

"Like whom?"

"Me," I almost bit my tongue. "I mean I don't know how to use guns, but I still think I could give them a run for their money."

"That could be arranged," he said. "There's a game for attitudes like yours."

"What game is that?" I asked.

"Paint ball, pure and simple," he answered. "You go into the forest, and shoot small paint balls from carbon dioxide pistols or rifles."

"Oh, I've heard of that," I said. "That's the game militia people play. Crazies like the Unabomber." I tried to sound as out-of-the-loop as possible.

"Yes. I know, I know. It's a game for the Lost Boys. But that's a typical misunderstanding. No, it's not a militia exercise, and we won't be reading passages from the Constitution between rounds. And, to my knowledge, Ted Kaczinski did not play paintball."

"I'd like to play. I like new games."

"You know," he said, and rose to his feet and leaned one hip on his desk, "I see why our friend Dale is smitten with you."

"You mean Michelle's boyfriend? I am sorry to hear they broke up. She did look kind of sad."

"That's why I asked her to talk to me this morning. She's a nice girl, and break-ups are no fun for anyone, no matter how strong they are."

"How long were they together?"

"Seven, eight months," he answered. "As you can see, when you work with students as closely as I do, you get involved with their personal lives. I like to be a mentor not only in academically related work." He smiled.

"She'll recover," I assured him.

"She'll handle it all right, but probably not like you would."

"Like me? What do you mean, Dennis?"

"Just little impressions. The way you walked in the water when you and I carried the boat. The way you reacted when the bear surprised us," he said

"What are you talking about? I was scared to death. It doesn't happen to me every day in Berlin, you know."

"Oh, you were very scared, but I was amazed that on a certain level you were still very calm, strikingly calm. Growing up the way I did made me very observant. No wonder Dale has a little crush on you. There is something wild about you, well hidden though."

"No thanks, I replied, "One—I'm taken, and two—I'm not taken with the jock type."

He abruptly changed the subject. "Well, have you given some thought to your thesis topic?"

"Yes, I have, but could I be open with you?" I spoke quietly.

"I think it's always the best way to go."

"Look, Rachel was a very close friend. We met because of a mutual interest in this subject of investment strategy. We spent hours reading and debating about what we were reading. We had a lot more in common than just that interest, as it turned out, but at the time that work was a mutual obsession. We both planned to continue here, in a formal academic program, but I confess I'm a bit shocked at how ambivalent I've been feeling about since her death. Maybe I'm just shell shocked. The work still interests me but not as in the past. The degree would be useful though. And Rachel's mother seems to look to me to carry on her daughter's work."

This was quite a speech, quite an act, really. I paused and glanced at McFarlane, as if I was seeking knowledge.

"Go on, Barbara. I can imagine how tough it's been for you."

That's just what I needed to hear. "Well to be honest, at this point I couldn't care less what subject my thesis is on. Some days I dream about becoming a veterinarian. Other times I think about physics. On other days, I want to play soccer with the penguins at the South Pole. I think I need a little assistance here. What if you give me some guidelines, and I take it from there?"

He took some time after that statement, and I was hoping he didn't find my humbug to be hopelessly confused. "Whatever is said here stays between you and me. This is a promise. I appreciate your sensitivity concerning Rachel's mom. Your honesty, although a bit unwise for your academic future, is also commendable." He hesitated. "Now it's my turn to be unusually forthcoming. Your academic record is certainly respectable, but not spectacular. Your GRE test scores are spectacular, however, and your field of interest—in spite of your present ambivalence—shows unusual sophistication about the matter of investments. The truth is that you're the kind of student that graduate programs consider themselves lucky to attract. I'd be happy to help you develop a thesis topic."

"Good job, Yael," I thought to myself.

"Rachel was, as we all know, intrigued by advantages of holding companies as far as how they maximize the profits of the shareholders," he said. "Follow me?"

"Of course."

"There are extremely different approaches to attaining that goal," he continued. Let me use two extreme examples: Buffett and Cisco. Buffett buys companies and rarely interferes in their management. He's big into companies with competent management that can run the show without him. A low-maintenance management approach, so to speak. Then you have Cisco, which buys companies and then actively manages them. It's hard to even call Cisco a holding company because they try to integrate the companies.

"There's a huge gap between these philosophies, and what your friend Rachel was interested in was the correlation between the various kinds of holding companies and the profitability to the owners, the stockholders."

"Did she leave anything in writing?" I asked.

"Not that I know. She died before anything was actually due. It's possible she had something with her personal belongings, but I couldn't get to something like that. I doubt you could, either, unless you go through her mother."

"I didn't realize she still had some things here," I said.

"Yeah, the police called a week ago and asked if she had some belongings here."

"Well, I'll call the mother and ask her to give me power of attorney," I said.

"Great idea, but remember, we can handle the project even if we don't find anything. Don't get your hopes up, and feel you need to depend on her work."

Incompetent Mossad, they should have told us about the items still in Missoula. I didn't need to find this out from a possible killer. What will happen when Harel and I retire in two months? Will our lovely country survive?

"I liked what you said about the South Pole and the penguins," he said suddenly, "if you ever . . ."

"If I ever what?" I asked

"Ah, forget it, just get to work."

I didn't forget it. Instead I said something I had no intention of saying. "That comment you made yesterday about genocide was interesting to me. I wanted to tell you that I know what my country did was horrible. I wasn't trying to say hunters are at the same level. I'm really sensitive about the Jewish issue and Germany."

"No offense was taken, Barbara. I was just teasing and poking fun. To tell you the truth, I'm pretty sensitive . . . well, let's just say, informed . . . about Jewish issues in general."

"Oh?" He'd caught me off guard again.

"When I lived in New York after my undergraduate degree, my girlfriend was Jewish, and one of her parents was an Israeli. She sensitized me to the subject, had me feeling like a radical Jewish intellectual. And then left me like the gullible American I am."

"She broke up with you?"

"No, I broke up with her and it broke my heart."

"Why did you do it?"

"I was ready to give up Montana for her, which, trust me, would have been a hell of a sacrifice, but I damn well loved her. I was just not ready to live in Manhattan for the rest of my life. That place is a hamster cage. I guess I'd say that about every large city, though. I would not mind Maine or upstate New York but not the big city. Any way, she refused any compromise, and in the end it seemed to me that New York was the lover that won."

He looked at me and smiled. "I don't know why I'm telling you all that, but now you know about a piece of my life and why I liked Rachel. Just hand in any proposal you wish and we can go from there."

Things were getting too personal on both sides—the last thing I needed. But Dennis McFarlane has some depth I rarely encounter. Something I thought I would never say about a hunter.

58

I met Michelle briefly, and asked her if we could meet again an hour later. I needed some exercise. She pointed to a trail right off the campus, and in less than ten minutes I was alone among some Ponderosas and patches of sagebrush. No one was on the trail for hundreds of yards in front or behind.

I stopped to take a breath, and pulled out my "handy." I know they're called cell phones here, but I like the German word better. I connected to our Embassy in D.C., entered the area code, and continued to dial. No one could know I was talking to Ari across town, unless someone was jacked into a specific Israeli military satellite. Even then, they would need to crack our Hebrew, and then crack the coding system that protects my voice and sends it to Ari, and then decode it for his receiver. This blender system is standard for top-secret communiqués.

I told him about Rachel's stuff, and he said he would take care of it right away. He cursed the Mossad too, and I couldn't help but smile. I wonder if they curse us as much. Not that we give them any reason.

"Check also if McFarlane once had a half-Israeli girl friend. It's too much of a coincidence. They lived in New York."

"Will do."

"I don't know what it will come to, but it's worth a try." I said.

I ran back to campus and found Michelle sitting in the room, waiting patiently. I didn't knock—a habit I knew I should change, but she was startled by it more than she should have been.

She recovered and said, "Okay, let's go. I'm so hungry I could faint."

The cafeteria was not far from the building. We covered the distance at our usual speedy pace, even though this campus was worth a slow walk. It's not unusual to spot an eagle above you or deer that come down from the mountain at twilight. The big news story last week was an incident at a woman's house in the University District. She called the police after a mountain lion had gotten into her bathroom. She was actually on the toilet when she saw it come through the first-story window. Fortunately, the door was closer to her than the cat. She got up, pants around her ankles, and slid out the door before the cat could get out of the damp bathtub under the window. I was relieved to read they didn't kill it. After a shot from a tranquilizer gun, they threw it in the back of a truck and carted it out to the hills.

The cafeteria was located in a three-level building. There were subtropical plants everywhere, some quite rare, making it look more like a greenhouse. "Believe it or not, there are special University personnel solely responsible for the indoor plants," Michelle explained.

I didn't tell her that as a kibbutznik I could appreciate how much work it takes to maintain such an arboretum. Because of our seclusion there, we developed our own ways of working with plants. One of the safest ways to combat many of the plant diseases, for instance, is to place garlic everywhere. It's not only the saving grace for humans. Harel's grandpa believes he is so healthy and old because he eats a fresh garlic clover every day, not one of those useless garlic pills.

"I wanted to apologize for my parents." She said.

"Why is that? They're nice."

"The way they put you on the spot about Israel."

"What do *you* feel about Israel?" I was genuinely curious.

"To be honest, I never cared or thought about it until I met Rachel," she said. "It seemed like she really loved her land. I'm not a political person, and sometimes I was envious that I didn't have something I cared about as passionately as she did."

"Maybe it's because you take this land and your freedom and safety for granted," I said as lightly as I could.

"Americans," I continued, "or, for that matter, we Germans have all this luxury and we don't give it a second thought. It's like taking air for granted until we sit in an airplane and a window breaks and we're gasping for oxygen."

"You're right. It's just that our everyday problems take over, and we don't even think about those things. Rachel told me that in Israel people hear every day about soldiers or civilians being killed." She smiled sadly. "I guess under those circumstances you don't have the time to think about your own pathetic little lives."

"Your parents are Jewish, so why all the animosity toward Israel?"

"Oh, just ignore them. They're old leftists."

It's always a no-win situation. I thought. The liberals say we are right-wingers, the right-wingers say we are communists. I got used to seeing anti-Israeli feelings among European Jews, but at least with them I can understand. They have insecurities about living on that continent and consciously or not, seem to seek alliance with gentiles, but when American Jews fall into this thinking, it just angers me.

♦ "So, what about your life?" It was time to change gears. "You've seemed sad the past two days, but since I don't know you well, I didn't want to bring it up."

"Dale left me, and I just don't get it," she said, "I mean, I could have understood if things hadn't been going well, but this came out of the blue."

"It always comes out of the blue," I told her. "I'm no expert, but I've seen break-ups before among friends. Truth is, it never really comes out of the blue."

"Well, I need a good vacation, that may help" She smiled.

"That's the best way to take it, Michelle," I said. "In two years, you'll look back and feel frustrated by every second you wasted over him."

She laughed, "More than missing him, I can't take the rejection."

"I think that's why so many people freak out after a break-up. It is not because they really cared about the other person. At least, that's one of the main reasons."

"What's the other?"

"The fear of being alone. Or the fear of not finding somebody as wonderful again."

"Well, then, I'm in real trouble, because he's the big star on the Grizzlies."

"The what?"

"The University football team," she reminded me. "Where have you been?"

We both laughed.

"Those big guys were never my type," I told her.

"Well, your boyfriend isn't exactly an effete intellectual. He looks almost as strong as Dale."

I leaned over the table and whispered, "Oh, he is just a big baby and he follows me everywhere. He cried when I told him I wanted it over, so I stayed in the relationship. He is kind, so I didn't have the heart to hurt him."

I love describing Harel as a crybaby. I also didn't tell her that football or no football, Harel would put down her Dale in less than a second.

"By the way, how did you meet Dale?"

"On a hunting trip."

"No way. You're not a hunter, too?" I asked.

"A very good one too, thank you. I think I impressed Dale when I dropped an elk with a single headshot. I suppose most men don't think women can do it."

Waste of talent, I thought. But I decided not to argue anymore about hunting in Montana.

"Well, I think I'll get moving. I got the guidelines for the thesis, and I understand that the graduate students are meeting next week to present their new proposals."

"Yes, but nobody will expect anything from you this soon."

"Oh, I'm quick," I assured her. Solomon will have to work his butt off the next several days I was thinking.

"Then you will be very busy. Too bad, because I thought you might help me tomorrow evening on something. But I can ask somebody else."

"What do you need?"

"I have some books and clothes at Dale's house, and I wanted to ask if you could come with me."

"Of course. I have the time for that. Are you afraid to confront him?"

"He has a temper, but I think in front of you he wouldn't show it."

"A temper?"

She didn't answer, and I guess she felt uncomfortable, perhaps ashamed.

"You mean he might get violent? Has he ever hit you?" I asked.

"Well, not really. But after the party last week he got wasted and pushed me to the floor. I'd never seen him like that."

It was hard to hold my tongue, but I knew from experience that Michelle needed support at such a time, not a tirade from me. But here I can say freely that I find male dogs to be more civilized than many human males. There's no excuse accepting abuse, although that doesn't stop even educated women from making excuses for a violent partner. I could never imagine women in our kibbutz taking physical abuse even once. To be fair, I could never see Harel or Eric or any of the men in our kibbutz ever even consider the use of physical force toward their partners. But that type of thinking, like its violent counterpart, has to be taught early. Violence is only justified as a means of self-preservation.

So I said nothing more, and we decided to meet each other the following day.

59

When I came home, everyone was sitting outside on the deck, eating homemade falafel, enjoying the sun and speaking Hebrew. I am the only one, it seems, who has to work for a living.

Ari had gotten fed up with being under observation and had instructed Rafi to destroy the camera in such a way that it would look as if a deer or a bear messed with it. If anyone came close enough, Rafi's equipment would detect it.

"It could be a trap, telling us she left stuff at Dale's apartment," Solomon suggested, after I reported what I had done. I didn't report on the last several minutes in McFarlane's office

"Maybe, but I don't think so," I said

"We still haven't given them a reason to move," Ari said, "but we'll take no chances. Matthew, you and Harel be in the neighborhood, and Rafi, arrange again for Yael to take a microphone."

"How are we going to provide them a reason?" Rafi asked.

"McFarlane has told Yael what he thinks her topic should be. We'll sleep on it tonight and think what might make them mad enough to try to lash out," Ari said.

"Are the updated reports here?" I asked.

"Yes, we already downloaded them. Tomorrow we'll discuss them, and afterwards Solomon can write a nice proposal."

"Can I see them?"

"Sure, they're downstairs. We've already read them, but go ahead and read them for yourself. Then it's holiday until tomorrow. Thinking about something else might give us some new ideas, put things in prospective. We don't want to stay here all summer, do we?"

I went down to read the reports.

Cromwell had an impressive record, no doubt about it. His undergraduate degree came from Humboldt State University in Arcata, California, but his Ph.D. in economics was from Stanford. He'd had a teaching position at Columbia and had authored many articles in the professional journals and he also co-authored two books. He was a bright guy.

He's on the board of many companies in different fields: pharmaceuticals, timber, and defense. These are called value companies—the companies you invest in if you don't want to speculate. He's also on the board of directors of several mutual funds. I suppose many companies love having a star academic on their boards. It looks nice on the annual report, and he's photogenic as well. The report left open what specifically brought him to Montana but pointed out that many people come here simply for the quality of life.

The next report was McFarlane's. He picked up his Bachelor's in history at UM, with a minor in economics. Good grades, but nothing remarkable. He then moved to New York, where he did an internship for a brokerage firm. That's where he met Cromwell, although the report didn't say how. I guess McFarlane became his protégé, because he enrolled in the Ph.D. program at Columbia's Economics' Department shortly afterwards. It took him less than two years to get the degree, a remarkable feat under then-chairman Cromwell. Then they moved to Montana, and McFarlane took a post as an Associate Professor. We had plenty of information.

Cromwell had recommended McFarlane several months ago for a tenured position. Many of the companies that had Cromwell on their boards had hired McFarlane as a consultant. He was highly compensated, with generous consulting fees and excellent benefits.

A handwritten note added that McFarlane's half Israeli girlfriend was real, and that she currently held a middle management position in a prestigious public relations firm in New York. No wonder she didn't want to move to the Wild West.

Dale was next in the lineup. Like McFarlane, he's from Libby, Montana. He's in the third year of his undergraduate degree, although he's listed as a senior. It seemed from the report that his study skills were negligible, at best. But then again, many universities in America give their top athletes major financial benefits; scholarships for example. In three of the companies where McFarlane had worked, Dale had been "hired" as a Manager's Assistant.

It looked as if Mossad had either hacked into the IRS and some bank records or had some inside people there. The reports contained amazing financial details, testimony to the low level of security in American banks. All three were definitely ready to retire.

Michelle's file, on the other hand, indicated the negative fiscal status one would expect of a student. She owes substantial amounts of money from student loans.

The reports gave more data about the companies on whose boards Cromwell served, but I put them aside for the time being. Tonight is the Seder, and Ari himself told us to relax. So I'll follow orders for a change.

60

There we were, six Israelis, at the beginning of the third millennium, in the middle of Montana, celebrating Passover in hiding as if we were still in bloody Europe.

Ari, Matthew, and Solomon did all the cooking and preparations for the big traditional meal. Ari was famous for his cooking talents, and he told us once that after he retires he would open a restaurant. On missions with Ari, we're always well fed.

Rafi was busy with his electronic equipment, and Harel and I were told to take it easy, so we took our guns apart. We disassembled them, one after the other, in case someone paid an unexpected visit. We oiled them generously, inside and outside, the magazines, too. They were so smooth. Then, a short shower, and we were ready for the holiday.

The long table—two tables put together—was covered by a white map, and I wondered where they had picked it up. All the dishes, including the silverware, were form the local Salvation Army store. Still, it was perfect. The *matzah*—the unleavened bread, the bitter herbs and *karpas*—reminders of the bitterness of slavery; the *charoset*—symbolizing the sweetness of freedom; a roasted lamb bone and roasted egg—reminders of sacrifices made in the Temple times.

All the men, including Matthew, wore *kippot*, skullcaps. I always smile when I see this big blonde Texan wearing a skullcap. Each of us held a simple military edition of the Haggadah, the Passover book. No frills, just the original words that the Jews had been reading for the last 2,000 years. This edition even retained the original Aramaic that was used to interpret the Hebrew.

Each of us waited our turn to read. The four times we were supposed to drink wine, we drank red grape juice instead. In the passage where God said he would take revenge on all those Gentiles who killed his people, the Jews, we all assured Matthew we'd put in a good word for him. Heck, Jesus read and said the same words long before the pogroms, the Arabs, and the Holocaust. I wonder sometimes how the Bible knew what was coming.

Two hours later, it was time for dinner. Vegetable soup with homemade Matzah balls, two huge Alaskan salmon with brown rice and fresh vegetables. For dessert, Ari made us tiramisu, an Italian delicacy that was probably not on the menu when the Haggadah was written.

After the meal, we spent another hour singing all those old hymns of praise. We did it all! I have no idea why I liked it so much, why even for agnostics like us, tradition in small doses still means something. Might it, after all, be the key to bringing meaning back into life? Why else does it always leave me with a renewed sense of hope?

61

The next morning, we sat down on the carpeted floor in the living room. We had to put the puppy in the other room after he scattered the dozens of reports we'd spread out. We had a lot of research and analysis ahead of us—back to the nitty-gritty of what spies really do. A little less dramatic than the producers of Mission Impossible have you believe.

"Let's summarize," Ari began. "We know what won't make them nervous about your research: The advantages or disadvantages a holding company has by buying companies and only being passively involved in their management or by buying and running those companies actively."

"In other words, we have almost nothing," Solomon said. "This is academic crap on which thousands of students waste their time. Most of them don't get killed."

"I agree. So the big question is, are there any other advantages a holding company gets by acquiring a particular company—advantages beyond the obvious one, which is increasing the value for the stockholders of the holding company?"

"Well, one huge advantage is that by buying into a company, you put yourself into a situation where you have a say about who would be on the board of directors," Solomon answered, "and it puts you in a position to know inside information."

"And how important is that?" Rafi asked.

"Well, let's say you sit on the board and you learn there's a big contract in the works that will jump the stock price up. Let's further assume that because of this good news, the price of your company's shares will go up ten dollars a share, once this information becomes public knowledge. So all you have to do is to buy a million shares. Several days later, when the price goes up ten dollars, you are ten million dollars richer. The only problem is that using inside knowledge is illegal."

"Is there a way around it?" Harel asked.

"Sure, you involve somebody to whom you are not related, preferably somebody abroad, and split the dough with them."

"Even after taxes, you are still left with five million, assuming you gave your partner a million and the IRS another four. Not bad for several days work," Matthew said.

"No Matthew, it won't be taxed at all. There's a loophole in the American tax law that says intangible assets, sent from abroad to an American citizen, are not subject to tax. You just ask your friend to wire you the money." Our wise Solomon was clearly in control. He knew his stuff.

"There is only one little problem here," Harel said. "It doesn't explain the murder. At least not the high professional level that it was carried out and the speed with which they executed the attack in Germany. Inside information, the way you describe it, sounds like fun and a lot of easy money. I'm sure a lot of 'insiders' in corporate America do it. But is that kind of big money enough to lead to assassination because somebody uncovers it? I don't think so."

We knew we were onto something. Someone had sent the orders to Berlin. It was also clear that Cromwell and McFarlane weren't totally clean. But we had nothing to indicate their involvement with Rachel's death. Not yet, at least.

At this point in my career, I can look back and regret many things, but one thing I don't have to regret is the killing of an innocent human being. I want to keep it that way.

"I think we're asking the wrong questions," Harel said. "Instead of asking how Cromwell is benefiting from being on the board; maybe we should first ask how he came to grab these positions of power in the first place—and in so many companies. Also, this guy sits on the boards of some of the biggest defense and biotech contractors in this country. I understand the insider trading issue and the money to be made with it, but it pales in comparison to the advantages one can have in these positions of power."

Ari broke in. "Okay, I agree with Harel. Let's look at this from some other angles. How does a person get in those positions of power and what can you do once you reached these positions? And don't tell me now that Cromwell got those positions because he is the Business School Chairman of a cowboy university."

"Well, if we approach it this way, then one of the surest ways to get a position on a corporate board is if a big shareholder demands it," Solomon said.

"Is there a way to find out who the biggest shareholders are in each of these companies where Cromwell is a board member?" Harel asked. "We might find a particular shareholder who has big stakes in all those companies."

"For this we don't even have to contact our library," Solomon answered while playing with the computer's keyboard. "The miracle called the Internet will give me the answer in less than five minutes. It's all public information."

It took him almost fifteen minutes, but the search produced printouts of all the shareholders who own at least one percent of the outstanding shares of these companies. "Doesn't sound like much," Solomon announced, "but because the shares are spread among thousands, or sometimes even millions, of shareholders, owning such a small percentage can give you a say. Not always control, but definitely a say."

The printed lists consisted mostly of the names of pension or mutual funds. Few were of individual shareholders. One percent control of a company's shares is worth $40 million, and that was only for small companies. General Dynamics, the main naval contractor, was an exception. Close to ten percent of its shares were held by one family.

The complete printout provided a list of more than two-hundred fifty names of mutual funds, pension funds, and a few individuals. We tried to select only those names that appeared at least twice, which would mean they owned one percent or more of the shares of at least two companies where Cromwell was on the board. It took us a good hour, and we were left with forty-six names.

At this point in the game we had no more individuals, only pension and mutual funds, which on Wall Street are called 'institutional investors.' The question was if any of them had a major position in all of Cromwell's companies. We checked and the answer was negative. So we asked ourselves the next logical question: Do any two, combined, have a major investment of at least one percent in Cromwell's companies.

We colored the lists with neon markers, and I imagined how childish it would have looked to an outsider—everyone on the floor having fun with colors.

Five minutes later we had it. Only one combination of two institutional investors had at least one percent in all those companies. Guess who was on their board? Yes, our friend Cromwell.

Both institutional investors were private pension funds from Montana, one of them was located in the biggest city of Montana, Billings, and its biggest shareholder was the pension fund of the timber industry. The other one was located in Helena, the capital of Montana, and the biggest shareholder there was the pension fund of the mining industry.

We then compared the big shareholders within those two, only one investment group came up. It was from California: The Eureka Rainbow Investments Fund. I'd noticed before that most of the institutional investment enterprises have reassuring names.

Solomon was back at the computer. "Sorry guys, we're stuck. The Eureka Rainbow Fund is a private company, so they're not required to give the names of the owners."

"So how will you find that out?" Rafi asked.

"Oh, it's very easy. Even the smallest restaurant in every town in America has to be registered in its local Chamber of Commerce. All we have to do is to send somebody to the Chamber of Commerce in Eureka, and we can find out immediately. This information is not always available on the Internet, but locally it's easy to get."

Before Solomon had finished the sentence, Ari was on the phone barking orders to our people in Seattle, Portland, and San Francisco. Then he clicked the phone off. "Our closest guy is in Portland, and he'd better be on his way." He looked at his watch. "Its 9:30 here and they're one hour earlier, so I think he should make it there by noon. Within twenty-four hours, we can have a full investigation of all the names he comes up with."

"Because it remained a private company, I would say there probably won't be too many names on the list," Solomon explained.

"I'm betting it will be just one person," Harel said, "unless there are some of his or her straw people too. That individual controls an obscure company, which, by leverage, controls two relatively little-known, but respectable pension funds in Montana, which once again, by leverage, have a say in, and partly control, the most important defense contractors in this country, including cutting-edge biotech companies."

In a deliberate voice Harel continued. "I still can't see what the financial implications are, but this individual could indirectly control companies that are worth billions. And what might turn out to be even more significant is that this control represents enormous financial, and more important, political power. Especially considering the nature of those companies."

I had a gut feeling Harel was on the right track. He and we were unfolding a mystery with just good, straight thinking and a little computer. With all their super computers, Mossad was still off base. It's hard not to get some satisfaction out of that.

Ari stood up, all smiles. "All right, guys, for the first time I feel we're making some progress. Good job, Harel, good job. Nothing to say to Harel, Yael?"

"Today is his day." I smiled and patted him on his shoulder.

"Then let's digest what we've talked about. By tomorrow at the least, we should have some preliminary reports about those guys in Eureka and then we can decide on our next move."

But no matter how good I felt about this breakthrough, I still thought we had, at most, only something to provoke them with. Whatever they were up to, it was most likely legal, because guys like this always have top lawyers. We still didn't know the actual motivation behind this concentration of power. We still had to find the connection between them and Rachel. And once we did, they would sure need more than smart lawyers.

62

I met Michelle as planned on the corner of Broadway and Ryman at 8 p.m. There's this nice vegetarian restaurant there called The Black Dog.

"It's one of the best restaurants in town," Michelle told me. "It used to be owned by a crazy biochemist that served superb organic food."

"Biochemist?" I laughed, "and a health nut?" I'd always thought that those were the guys who poisoned us with all the food additives.

"He was a super health nut and a real Ph.D. from Harvard. He and his girlfriend, also a chemist, took a trip from the East Coast to Seattle and fell in love with Montana along the way. There were no laboratories here, so they opened the Black Dog."

"How did you get to know them?"

"I didn't. Rachel got to know him because he spoke Hebrew. Not many people speak it here, as you can guess."

"Was he Israeli?"

"No, he told us that his parents came to Israel as refugees from Prague, and after three years they immigrated to the States. As doctors they earned ten times as much here. Anyway, after he sold the restaurant, he decided to go back to school to study accounting."

It always amazes me how many Israelis live here in America—more than half a million of them. It was interesting to hear another story about the pressures that force Israelis to leave our Jewish homeland.

After dinner, we left for Dale's house in the University District, a fifteen-minute walk. Rachel's "accident" must have occurred only several blocks from where we were heading. We weren't taking any chances. Harel and Matthew followed Michelle and me pretty closely, and I was also equipped with one of Rafi's microphones. Harel and Matthew could hear us clearly.

We walked to the front door, and Michelle wasted no time opening the screen door, knocking, and then closing it again. Seemed odd to me, but it could have been a Missoula custom. A brawny, football type opened the door and peaked through the mesh. Peering at us through bloodshot eyes, he greeted us with a "Whozit?" It was clear he was drunk.

"It's me, Hank," Michelle said. "Is Dale here?"

"No, I guess he had some extra training tonight. Hey, come in ladies. You look like you could use a beer."

"Thanks, but we just came to pick up some of my books. This is Barbara."

"We-l-l-l Hell-ooo, Bar-bar-a," he said.

Another big guy came out of the kitchen.

"Hi, Terry," Michelle greeted him. "This is Barbara. Barbara, Terry. And the other guy's Billy. They're Dale's roommates."

Terry was numbed, as well. We got away and went up to the second floor. Michelle opened the door into what I thought would be a simple room with a table, bed and chair. Instead it was a full-size studio with the amenities college students shouldn't have. A Bang & Olafssen stereo system, a 150-gallon tropical fish tank with piranha, and the furniture was for sure not from a cheap shop. Maybe the University was taking excellent care of its football stars or our friend from California was a generous provider for his or her people. I guess the latter, since I can't believe Dale or the University would purchase a Bang & Olafssen for any reason. Cromwell would.

Michelle collected her stuff. It wasn't much. Some books, a colored glass jar of flowers, and a yellowish old teddy bear.

"That's sweet that you take your bear everywhere," I told her. "I have one too, but I keep it at home."

"I've had it since I was a baby. I just love him, and he has to comfort me now that my boyfriend deserted us." She smiled. She didn't seem too devastated.

Hank and Terry swaggered in tandem through the door.

"Hey gals, ya' wanna join us for a little party we're having?"

"Oh, maybe another time, Hank," Michelle tried to evade him. "We've got papers to write tonight."

The way she said it was the way she opened the outside door. Very carefully.

"Then stay just for a drink," Hank said.

"OK, but then we have to go," Michelle gave in.

"Just stay here, gals. We'll bring up the drinks." They went to grab some wine.

When they left, I looked at Michelle.

"Why are we staying here?"

"Let me handle it," she whispered. "They're drunk, and I don't want to make those guys mad."

"They can go straight to hell," I told her.

I was sure that Harel and Matthew, probably just outside, were having a great time listening to our talk with the meatheads.

"Barbara, I don't think you get it. I've seen these guys get nasty. They're incredible boozers. I don't know why Dale doesn't make them move out."

She wanted to say something else, but they were back with a bottle and some glasses. Hank put on some music. Terry was looking me over in the classic style of drunken morons.

I looked at Michelle, ignoring the amorous athletes. "Well, I'm from Bavaria, and we have different rules there."

"What are you talking about? Bavaria?" Terry asked while offering me a glass of wine.

I took the glass and said, "Oh, I was just explaining to Michelle that in Germany we don't take shit from men. What do you think about that?"

"Oh! I think I like German women. You look wild, honey. You're my type of lady."

"That's funny, because you're not mine."

I guess they didn't know how to take me. I wasn't helping by being an instigator, as if I cared about that. They were hesitating. Michelle was getting more nervous.

She stepped towards me, and then turned to them, "Guys, she's not from here. Please just leave her alone."

That was a mistake. They didn't know how to handle a strong woman, but they were in familiar territory with a woman pleading for mercy.

I knew she was on the wrong track, but I was still impressed with how she tried to protect me. My first impression was right. Michelle is a decent person.

If I had wanted, I could have said some code words, and Harel and Matthew would have been there in a second. But I don't like to ask for help, and I knew I could handle these clowns.

Hank touched Michelle's breast. I shoved myself between them, and Michelle dropped instinctively behind me.

"She thinks she's smart," Hank looked at me, speaking over his shoulder to Terry.

I decided I'd waited long enough for this pathetic drama to play out. "Look here!" I told Hank, and when he looked, I shoved the wine glass directly into his eyes.

He yelled and wiped his eyes with his hand, indicating his temporary blindness. Ten seconds was all I needed. Terry's reflexes being what they were, I hit him easily with the heel of my hand in the middle of his forehead. It's not the blow itself, but the quickness of the hit that forces the brain to shake. He lost consciousness, and I must admit I felt good about it. I'd practiced that move a million times, but never on a real person.

Hank was recovering, so I grabbed the crotch of his training pants, and searched for something moderately solid. I gave what I had a good twist, not too strong because I didn't want to kill him. He hit the floor screaming.

I had planned to do the same to Terry, although he was unconscious, there was no need. I'd have done it purely on principle. It didn't matter, because the downstairs door opened and up came Dale with a friend.

"What the fuck is going on here?" Dale cried, each word rising in volume.

I stopped and looked at Michelle, now catatonic, then to Dale. "Your buddies here need some help." He wasn't sure what to think or say, and to my relief, Matthew's voice filtered in from behind them. They knew we were upstairs.

"Martin and I can't wait for you both all night," he said. "You told us that it would take you two minutes to pick up the stuff."

He and Harel came in.

Dale and his friend turned to them, and I used the opportunity to put my finger on my mouth, signaling to Michelle not to say anything. She wasn't quite ready anyway.

Dale was still confused. You could see the puddle of wine now settled on the shiny floor and the rest on Hank's shirt when he lifted his upper body. It was clear that just this simple movement gave him much pain.

Terry was still out cold, lying on his stomach with his hands underneath his body. It was an amusing pose.

Dale looked at his friend and said, "Take care of those morons."

Then he turned to us, "I don't know what the hell happened here, but if those guys hurt you, I'm really, really sorry."

He touched Michelle softly on her arm, and I was surprised how much tenderness was still in his eyes. "I am really very sorry."

"I might press charges," I said. "Rather, we might press charges. We were lucky that they were so drunk and clumsy."

"Could we go downstairs and talk?" He asked.

The big kitchen, was much lighter. I could see that Dale looked a bit scared, but he was trying to keep his cool.

"I can understand why you want to press charges, but if it went public that crap like this was going on in my house . . . I've got an image to think about."

"That's bullshit," Michelle snapped at him. "The University won't touch you. They didn't give a damn when your teammates raped that teenager."

Harel pressed his hand lightly against Michelle's cheek, but she brushed it away defiantly.

We couldn't tell her that Dale wasn't scared of his athletic career being tarnished. He had other; more lucrative issues to worry abut. The headline he didn't want to see: Graduate student from Germany, carrying the torch for a fallen friend, presses charges for attempting rape. Barbara Skibbe would be untouchable.

"It makes me sick Michelle," I assured her. "You've got every right to be angry."

"Listen," Dale directed his speech toward me. "If you want them punished, I can do it better than the University or the local police or even the local judges."

"How is that?" I asked.

"I personally will see to it that they won't play on the team ever again.

Believe me, for these guys, that is as bad as it can get."

"What do you think?" I asked Michelle.

"He's right. In this town nothing would happen to them." She turned her head.

"Bullshit, I'm going to the police," I said, forcing him to demean himself.

"I'm begging you, Barbara." Dale said quickly.

I waited for fifteen or twenty seconds, and then said, "I'll take your word for it." Immediate relief swept over his face.

"But I insist that you make good on your promise," I said.

"If he doesn't, we can demand that our German Consulate intervene," Harel threw in for good measure.

I'd never expected to deal with this athlete-above-the-law stuff. I don't think it exists anywhere but here.

63

I got to McFarlane's office early Friday, proposal in hand. Solomon had worked on it nonstop for the last several days.

"It is your death certificate," he kidded me.

No kidding. Indeed, it might be.

The tension among us is almost palpable these days. Matthew, Harel, and I spend our time training like mad, as a way to relax. Our bodies almost scream from exhaustion and, at least momentarily, we flush out every drop of tension.

A couple of days ago, to break up the monotony, we went south of town to a densely forested area. We bought beer on our way out to make it look like a respectable road trip. Montanans have been known to measure the length of a drive by the number of six packs consumed en route, but we had another use in mind. Harel opened the first can with a bullet from 45 feet away, no direct aim. Those twenty-four cans of beer received punishment from all angles, all directions.

Back in town, we had discussed the document one more time before Solomon wrote the proposal. A proposal; which he called his "most recent masterpiece."

Our Mossad man on the Eureka end had also done his homework. A sixty-year-old man named Van Engen turned out to be the owner of The Rainbow Investment Fund. What understandably was not included in the Eureka Chamber of Commerce report was that he was a straw man. For the last ten years, his multiple sclerosis had put him virtually out of the picture. His wife, twenty years his junior, and her brother were the real bosses. They lived in a renovated old mansion near a small town called Ferndale in Northern California.

Mossad had been doing some good work. I was feeling an unexpected and worrisome tenderness toward them. But before I get carried away, we'll have to see how long they can keep it up.

According to Solomon, there were several reasons why this firm could keep such a low profile. First, they were private. Second, the capital, which they to invest in the two Montana funds in order to get control, was way less than a quarter of a billion. Nothing compared to the real big funds.

Once they gained access to those two mutual funds, they used the new resources of the funds they controlled, to invest in those particular companies. It's amazing how much control you can have in American companies by putting together a small amount of money, relatively speaking, and concentrating it in a select number of companies.

The third point was the fact that the investment didn't grow so much. It was enough to keep the local Montana investors happy, mainly local unions, yet not enough to make the Wall Street watchdogs take notice. The fact that their headquarters were in far away Montana was a calculated advantage, far from the unwanted attention of curious financial journalists or analysts.

It was clear that something corrupt and big was going on; the question was what exactly it was. Rachel was not killed because she found out that Cromwell does inside trading to keep a Porsche for his secretary (mistress, we think). Cromwell, McFarlane, and maybe Dale are only pawns, no matter how big-time they appear in the backwoods of Montana. But since we didn't know the full story, we could only suggest in the proposal the guidelines to follow. Solomon's proposal focused on the benefits received by holding companies that were beyond mere money rewards for the owners.

It further suggested that instead of analyzing the mutual fund themselves, what should be analyzed are the major owners and their motivations. The nail in the coffin was the suggestion that since we were in Montana, I, Barbara Skibbe, should immediately begin my research on the local financial community. I couldn't have been blunter.

All that's left for me to do is to survive the next several weeks. If this proposal doesn't provoke them, I don't know what will. Of course, if our investigation in Eureka comes up with something new, our presences here won't be required. But Ari told us to not count on it. He sounded a bit mysterious, but he didn't elaborate.

64

At the office, McFarlane wasn't waiting alone. Cromwell himself was there. Smiling as always, he got up to greet me.

"I see you brought your proposal, Barbara," he said. "You're faster than most students we have here. In fact, Rachel was the same way."

"You'll be surprised how similar our material is too," I wanted to tell him, as I handed them the proposal, tucked inside a nice tanned leather notebook. They didn't open it, and I was somehow relieved.

"I learned a lot from her," I said. "As a matter of fact, because of her, I began to take my studies as seriously as I should. She had a very creative way of thinking."

"Yes, she sure did," McFarlane said.

I think Cromwell didn't like the way McFarlane agreed. He changed the subject, "Dr. McFarlane and I are very appreciative that you didn't take what happened the other night any further, Barbara."

"I was not sure what I should do," I said.

"For the school's sake, you did the right thing." He continued.

"As Dale explained to me, going to the police or the University wouldn't have helped." I said.

"If I become president of this University next year, those kinds of shenanigans will not be tolerated," Cromwell declared forcefully.

"And I am going to be your greatest fan when you do it." A little buttering up couldn't hurt I decided.

"But I also won't forget, Barbara, how maturely and how responsibly you've handled this affair," he added. In other words, it's good to have the president owe you a favor.

"Sir, I have never been in such a situation before, and I trust you to know how to handle what happened in the best way," I told him, trying to sound like a nice, submissive German graduate student.

"You won't regret it," he said, seemingly satisfied with my answer. "I better run. I'm flying to Washington, DC, today for a two-day conference." He gave us one of his splendid smiles and left.

From the second he walked out the door, McFarlane looked more relaxed. "I heard you beat the crap out of those guys," he said with a wink.

"Well, they were so drunk, they could barely stand," I said. "Besides, what do you think we learn in the summer camps in Bavaria?" We both laughed.

He couldn't hide the fact that he liked me. I guess Montana men like strong females. Maybe this has its roots in settler times, when a man without a strong woman to support him couldn't survive in this rough land.

"Have you known your boyfriend for a long time?" He asked out of the blue.

"Why do you ask? That's a very personal question, Dennis," I said softly.

"I'm sorry; I didn't mean to be intrusive."

"That's okay," I said. "And yes, I have."

There could have easily been a "but" at the end of my statement. I left it out. He smiled when I handed him my proposal.

"Enjoy it." I said and smiled back

65

I found Michelle in our on-campus room. She was typing on the computer as I came in. The minute she saw me, she gave me a big happy smile.

"You look excited," I told her, "what's the occasion?"

"Guess what, we're back together. Can you believe it?" She sounded thrilled.

"You mean you and Dale?"

"Of course, who else?"

"I hope you know what you're doing."

"He really wants to give it another try, and he apologized for what happened."

"You mean for the fact that he shoved you?"

"No, for what happened with his roommates," she answered, a little taken a back, realizing the real issue hadn't been resolved. It was clear she hadn't thought things through. People in love don't think with their heads.

"What about the things he should apologize for?" I didn't let her off the hook.

"We can't go through life without sometimes forgiving, Barbara. Especially you as a German should know that. We forgave your parents' generation for what happened and accepted Germany back as an ally," she answered in defiance.

That was pretty original I must admit, and in this circumstance, almost amusing. Here we had a healthy American Jewish woman, not bad looking, exceedingly good in sports, and at least intelligent enough to make it through a provincial university. And she defends a guy who beats her. And on top of that uses this 'German issue.'

"First of all, Michelle, you like many Americans, like to cheapen the word forgiveness. There is no forgiveness without deep remorse and no Hollywood-style 'sorry,' with or without tears, is sufficient.

"Now, as far as Germans, neither you nor I, young as we are, is in any position to forgive. Only the victims have the right. And by the way, let me tell you something else I learned from Rachel. Only the Israelis as a whole *still* pay with their blood for the Holocaust, so if at all, we the Germans should ask for forgiveness, it won't be from you people." It came out a little harsher than I would have preferred.

"I didn't realize you were so close to Rachel." She seemed a bit shaken.

"You better believe it. I was very close to her and to what she stood for."

"Damn it, Barbara, I know I may seem stupid, but Dale is not as bad as I described him. God, Barbara, I've never seen you like this."

"We can talk about it another time, Michelle. The real point here is that you're going beck to a man who abused you. I may not have the entire picture, but nothing justifies taking any abuse."

"But whatever happens, are you going to give me a shoulder to cry on if I need one?" She gave me a rueful smile.

Before I could answer, McFarlane stormed into the room. He didn't even acknowledge Michelle.

"I want to talk with you, now!" There were no preliminaries.

"Sure," I said. "In your office?"

"No, let's take a walk."

I wondered what he had in mind, but I also wondered what Michelle must have thought. He had my proposal under his arm with my name in full sight. Michelle signaled that she would call me.

We took a short hike on one of the many hills that surrounded the campus. He made very sure we were alone and didn't even try to hide that concern from me. Here and there one could see smooth gray rocks that looked as if they were carved by a giant sculptor. I think these strange rocks are the footsteps of the glaciers that formed this valley.

We sat down on a piece of clear, sandy hillside. He didn't say anything for a while, a very long while.

At last he said, "What is this?" He shoved the brown notebook towards me.

"That's my proposal, Dennis. I've spent the last several days writing it."

"But this isn't what we decided on," he sounding defeated.

"That is what Rachel and I worked on."

"Listen, Cromwell expects me to be in his office to show him your proposal. I can't bring him that."

"Why, isn't it well written?"

He took again a long time to respond. "Okay. Let's cut the bullshit. I know you're not Barbara, and I know you didn't write this. So the question is, who, exactly, are you and what do you want?"

"Sorry?" I didn't expect that.

"You look something like Barbara, but not close enough. I came across a photo of Rachel and Barbara. Rachel herself gave it to me. You're not her. I looked at it carefully. You have a strong resemblance to Barbara, but you're not her."

• "Oh, so you've gone around telling everyone I'm an imposter," I said, trying to find out what he'd divulged and to whom.

"Of course not, and you are lucky that Michelle who has the same photo is not that observant, but as soon as I give this proposal to Cromwell, it's over for you."

I decided to take a chance, "Like it was 'over' for Rachel?"

He seemed to not even register the comment. I guess he was plotting his next move. He gave me a very long, penetrating look. "Tell you what. I'll give this proposal to Cromwell, because it's clear that whoever you are, and I have my own ideas about that, you really want him to read it. But I advise otherwise. And I'm telling you that this discussion between us never took place."

"It never took place, and I have no idea what you tried to tell me," I touched him softly on his cheek, something Americans don't do. "You're quite a decent man, Dennis."

"Barbara, or whoever you are, I like you. I don't know why, but I damn well like you, maybe more than that. Listen to me, and listen real well. Things can get very rough here and there could come a point in time when I can no longer help or at least warn you. My advice to you is to get the hell out of here. You're getting involved in things that are way over your head, whoever you are."

"Did you say the same thing to Rachel? Do you want to be more specific?"

"I said the same thing to Rachel—except the part about 'liking you.' And I didn't expect her to be killed. I need several days to do some thinking. Don't go any place without letting me know. God, I don't know why I'm putting myself through this." And with that, he turned without looking back and left me sitting there.

66

The ball was in their court now, and it was back to a waiting game.

In my gut I felt McFarlane was not against us. I mean, he didn't have to tell me he knew I'm not who I say I am. But then again, we've been taught not to trust our gut. Not that I agree with everything they taught us, especially not with that. I regret not reporting the little flirtation with him to my colleagues. Well, it was just a little teasing. No big deal. We've also been taught to be selective and concise in our reports. Besides, can you imagine how Ari would scream at me if I tell him now?

Oh, I forgot, Michelle called me early today on my 'home' phone. Ari, seated across the room, listened on the other line.

"Hi, Barbara. Guess what, Dale came and begged me to forgive him, for everything." She sounded excited.

"Let me guess. You forgave him, and everything is hunky dory for the third time."

"Oh, Barbara, don't make me feel so guilty. He apologized for everything—and I mean everything. I can't help it. I love being with him. Maybe I just take advantage of him." She giggled. "I'd like you to get to know him. He's different from what everyone thinks about him."

"I can't wait."

"Will you stop it, Barbara? God, are you always so difficult?"

I knew I was being too harsh with her, "Almost always and only with people I like. But you may be right. No outsider can really judge what is going on between a couple, and I hate it when people volunteer their opinion about how I should be living my life. So it's stupid of me to do the same. I hope it works out between you two. Maybe the four of us could get together sometime."

"That's exactly what Dale suggested. He and some of his friends from school have arranged a paint-ball war for tomorrow in the Bitterroot. McFarlane might come too and bring some of the graduate students. Would you and Martin like to join us?"

I looked at Ari, because I was inclined to say no. Sounded like it could be a great time, but I was too tired and tense to play games. But Ari gave thumbs up and mouthed a 'Yes!'

"We'd love to come." I heard myself saying.

"Okay, but keep it a secret. Too many people spoil the fun. And Dale asked me to invite both of you to dinner after the game."

"As long as he doesn't bring his roommates."

"You're very funny."

We decided to meet at 8 a.m., on the block south of 'Malfunction Junction,' the town's biggest crossroad. It's always jammed with cars, giving the locals the illusion that Missoula is a major metropolis. Tomorrow, though, there won't be any traffic. On weekends and holidays the town is dead unless there's a football game. Michelle said we needed to meet early because the game site was ninety minutes away.

"I wanted to relax," I told Ari after I hung up the phone.

"The game is relaxing, and I don't think it's a bad idea to get to know Dale a bit more." He laughed after saying that. "I have the feeling that the next weeks will be rough ones. Have fun while you still can."

The next day was predicted to be a bit cooler, so we would need some warm clothes. The kind you would not mind ruining with paint. So Harel and I took a trip to the local Goodwill and I found several old pairs of military fatigues in perfect condition. For all of it we paid less than ten bucks. These shops don't exist in Israel or Germany: "only in America," like the old saying goes. Marcus can't complain that we are draining the budget.

67

We showed up without paint guns, of course. We'd get the equipment free of charge there, since Dale's friend owns a shop that specializes in these kinds of games. Football stars seem to always have a lot of good connections.

Dale, Michelle, and another guy waited for us as planned, and we decided to go in two different cars. His other friend, the one organizing the game, was already on location. McFarlane was going to join us an hour later with some other students.

We followed them southeast on Highway 93 and could see snow-covered Lolo Peak, the highest mountain around Missoula. The weather was gray, but still dry. Everyone seemed worried about possible rain.

Our guns were, as always, strapped tight to our left legs. We never leave home without them. No microphones, though, and the cell phones would be left in the car. Nobody's going to assassinate me in front of all the cute Montana students! Harel brought a small pair of binoculars.

In the middle of a little lumber town called Lolo, we turned right on a narrow road and after another half an hour or so, we turned again, onto an even smaller muddy dirt road.

"I guess the only people still using it are hunters or people like us coming to have fun in the sun," Harel said.

"No sun today, that's for sure." I looked at the almost black heavy clouds in the east.

The road began to wind up the mountain, and we had to slow down. The car in front of us was still driving very fast. I guess Dale knew the place well, and besides, his car was smaller and faster than ours.

We drove at least another hour, climbing nearly all the way to the peak. There was nothing to see but trees and more trees. I guess we were quite high up, since there were patches of snow along the ground, especially under the shade of the trees. Finally we made it. Along with Dale's car, there was a pickup like ours and another big sport utility car. Dale was already talking with a small group of people, all in camouflage outfits. Even their faces were camouflaged. It seemed that in Montana people take this game very seriously.

As we arrived, Dale came to greet us, "I guess today is not our lucky day. McFarlane called, and he and the rest were not sure where to turn. Some idiot tore down the sign. I'll go back and pick them up. It won't take long."

He jumped back in his car and, with tires screaming, drove away. Jocks! We walked toward the group that was filling the carbon-dioxide cartridges with compressed air. Two people were already pelting a group of nearby bushes with the tiny colored balls. One of them was the guy that came with Michelle and Dale.

A tall, thin, rough looking guy, whom I presumed was the organizer, looked at us as if we were in the wrong place. "Ever played before?"

"Only once," Harel told him.

I didn't like the tone of his voice. Ari was right. We could have some fun with these country boys.

Michelle joined us, already holding a gun and pair of goggles. "We're going to have a short game before the rest come. Are you coming?" Apparently she'd had some experience.

"Sure, as soon as we get the equipment," I told her.

"It will be ready in a sec," the man with the guns told me.

"I've got to collect some flowers," I told him.

"What?" He looked at me quickly, and then turned his head. I should ask Michelle how to say that politely in America.

"I mean, I must go to the bathroom. I'm a bit nervous, and it's a bit cold." I smiled at him, and he didn't smile back. I guess these tough mountain boys don't have much patience for humor.

As I went to find a tree, I thought I heard dogs barking. I stopped to have a look and saw two big bloodhounds and three pit bulls in two small cages in the other pickup. I didn't like what I saw. That's no way to handle dogs.

Harel and I know dogs. Our kibbutz takes in a lot of homeless animals, and I've done work with the Israeli Humane Society. Some years ago, we rescued a puppy from a group of teenagers who were in the process of hanging her, after having blinded her with burning cigarettes. Can you believe how cruel humans can be? This happened in broad daylight near a big drugstore in Jerusalem, and nobody stopped them. We were there in seconds. The dog has been with us ever since and can completely compensate for her blindness.

We're familiar with the two breeds in the pickup. Bloodhounds, despite their name and size, are loving animals. You couldn't make them aggressive if you tried.

The powerful pit bulls are sometimes mean to other dogs, but unless trained to be vicious against people, they're gentle animals. These dogs didn't look well cared for.

When I came back, Harel was holding his gun, talking with Michelle. The other four guys were still standing, shooting at the bushes.

"What are the dogs doing here?" I asked the guy who handled the equipment. Apparently they were his dogs.

"In the second part of the game, we'll try to locate you with the dogs," he answered matter-of-factly.

"Pit bulls are not the right dogs to track people, only bloodhounds," I told him.

"The pit bulls aren't for the game; they're trained for mountain lion hunting," he told me as he spit. "They attack the cat and don't mind being killed in the process, but the lion usually doesn't fight. It climbs up a tree and we shoot it. We've done it many times. Maybe we'll hunt tomorrow. That's why we brought them and the tents."

What a pig, I thought, but I didn't let it cloud my vision. I took my gun and goggles, and he led us to an elevated spot. "Okay, these are the rules. First, you never ever take off the goggles, no matter what. The paint balls can inflict some light pain, but no more than that. Without the goggles, a shot in the eyes could blind you."

He looked at us as if to see if we got it and then continued, "Now, you three will have exactly twenty minutes to hide and prepare for the four guys here who will come and try to get you. You've got Michelle to help, if you have any questions. I'll be on their side of the field for the beginning of the game, but I'm nothing more than a referee. Now, if you're shot, you must put this white band I'm giving you on your head. Leave the area and go straight back to the parking lot. Don't take your goggles off until you reach the cars."

"What are the borders of the game field?" Harel asked. "We've never been here before."

"It's very simple. All the way down the slope to the small creek there, on the east side. To the west, it's the end of the forest. There's a clearing there. Half a mile further on each side, you'll see some new growth. Don't go past there."

"We are not allowed to cross the creek?" Harel asked.

"No. First of all, the water is still damned icy, and around three hundred yards later, there are quite a few steep cliffs. They can be dangerous."

He looked at his watch, "In twenty minutes, they will come and get you. The clock is ticking."

We walked into the woods.

"I told you to put the goggles on," the man shouted behind us. We complied; but as soon as we were in the forest, Harel took them off.

"What are you doing? You should keep them on." Michelle said.

Harel ignored her, and I took mine off, too. He looked around him and then back in the direction we had come from. "Let's go there, fast," he said pointing at an elevated place where a clearing in the forest began.

Michelle wanted to say something, but I hushed her with my expression. She took her goggles off too and followed us. We were more running than walking, remaining silent. We got to the end of the old forest and we climbed uphill to a more open area. Old timber and tree stumps in every direction. Harel slowed down and gave us the bend-down signal.

We came to a point from which we could watch the five men. We crawled behind a rock and a tree, and I noticed how the tree was growing straight out of the rock. Its will to survive intrigued me. Our enemies were far enough away that I couldn't see anything special. They were all holding their guns and talking with each other.

"What is going on with you guys?" Michelle broke the silence. "You're beginning to freak me out."

Harel, still ignoring her, gave me his tiny binoculars without saying a word. They were all carrying real guns. One of them had an AK-47, the other had an Uzi. These were not Montana-boy paint ball rifles. I gave Michelle the binoculars and watched her jaw drop after she'd looked through them. God they were fast. I'd handed in the proposal only two days ago.

"I saw Uzi magazines inside one of the cars, which also have out-of-state license plates, and I also wondered why Dale was in such hurry," Harel said. "I thought they would use Uzis for illegal hunting. Surprise, surprise."

We moved back down to the trees. We didn't have much time to plan our next move. We both drew our real guns and cocked them. They're good for short-range city combat, but no match for the high-power long-range weapons those guys had. Michelle looked at us, her eyes wide.

"Well, my dear," I smiled to her, "Now you have an idea of what a deer feels like every fall."

She ignored my proselytizing. "Who are you people?"

"Israelis. And those guys are here to kill us. And you, too."

She had something to say, but I stopped her. "No time now. These people also killed Rachel."

I spoke in Hebrew to Harel. "Do you have any idea how to improve our position?"

"We have to cross this open area because around here, it's too small to maneuver . . . Once we're there, we'll try to tackle them from shorter range on terms that we can dictate."

He looked at Michelle, "Are you a good runner?"

"I came in third in the city 5K."

"Excellent," Harel told her, softening his voice. "You follow us and do exactly as we tell you, and all three of us will be alive tomorrow."

"We are going to cross the next half a mile in the open area," I told her. "They will see us, but even with their telescopic sights, they won't be able to hit us as long as we move fast. They're too far away, and if they want to come closer to us, they'll have to move through the forest, too. They'd lose us then for at least ten minutes. And we need to sprint, okay?"

She got up to move, and Harel and I instinctively put our guns away. We didn't want them to see through their scopes that we were armed. Why spoil the surprise?

"Wait a minute," Harel said, "Let's take off after they enter the forest. It will give us a few more minutes." He crawled up again and watched them.

Those guys must have been really confident. In an act of bizarre honesty, they actually waited the full twenty minutes.

"They put their goggles on, too," Harel told us. "They really thought we'd reveal our location by shooting them with paint. It's tempting to ambush them and shoot them with something else, but I'm worried what would happen if they've split up. We could get most of them, but it's hard to avoid bullets in this small area."

I guess they had that planned out before the game. These guys were somewhat more professional than the crack unit in Berlin. Maybe without Michelle, we would have attempted to confront them head on. But we didn't want to risk her life.

"Be ready." Harel said.

Michelle and I got up. "Hey," I told her, "We've done these kinds of things many times. Just trust us."

She looked a bit more encouraged, though still stiff with fear.

"Really?"

"Sure," I assured her. I guess the fact that Harel and I remained nonchalant calmed her down. I wanted to keep it that way.

"Go!" Harel said, only loud enough to be clear. Michelle was fast, very fast indeed. She was running for her life, no doubt about that. The problem was the rough terrain; it was everything but the smooth track she was accustomed to in the University's stadium. It's like the difference between exercising with gym equipment or free weights. The latter are always the true test.

Harel and I could have easily out run her, but this was not an exercise in natural selection. If she had tried to keep up with us in full speed, she could have a broken leg. We were only twenty seconds from the forest when we heard shots. "Keep going!" I shouted, as I hit the ground to assess the situation.

There was only one man there, and I guess his shooting was more to draw attention of the others than to make an attempt on us. We were way out of their effective range. We entered the thick woods.

"As long as we move fast—not run, but walk fast—we are out of danger, at least for the time being." Harel said.

"The question is, in what direction?" I thought aloud.

We couldn't see the sun through the clouds, and the tall trees made things even darker. By that time, too, the rain had started to gently fall.

"Can't we just hide?" Michelle asked. "They won't find us in this huge forest."

"They have bloodhounds. It's a no-hide situation."

"We'll have to continue and hope to find a place to ambush them", Harel said. "But we've got to do it before nightfall. I'm sure those guys have night vision equipment. We don't."

We could hear the unique howl of the bloodhound.

"Will they let the dogs loose against us?" Michelle asked me.

"The bloodhounds, no, the pit bulls, yes."

"How many were there?" Harel asked.

"Three."

We kept a brisk walking pace. We had to cross through heavy brush, and large areas of deadfall continually forced us to alter our course. They must have been gaining on us.

"I once saw a live show on pit bulls and they ripped an elk in half." Michelle sounded worried.

"We're not going to climb a tree and be shot like mountain lions," I said. "Only useful comments now, please."

"Shoot them! You've got guns."

"Personally, you people make me sick," I said to her without any spite in my voice. I had more to say—something about how gentle, pacifist types readily turn to violence when their own necks are at stake—but I could sense she was breathing pretty heavily. Stress and physical exertion weren't the winning combination. I wasn't helping.

"Sorry," I muttered. I suppose she figured I was unstable.

After twenty more minutes of cutting through the brush, we could hear the barking of the pit bulls in the distance.

"They'll be here in less than two minutes," Harel said quickly.

"You've got to shoot them, you've got to!" Michelle bordered on the hysterical.

"Take your jacket off fast," I told her as Harel and I were taking off ours. "If we shoot them, your hunter friends will know that we also have guns. There will be no ambush."

We put the jackets around our left arms and told her to do the same.

"When they come, show them your left arm and whatever happens don't let them take you to the ground, because they'll go for your throat," I said. Harel and I moved forward.

The dogs appeared even sooner than we had expected, and even though I'm trained in dealing with almost anything, I was frightened. They were big, powerful, and fast.

"Hold yourself with your right arm to the tree and make movements with your left one, they never go for the body." I shouted to Michelle before the first dog reached me.

I had the dagger ready in my right hand. God bless Marcus for ordering us never to go without them.

The first dog passed me, and I heard a scream from behind. Then another one had my left arm. His teeth didn't go through, but I could feel my arm being pressed with such power that five more seconds and his teeth would have penetrated my skin or crushed my arm bones.

I pushed my dagger in and out of the animal's neck several times. Blood sprayed out, covering my face. I must have hit an artery. I don't know how many times it took before the dog released its jaws. In fact, Harel had to pull the thing off of me. Stabbing live moving flesh sickened me, but I couldn't think about it.

Michelle was crying on a patch of grass ten yards away, a dead dog near her.

"She's okay," Harel told me, "She got thrown to the ground, but before the dog got her neck, I got him."

Words didn't help to calm her down, and it took two slaps to get her to look at me.

"We don't have all day, you are okay, you are okay, and we are all okay!" I shouted to drown out her sobbing. "Now, shut up and be quiet," I tried to sound as detached as possible.

Harel tore a branch from the tree and broke it. He then pushed the broken part into the neck of one of the dead animals.

"What are you doing?" Michelle asked. I think she thought we were performing an Israeli dead-dog ritual of some sort.

"We're trying to give our followers some clue to how we killed the dogs," Harel answered. "I don't want them to suspect we have even knives."

"At least," I smiled to both of them, "they will realize that we are not such easy prey. They wanted fun, and they're going to get it."

"Your face is covered in blood," Harel said and grimaced while pretending to move some hair that didn't exist from my eyes.

We got on the move again. The encounter with the dogs had cost us time, and the hunters were closing in on us. Those noisy bloodhounds were actually a great help to us. We could estimate their position, and with the rain pouring harder, it was important for us to hear them.

By this time the rain was pouring down through the trees. With it came the wind. The moving mass of trees sounded like a giant waterfall. Branches were falling, and we could hear trees cracking. Nature exploded its thunder, and it was difficult to steady ourselves.

"It's about time to plan the ambush," Harel shouted with a hint of desperation in his voice.

"We need water to shake the hounds," I shouted back. The fact that we were going down most of the time almost guaranteed we'd hit some.

I noticed that Harel was getting more worried about Michelle by the minute. She was still walking fast, but her movements were robotic. The violent encounter with the dogs had drained her. Fortunately it wasn't as cold as it could have been. I went up to her and hugged her as a coach might.

"It's going to be all right," I said. "Just a bit more and it will be over."

She answered with a cold look, her eyes deep in their sockets. She seemed to have little will to continue. I grabbed her hands and couldn't believe how frigid they were.

Harel stopped suddenly, and I stopped behind him.

"What's going on?" I asked.

"Look." He whispered.

"No, don't tell me a bear, not now?" I said. It seemed like the logical progression of events.

"No, look there," he said, pointing with his finger. A huge moose stood fifty yards ahead of us eating grass. He lifted his big head out of curiosity.

"It's big, but cute. Why are we stopping?" I whispered back.

"Nothing so big can be cute," he smiled to me.

Michelle pulled my hand. "Let's just go around it, they're usually not aggressive."

I remembered what McFarlane and Dale told me about this big animal. Carefully, quietly, looking at its eyes but without the slightest disrespect, we walked around him. As we went on, we could no longer hear the hounds, and when we finally found the creek we'd been looking for, we walked beside it.

Michelle was in a state of near-collapse, just like a first-year military trainee. We decided to take stock. They were five people, all with long-range weapons. Our only advantage was that we could choose the location for the showdown. They didn't know we had guns, and would probably underestimate our marksmanship even if they suspected we were armed. We could not ambush dogs, however.

Our only chance was to confront them from short range, assuming they would walk in two groups: The first with two men and the dogs, the second with the other men.

If they were professional, that's how they would do it. We had to assume they were.

So even if we killed the first two, the other three would shoot at us from outside our guns' effective range. This was of course the most unlikely and worst scenario possible. They would probably be walking in one group and telling each other dirty jokes and dreaming what they would do with the blood money. Why be cautious with the unarmed?

But then again, if they were good, they wouldn't take any chances. Just the fact we killed the dogs should have been enough to make them wary.

We ignored Michelle entirely now, planning our move in Hebrew. She was in bad shape. I could almost see her life ebbing away.

68

The rain would make it more difficult for the dogs, but we had no illusions: Bloodhounds can smell an odor in a concentration of one to a million. Our knowledge of dogs was an advantage, but our training hadn't prepared us for thinking like foxes.

We decided to ambush the hunters along the creek in two different places, just in case they were pursuing us in two teams. We assumed they would operate professionally.

The only way to fool the dogs would be to follow the river to a place where Harel could wait between the bushes. Michelle would walk two hundred yards further and hide there. I would go upstream, back around one hundred yards, my body submersed in water. The dogs couldn't sense me then. The idea was simple: if they all were walking together, Harel and I would ambush them together. He'd wait until they were only ten yards from him, then open fire. I would shoot from behind. If they walked in two groups, we'd split them up. We planned the crossfire for the two scenarios so we wouldn't shoot each other. This was all we could do with Michelle in the condition she was in.

But even this was easier said than done. The fresh mountain water was only a few degrees above the freezing point. I took off all my clothes, and Harel poured all the olive oil we had on my body and massaged it in. He kept only his flannel shirt and pants, giving me his long underwear. I then piled everything else, including his socks, on top of mine.

I ate all the muesli bars we'd brought with us, knowing I'd need every calorie. We didn't try to keep the water from my body. On the contrary, once the water touched my oily skin, the many layers would keep it there and the body-warmed water would become a protective layer itself. It's an old trick. Far from perfect, but the best we could do under the circumstances.

"The dogs will lead them directly to me, and I will shoot at the very last second," Harel said.

"You mean, if they go in two groups, right?" I asked, anticipating the cold water. "But if they go, hopefully in one bunch, start shooting earlier and we'll crossfire."

Harel gave me a quick kiss on my oily forehead, "Think about the warm bath you'll take tonight. We will all fight for the honor of scrubbing your back."

I tried to smile back, but the synapses weren't working. We'd planned all we could. The rest we'd have to play by ear.

"See you in ten minutes." I said, checking my gun one more time, oiling it with my oily hands.

The water was not deep, barely reaching my hips. It was cold, paralyzing cold. It was also surprisingly fast, which made it all the more disorienting. At least my smell would be carried downstream. I moved slowly, looking back once in a while to estimate where Harel would ambush them, making sure he would be out of my shooting direction. Branches, hanging above the water, scratched my face. The rocks on the creek bed were slick with weeds and moss. I fell down at least twice on my way, cursing everything and everyone.

One hundred yards upstream, I began to search for a good stopping place. The water was noisy, but with effort I could hear the hounds again. Perhaps five minutes away.

I located a half-submerged rock that jutted out from the shore, covered by low-hanging brush. It seemed perfect for hiding behind, and maybe even for a bit of protection if something went wrong. I submersed myself, so only my head and the hand that held my gun were out of the water. Both had to stay warm and functional.

I seemed okay temperature wise, which meant two possible things: the olive oil was working or my body was numb. I focused on the first. I still couldn't see the men, but the barking and howling grew louder. I couldn't afford to stay in this position more than five minutes, but I didn't have a choice. It was the only way to make sure the dogs couldn't smell me.

I held my gun in my left hand. With my right, I did finger gymnastics to ensure the flow of blood. I reached a point of deep concentration on the task at hand, and, as the seconds passed, the cold dissolved into nothing.

I could see the dogs, with the men strung out behind. The two men with the dogs were now holding magnum revolvers. They're deadly at long range, but heavy and awkward. Submachine guns would have been way more effective. Now most of my head was below the water. Not even the dogs would have a clue that I was nearby.

Few have the stamina that training has developed in Harel and me. We had a huge advantage under these conditions. I saw that our pursuers were impatient in the wind and cold. They looked tired and stiff, so maybe they weren't good old Montana boys. The predators had suddenly became the prey, and they were completely unaware of their change in status. In less than sixty seconds, Harel would begin shooting. I'd have to watch, and then kill the remaining gunmen before they got Harel.

The second group appeared, but they were only two. We had clearly counted five men. Had one returned to the car, or did he follow as a third reinforcement for the second group? Not something we could have anticipated. The first two would be killed for sure, but if I didn't kill the second team, Harel might be exposed. If I got them, I would be exposed to the fifth man. Several seconds passed. I wondered if Harel realized what was going on.

It didn't really matter in the end. I heard the familiar sound of Harel's gun and I didn't need to look to see if he'd gotten them. It's a given. I raised myself from the water and saw the men in the following group already raising their shotguns. I shot them on the diagonal—one bullet each, body center. Unlike in the movies, there were no shouts or long pre-death antics. They were dead before their faces touched the muddy ground.

There was no time to think before I sought cover behind the rock from the fifth guy, submerging myself again in the water. Because bullets move faster than sound, I knew I wasn't hit by his first three shots. I didn't dare raise my head. If the fifth guy had a telescopic sight, I was safe only as long as I was behind the rock. Everywhere else was a killing field. I hoped Harel had read the situation clearly and would go after him, but I knew he could be in the same position as me.

"You both are covered," somebody shouted, "So come out with your hands up, and your lives will be spared."

"Yeah, sure, I thought." By then, he should have known he was dealing with professionals. Several minutes passed.

"Okay, take your time," the voice said confidently, "I've got night vision here and loads of food. I'll wait for hours if I need to. Take your time, friends."

We didn't have hours. I didn't even have fifteen minutes. My oil layer was wearing off, and I could feel the icy water. Harel, I'm sure, had it in mind. I decided to check the gunman's alertness. I took a stick lying behind the rock and lifted it. Two inches up, and the guy shot right past it. He had a Russian Kalashnikov. He was less than fifty yards away, and I had to assume he had a telescopic sight.

I shot in the air to let Harel know I was okay and a second later, he shot back to greet me. We both were trapped, unable to change our positions.

The whole time we could hear the dogs yelping. I wasn't sure if they were hurt or not. They had probably been wound up in the corpses by their leashes. I was beginning to play with the idea of diving close to the shore and making my way out, but it wasn't realistic.

A volley of shots broke my thoughts, and I made myself even smaller behind the rock. It lasted at least half a minute. Then the sound stopped, and there was nothing but the hum of the wind.

"Are you okay, Barbara?" It was McFarlane's voice.

I didn't answer, fearing a trap.

"We got this guy with the Russian rifle. Now we're going to come over to you with our hands up. For god sake, don't shoot."

"What are you doing here?" I shouted maybe screamed, back. I didn't have much control over my voice at the time. I was shaking from the cold.

"Dale and I came out as fast as we could. We are not gunning for you, I promise."

"Okay, expose yourselves. You'll be dead, I swear it, and you both will be dead if you try anything."

"All right, give us a chance here. We are coming." McFarlane's voice was almost too calm for what was going on. But then again, he was not in the water.

"How do you know I won't lie?" I shouted back.

"Because, Barbara, or whatever your name is, it's not nice to shoot the good guys," he screamed back. That was pretty funny, given the situation.

"Walk forward then, and sing very loudly and while you're doing it, hands in the air," I shouted. I wanted to know their positions at all times.

"Any requests?"

"Your national anthem."

"The Montanan sounds better."

"Dennis, don't make me mad, I'm not in the mood right now."

They were singing at the top of their lungs all the way up to me. They passed me at first, and then stopped with their arms above their heads. They looked like they'd been through hell, too. Their faces were scratched and bleeding from the bushes, which told me they had to run to find us. Or maybe kill us, couldn't tell yet.

"Can we take down our hands?" McFarlane asked.

"Yes, and do some convincing, quickly. I'm damn cold." I told him, with both men locked in my sights.

"You'd have already been dead if we were with them, my dear. The guy would have pinned you in this spot, and we would have flanked you," McFarlane said. "You can tell your friends to come out now. It's safe."

Dale cut in. "Besides, you're so lucky that those were Californian boys playing hunters. You wouldn't have had a chance against Dennis and me."

"You both are quite brave or quite stupid to talk to somebody holding a gun at you," I informed them, while getting out of the water. "So why did you both suddenly come to the rescue? Did you have a change of heart?"

"This is something we can discuss a bit later," McFarlane said. "I'm no angel, but the deal that Cromwell offered to me several years ago didn't include murder. When Rachel was murdered, even Cromwell was surprised and scared. We don't want any more deaths. We saw this one coming today and nearly acted too late. I was waiting for Dale not far from here. We knew they won't kill you on the spot."

"Hey," Dale interrupted. "Where is Michelle?" Harel walked now toward us, his gun steady, with Michelle draped over his shoulder. The bloodhounds, now released, walked behind him.

"*Hu beseder.* I think its okay," I told him in Hebrew.

"Really?" He was still not convinced.

McFarlane interfered, divining that we weren't sure about the rescue. "Look guys, every beginning hunter can tell you that those dogs not only lead you to the game, but also change their behavior when they close in. Those guys didn't even know that."

"How do you know that?" Harel asked.

"If they had known, they would not have come as close as they did so unprepared. Anyway, now that we're here, we're running out of time. Once the people in California know what happened, it's going to get very sticky. When we killed that son of a gun, we chose our side."

Dale gave us his dry underwear, and McFarlane offered his heavy jacket and pants. "I never thought that I'd walk in these mountains in only my underwear," he smiled.

"We can use their clothes, too," said Harel, pointing at the dead people.

"If they had killed us, who would they report to?" I asked still trembling.

"They would report to Cromwell, through me. They really wanted to stay here for several days to hunt black bears. But, um, shouldn't we talk about this when we get to dry country or at least to the cars?"

Harel disregarded the comment. "Good, then we may have a window of opportunity. Should we bury the corpses, or let the animals take care of it?"

"Let's take them about fifty yards away and shove them into some bushes," McFarlane answered. "We're not going to get much digging done with the ground this hard and frozen."

Dale, now holding Michelle, added, "Hunting season is still six months away, and it's pretty likely that most people won't see this area before then. The people around here might not report anything anyway. They mind their own business."

"They have an extreme aversion to authority." McFarlane made it sound better.

"You like to sound smart, don't you?" I asked.

"It is my last chance because I've pretty much screwed myself at the University now." He looked at us. "Israelis, eh?"

It took me a second. "Good guess, was it the Hebrew?"

"After three years in New York, I developed an ear for it. Besides, I've had a few Israeli buddies in my life living in the big city."

"Ah. Some of my best friends are black? That sort of thing?" I asked, forgetting for a moment the Israeli woman in his past.

"I can be accused of many things. Racism for sure is not one of them."

Harel nodded, ready to get on with the grisly task at hand. "Come on, let's move the bodies," he said.

Michelle and I released the dogs from their leashes. We let Harel, Dale, and McFarlane take care of the corpses.

Harel collected everything of worth from the men, especially cellular phones and papers. We carried all of it back with us, figuring it could somehow be of use to Rafi. Finding machine guns in the forest wouldn't be a good thing for local teenagers, either.

Dennis and Dale led the way. Now, Ari will have to decide if he trusts them.

69

Everything was the way we'd left it at the paint ball base. We contacted Ari, and after discussing the matter briefly, it was decided that we should all return to the house. He and Matthew would interrogate them.

Back home two hours later I had four glasses of hot chocolate milk with tons of vanilla and I could have had five more. Michelle, Dale, and Dennis weren't allowed at first to eat anything, because Ari thought he might have to drug them to get information out of them.

Thirty minutes later, he came back with three of them, fresh from the first part of the interrogation, and seemed reassured by what he's heard. "We still have to do some security check-ups on you, but we're running out of time. We'll need your help."

"Can you tell us who you are?" Dale asked hesitantly.

Harel and I hadn't offered them much information on the trip back from the Bitterroot.

"Not now. Later," Harel answered brusquely. "We're waiving the use of drugs on you guys; because frankly we need your help immediately, if you choose to help us."

"Exactly as I told Barbara, you have to trust us," Dennis said.

"Distrust is our second nature," Ari responded. "That's why we still put you in three different rooms as the three of us," he pointed at Solomon and Matthew, "ask you a lot of what may seem like stupid questions. Take them seriously, and answer them as honestly as you can, and in twenty more minutes, I can tell you if you're to be trusted."

"Sounds fair to me, but what happens if we don't pass?" Dennis said while smiling at me.

We ignored the question, maybe because that possibility was too painful to contemplate.

"Remember, answer with total honesty, no matter what we ask. If we ask how many times a week you masturbate, for example, just answer straight. It will save us a lot of time. Is that clear?" Matthew reminded them again.

Their three heads nodded quickly and in unison. Even Michelle was back in the game. They took them downstairs. Rafi joined them to record the proceedings.

We had trained extensively in how to give these kinds of interrogations. A one-person session can be difficult. But with two people, especially three, cross questioning can produce results quickly. Ari is a master in this area.

They were back in about an hour. The obvious chemistry between them and Ari, Matthew, and Solomon made it clear that trust was established. They joined us for dinner, happy to turn their attention to salmon and baked potatoes.

"Before we proceed," Ari said, "I want you, Dennis, to call Cromwell to update him, exactly as we decided. The guy will be losing his mind by now." He handed Dennis the phone. Rafi and Matthew were listening on attached lines.

"Quiet," Ari reminded us.

Dennis dialed, and Cromwell answered on the first ring. I'm sure he was nervous, probably because it shouldn't take all day to kill two nerdy graduate students and a boyfriend.

"Hi James. Sorry for the late call. I just wanted to inform you that we all had a nice game." Dennis winked at me after he said this. This guy continued to amaze me. He's got nerve.

"I tried to call you an hour ago, but couldn't get through,' Dennis continued. "We had a little trouble for awhile. Do you still want me to drop by with Dale for a drink?'

Matthew seemed satisfied with what he heard. When Dennis hung up, Ari began immediately to delegate responsibilities.

"We'll go there with two cars. Dale, we'll need your second car. Nothing should look out of the ordinary. What kind of car did you say it was?"

"Audi sport," Dale said.

"Oh boy, it's not exactly roomy. Well, you and Dennis go there in the Audi with Yael and Harel in the back. Once you enter the house and everything is clear, Matthew and I will join you."

He looked again to Dennis and Dale, "You said you're sure there are no alarms? That's odd. The guy is very wealthy."

"We should know," Dale assured us.

"Besides," Dennis said. "This is Montana. People leave their keys in their cars. He doesn't even have a dog."

"And guns?" Harel asked.

"He has several, and he is very proud of them," Dale said.

"How about a wife?"

"The secretary is more likely. He and his wife don't live together—it's a relationship they maintain for appearance. But I bet he is alone tonight."

"All right let's go," Ari said, looking at his watch, "Rafi, bring your gear, as well."

"Already got it," Rafi answered.

I checked my gun and noticed that Dennis was watching me. Our eyes met, but I looked away. It was hardly the time to flirt, although I admit I didn't mind watching him watching me.

"Do you think it's a good idea to get so cozy with them in the car?" I asked Ari in Hebrew.

"If I had to bet my life, I would say that they are clean and definitely on our side. They were in a position to kill you. Or at least they think they were. McFarlane also described precisely what he did in Switzerland," Ari said, also in Hebrew. "He transferred huge amounts of money he received from people he didn't know into various secret bank accounts. And he understood, although late in the game, that what Cromwell offered him was more than just normal Wall Street fun. We're talking about cash payments of thirty or forty million dollars each.

"He began to document the dates, account numbers, and the names of the different banks—as insurance against Cromwell's bosses. He says he has the information in a deposit box in a local bank. We'll check it out tomorrow. When Rachel was murdered, he could no longer deceive himself about how deeply involved he and Dale were."

"So you don't think the money was given in exchange for inside information?" I asked.

"No. We're going to find out very soon, perhaps tonight, what it was for. I think I already have an idea, and I think McFarlane has one, too." He didn't elaborate.

Ari looked in the direction where Dennis and Dale were checking the guns we gave them.

"Just in case, we gave them nonfunctioning bullets—not that I expect any problems," Ari said. "Now, you two, protect them."

"Is there any reason why they didn't just quit the game?" I asked. "They're tough boys. Look what they did for us."

"They're tough, but not tough enough to protect their family members in Libby. McFarlane has two sisters there and Dale a younger retarded brother. And they both have elderly parents."

Harel cocked his gun and said with total confidence, "We might be the ultimate solution to their problems."

"They realize that, too," Ari said.

70

Before we entered the house, Dennis turned around to us. "Bye-bye to my tenure, my future, and my home. Not that I regret it, of course."

"Tell me about it," said Dale.

"Don't be so pessimistic, guys," I said. "Look at the bright side. We didn't have to kill you. You're still alive and well."

We bent down before Dale parked the Audi in front of the closed garage. The lights in the front turned on, the oversized front door opened, and Cromwell popped out dressed in an expensive silk robe.

"Shit, he's coming over here," Dale said.

"Step out of the car and close the door behind you so the light goes off," Harel said quietly. They stepped out, careful to close the doors behind them.

"It's over," I heard McFarlane say in a sober voice.

"Michelle's dead, too," Dale's voice was not as steady as Dennis. "Why the fuck did she have to die, too?"

"I regret it, Dale; it was done against my will. In fact, every goddamn thing that's been done around here in the last several years has been against my will. You both know it. We discussed it."

"What about poor me, Cromwell" I asked, as I stepped out of the car, my gun pointed at his torso. He turned, but even in the dim light I could see him shake. I came closer to him. "You're sorry about Michelle? What about Rachel?"

He was still frozen, and I planted the tip of my boot into his scrotum. He bent over in pain, and I pulled his head up. My gun filled his mouth. "A good friend of mine will ask you some questions in several minutes, and you better answer them, got it?"

He moved his head, still in pain. Harel lifted him with one swing of his right arm and roughly carried him into the house.

"Wow, talking about being in a bad mood," Dennis commented.

"No, Dennis. As a matter of fact, I'm in a very good mood because we've made some progress. I just want to make sure that we get some straight answers. Soften him up, so to speak."

"I'd hate to be on your bad side. By the way, do you have a real boyfriend back home?"

"Is that why you came to our rescue?" I asked.

"So you admit we saved you?"

"You helped a little. If you hadn't, I would have pushed my gun in your mouth, too."

"Are you always so difficult? Not that it's a problem. I like women with an edge."

"I thought you were one of those hard-boiled Scots, not a sweet-talking Italian. Better cool it, Dennis."

"Okay. Just note that I'm Irish, not Scottish. But I could hardly expect a provincial Israeli to make that distinction."

Rafi announced that the house was bug-free. Five minutes later Ari and Matthew joined us inside. Harel stood directly over Cromwell, who sat motionless on a kitchen chair.

Ari grabbed a chair and put its back directly in front of Cromwell so that they were sitting with their faces inches apart. "Mr. Cromwell, we may be running out of time, so I will say what I have to say only once. It will be up to you if you want to collaborate." Ari talked as matter-of-factly as he might to a broker about the latest trend on Wall Street. "If you do, we won't hurt you physically, or otherwise, and you will most likely be in a position to continue with your job and the rest of your life. We intend to destroy the organization you work for within the next forty eight hours. You'll have no further problems from them. Do you grasp what I'm saying?"

Cromwell, still almost motionless, said nothing but nodded his head.

"Good, I'm happy we are on the same wavelength. Should you need another reason to think rationally, just a reminder that without your cooperation you might find yourself in a federal penitentiary for disclosing sensitive military information. That's twenty years, if not life. I believe I'm one of the few people to know about this outside of your network. We can keep it that way."

"Who are you?" Cromwell seemed in shock, but his brain was definitely working.

"We're from the Israeli Secret Service. Heard of the Mossad?"

"Yes."

"All right, so we can leak information about you to the American government or kill you. The second is more probable considering that Rachel was murdered."

"The last thing I wanted was Rachel dead," Cromwell said quickly. "I'm not stupid. You've got to understand I've wanted out. All three of us wanted out. But you can't just get out of this business when you know so much. I'm sure you realize that better than I do. If we had just left, they would have killed us. Had Dennis or I complained to the FBI, they would have killed us too, because with their lawyers nobody could touch them. On paper they've done nothing wrong, at least nothing one can prove against them in court."

Why is it that all these tall, noble-looking Anglo-Saxons know how to lose with grace? I thought to myself. Maybe because of it, they usually don't end up losing in the first place. I once read that tall people, especially tall white people with symmetrical faces, are more successful in life than other groups. It drives me crazy to observe how true it is. He's slick. He'll probably end up being our pal.

Cromwell looked at me and appeared to be reading my mind. Then he turned back to Ari. "You're the only one with the power and motivation to help us out of this mess. I'm fully aware of that. You will have my total cooperation."

"We're going to ask you some questions, then medicate you, and ask them again," Ari said.

"What am I going to be medicated with? I have certain health conditions."

See what I mean? He was setting terms. Well, why am I surprised? His face is very symmetrical.

"Don't worry about that. Now tell us about Rachel's death."

"It was a message," Cromwell said. "They wanted to talk over her research with her and she said no. I didn't expect them to kill her."

"A message?"

"Yes, to let us know what might happen if we thought about bailing out."

"Who gives them the information from Missoula?"

"I do."

Did you call them tonight?"

"Yes, and I told them the job was done after Dennis had called."

"Weren't those guys themselves supposed to report directly to them?"

"They didn't know who they were working for. Before the killing I was told to transfer money from an account in Luxembourg directly into a joint account set up for the assassins. They made me set it up to link *me* with the killers."

"How much?"

"Quarter million."

"We plan on hearing more details later," Ari said.

"You were not always straight with us Jim," Dennis sounded angry.

"When I drafted you in the business, we were still doing only routine Wall Street stuff . . ."

Ari interrupted, "Everybody shut up. This is not a therapy session. We're here to solve bigger problems." He turned to Cromwell, "Can you arrange yourself a visit to California?"

"I have to be there two days after tomorrow to get a new disk, with the latest instructions."

"Do you always fly there?"

"Yes, I rent a car at the airport when I land and stop at the local university in Arcata to justify my trips. I teach a class there. Then I drive to dinner with her . . . the woman who heads the Fund. She always has a ten-man staff, if not bigger, around her. They look more like henchmen."

It seemed that Ari had made up his mind about Cromwell. He wasn't exactly decent, but he wasn't evil either. Cromwell was a brilliant opportunist that got into something way over his head. He was desperate, and we might turn out to be what Americans call his magic bullet.

"You are coming with us, Mr. Cromwell, and you will tell us everything else you know. Things are getting more complicated as we speak, but with some luck, we might manage to handle the mess." Ari turned now in our direction. "Go home and get to bed. We're going to California tomorrow evening. I need you rested."

He looked at Dale. "Are you good with guns, or are you only good in shoving your little Michelle?"

Dale looked down and didn't answer.

Dennis looked at Ari, a bit offended by the abrupt comment. "He's a Montana boy like me, and he's a very good man."

"Good men don't hit women. Being from Montana doesn't change that," I shot at him.

"I agree," Dennis answered, "But he didn't have a choice. We both realized that Michelle's life was in danger, and we thought that by him breaking up with her the way he did they would leave her alone. There was no other way to break up an otherwise loving relationship."

I walked to Ari and said in Hebrew, "Could I have a word with you?"

"Sure, *reggah*. One minute."

He organized the return to the house, what was to be brought from Cromwell's, and what would be done that night. Then he turned back to me. "I bet I know what you want to ask."

"We have enough people. Even the losers from Mossad are better than civilians," I said. "Dennis and Dale are civilians."

"Don't you think I realize it? We just don't have a choice." Ari was curt.

"What do you mean by that?"

"There is a new order from Jerusalem, an official order from the foreign Ministry. Our project has been cancelled, terminated and we are to return home immediately."

"What!"

"Yes. I've called Marcus and he arranged for us to continue with surveillance, but nothing more than that!"

"Which means?"

"Which means that if we go in, we're on our own. If we need any help, Dennis and Dale, besides ourselves, are all we got."

"Why don't they want us to finish the job?'

"Marcus couldn't tell me; maybe because they can listen to our communications. But right now, this is the situation and unless things change, I will assume that I can count on nobody but us. Keep this under wraps for the time being. That is an order."

It was an hour after midnight when we left Cromwell's place.

71

I was still deep asleep when Matthew woke me up. It was already after nine and to reach me, poor Matthew had to go through the two bloodhounds and the puppy that slept with me on the king-size mattress. It reminded me that I needed to ask everybody for possible names for our new friends.

Everyone was already waiting at the breakfast table. Maps and papers were scattered everywhere. Underneath, I could see a couple of half-empty cereal bowls. Ari sat at the head of the table. If he'd been awake all night, it wasn't apparent.

At his side was Cromwell, unshaven, wearing jeans and a plaid shirt. It was an odd sight—without his exterior social games and the upper-crust façade, he looked much more pleasant. Not my type, necessarily, but I think most Israeli women would find him smashingly attractive.

He was busy talking with Rafi, Ari, and Dennis. Harel, Dale and Michelle were in another group, also deep in conversation. Solomon's head was sunk into a large topographical map. Matthew got on the phone, and since he was speaking proper Hebrew, without cursing, I suspected he was talking with Marcus.

Before I sat down, I poured out warm oatmeal for the dogs. It was gone in a second. I then helped myself to some freshly pressed blood orange juice. Ari looked extremely relaxed, his dark brown eyes shining. It was his preaction glow. We all waited for Matthew to end his call.

Matthew hung up and said in English, "Our boss gives us all his unofficial blessings. When it's all over, he would like to meet you all."

"And to this I might add," Ari said, "that except for Cromwell, if any of you want to avoid the excitement of the next few days, you are more than welcome to get out now. It won't be a walk in the park, and it could be fatal."

"Dale and I might get offended if you make that offer again," Dennis said as he turned to Dale, who nodded in agreement.

"What about you, Michelle" Ari asked.

"I was being hunted too," Michelle said. "And in the case anyone's forgotten, Rachel was also my friend."

"Good," Ari said, "so we join forces now."

Yeah, sure, I thought. If they hadn't joined us voluntarily, we would have had to put them under some kind of house arrest. That would have meant pleading with West Coast agents to help us.

"Let me say something," Cromwell Spoke. "Solomon, Rafi, Ari, and I didn't sleep much last night. I just wanted to say that I realize that it's an opportunity for me to be extricated from a mess that began many years ago because of my ignorance and well . . . greed. I guess that holds true for my friends here, Dennis and Dale, too."

He looked at me and grinned. "I'm not on drugs, Yael. Why did you give me a funny look when I said that? In any case, I would have acted exactly like you did last night. It's no wonder all the local guys are fascinated by a tough girl—sorry woman—like you."

He continued, "I was involved with more people in influential positions than most folks, and I want to say that in the last twelve hours I have been impressed by two things. With your analytical abilities, you could make millions in this country. The second thing is going to seem a little schmaltzy—you're an amazing bunch. I've never seen anyone work together like you guys do. I appreciate your trusting me enough to bring me in on this. Amazing, considering I was still enemy number one yesterday."

Ari waited a second, then said, "Thank you, James, for the kind words. You'll be surprised to hear we rarely get praise for our job.

"Now, the schedule will run as follows: In fifteen minutes, Dale and Dennis, you take Yael, Harel, and Matthew to a secluded place for target practice. Matthew, please report on our new team members' abilities."

"We're good," Dale said.

"Show us, then," Ari countered. "And when you're done, come back and we'll eat. Then all of us will drive to Spokane. A chartered plane will take us directly from there to Arcata—north of Eureka, California. We'll relax there for twenty-four hours, and then follow our plan, which is still being developed. Our satellites are already taking pictures, and we've got the house under ground surveillance.

"We're also checking, based on what James told us, the involvement of other foreign governments. No question about it, we're going to step on a lot of toes when we put an end to this ring. This could be the most serious espionage in this country since the end of the Cold War.

"But finally, I must say the only way to mobilize this operation was to convince our government that we just wanted to observe and substantiate certain suspicions we have. When and if I give the order to move in, we will be totally on our own. Everyone clear on that?"

Ari looked around the room. "Any questions?"

Nobody said a word, and then Michelle asked in a low voice, "Why don't we just let our governments take care of it? We could just collect all the evidence."

"Tonight or tomorrow I will give you the story on what this holding company in Eureka was really involved in," Ari said. "But to answer you directly, Michelle, if we involve our government or your government, the spying would be stopped. However, the other goals I mentioned would not be achieved.

"First, the people that gave the order to kill Rachel would get off completely because they are so wealthy. You and I know what that means in this country. In court, or beforehand, they'd work a deal.

"Second, if we're in good shape now, it's due to Dale, Dennis, and James. If the American government gets involved at this point, they may use them as scapegoats. Somebody has to pay, and if it isn't the people from Eureka, then it will be them.

"And third, let me also tell you from many years of experience that spying always reflects negatively on the government that was not able to stop it. The last thing on earth they would care about would be ensuring that you or Israel receive a sound and fair judgment"

Ari paused for a moment, and then smiled, "Justice for three cowboys from Montana? Not a chance."

Nobody said a word until Ari said, "Let's go."

He grabbed me by my shoulder on the way out and asked if we could talk for a second on the deck. I followed him there, and we were joined by the dogs—already loyal converts.

We sat on a big tree trunk off to the side of the deck. New branches had begun to grow from it. Montana gets its fair share of lighting storms, and it looked like this tree had been hit recently.

Ari looked serious. "Tell me what's going on with you and Dennis."

If I had considered him only as my boss, I'd have told him to piss off. But we're close friends, and I understand how these things can affect performance. "Don't you think that we have more important things to deal with?" I answered.

"Don't avoid my question. Besides, paying attention to these little human dramas is one of the reasons we're so good. As you noticed, I also encouraged Cromwell to express his feelings. Despite the stupid games he's been programmed for, he'll turn out all right."

Ari said the last part, half-realizing that it wasn't the point of the discussion. "Now again, what do you feel about Dennis, because he's clearly interested in you."

"How do you know that?"

"You can see it from ten miles away. Don't act like you can't see it. We're both smarter than that. Now, I care more about you than about him, so where do you stand on it?" He was really putting it to me.

"Ari, I'm married to Eric and, if Eric stays, I will never betray him."

"You still didn't say what you feel about Dennis," Ari said.

"If I weren't committed to Eric, I would say that I like him—maybe. But that's irrelevant. Married people always meet someone else with whom they could have an affair. Eric's not a used car. I care about him very much, and I won't hurt him."

"No divorce for the rest of times?" Ari asked.

"No, but under certain conditions, I'd divorce him without thinking twice."

"Oh, what conditions are those?" he asked curiously.

"Well, if he betrayed me, or left me, or got addicted to drugs or alcohol, or hit me. Well, hitting would be an impossibility."

"What do you mean? Harel told me that Eric does two hours of Brazilian jiu-jitsu a day," Ari grinned.

"He can practice it all day, and I could still beat him. I wouldn't want to do it, though. There's his male ego to consider," I smiled back.

"So what do you want me to do about Eric? Should I ask to send him here, like you asked me to do?"

Ari waited for my answer. My big revelation of two weeks ago—bringing Eric here in our last mission, letting him witness what I've had to go through the last several years and bolstering our marriage in the process—seemed a crazy thought from another era.

"No," I said. "I don't think it would be fair to bring Eric here." I looked at Ari for a moment. "What do you think about Dennis?"

"If I say something good about him, will that change anything?" Ari looked at me.

"I'd like to know because men judge other men better, just like women judge other women better," I answered, not sure if I believed it.

"If you remember, when you told me the first time about Eric, I objected to the relationship. It was partly because I felt that as a newcomer to the Department, you should stay unmarried for awhile. And, to be honest, I prefer keeping things Jewish. However, I was fair enough to tell you that after I actually met Eric, I thought you'd be crazy to let him go, remember?"

"That was a surprise," I admitted.

"In the final analysis, you're more important to me as a friend than as an agent." He touched me lightly on the cheek.

"So what do you think about Dennis?" I asked again.

"Dennis is a good man. He doesn't seem as green as Eric. I think when he got involved with Cromwell he was exposed to a world where moral issues are not so simple. He can probably understand our situation better because of that."

"Don't bring Eric, then," I decided again.

"So you've decided to give Dennis a chance?" Ari asked.

"Not at all. I've just decided that after almost three years in Israel, if Eric still doesn't get it and doesn't want to stay with me, I'd better accept it. And as far as Dennis is concerned, I don't think it would be fair to him. And it would be stupid for me to do anything until at least six months after Eric leaves. And I hope he won't."

The truth was I didn't know what I wanted, but I didn't say it to Ari.

"You sound too logical to me, so when you feel mortal again and come down to earth, maybe we can have another conversation," Ari said not laughing.

"I'm all right," I said, figuring this conversation had run its course. I kissed him on the cheek. "You are a very good guy Ari."

"I know," he said.

72

"O.k., you two," Matthew addressed Dennis and Dale, "We're not trying to show you how much better we are or how much you still have to learn. But we must make sure that we know what you can do, you know what we can do, and that when we go in, you follow our instructions. We want all of us to come out alive."

We were standing in an isolated meadow less than thirty minutes away from Missoula. Eighteen full cans of beer were standing on an old wooden fence about thirty feet from us.

"Each of you has nine bullets in your gun. Let's see how many you hit and how long it will take you."

Dennis didn't say a word.

Dale was grinning. "I don't doubt that you guys are good, but I was born shooting cans of beer."

They were good. Shooting, and then aiming immediately at the next target. Good standing position, stable, two-hand hold. They were better than most FBI agents I'd seen and not bad from a Mossad perspective, either.

Only three cans were still standing. Dennis and Dale were smiling modestly, not able to fully hide their pride.

"Are we qualified?" Dale half-asked, half-stated.

"You are amazingly good for your lack of formal training," Matthew complimented them as Harel walked out and set up new cans of beer. "But in a real-life situation you would have already been dead."

"What is that supposed to mean?" Dennis asked, looking at me, then back to Matthew. "Could you be more specific?"

"Sure," Matthew answered, "You wouldn't have time to aim, for one thing, and you never shoot while you are standing. You're too big of a target."

"Generally speaking," Harel added, "the point is that in training everyone always concentrates on the targeting, forgetting that at the same time, you are targeted, too."

Dale and Dennis were not defensive about the comments. They stood and listened, instead, which in my book is a sign of confidence and intelligence.

"Watch Harel and me," Matthew said, "We'll walk while shooting, and we won't aim, although our eyes will stay focused on the target. During the walk, we're bending forward to minimize the chances of being hit."

Without giving further warning, they began shooting while walking parallel to the cans. Eighteen bullets were shot, and not a can was left standing. It took them less than half the time it took Dale and Dennis.

"That was beautiful," Dennis said. "I can't say these trees have seen much action like that."

"They didn't do it in order to show off," I said. "We wanted to make sure you trusted us. Situations could arise that we weren't able to predict. If that happens, let us play the heroes."

Dennis looked at me, "How good are you, Yael? Can you match those supermen?"

"Do you really want to know?" I asked.

"Sure, we want to know," Dale interjected.

"Then go and put new nine cans on the fence." I told him. Dennis walked over instead and put new cans up.

I got up, waiting for him to come back. Harel and Matthew stood there with Dale just watching me. When everyone was out of the way, I began to shoot. I went down to the grass then rolled once on my back, while firing. I got up on my feet for the last two cans. Nine bullets and nine cans were down, and I was already putting in a new magazine.

"Okay" Dennis said.

"Yep, okay," Dale echoed, and clapped his hands.

We were all better ready now for the days to come.

73

We left Missoula around 10 p.m. that night, way later than planned. We couldn't leave before the two guys from Seattle had landed. They came to uninstall our electronic gear and get rid of everything else we had left behind.

The only things we took with us were our guns, the two bloodhounds, the puppy, and a young black kitten that had lost her home and wandered to our house. She wore a band around her neck, but it didn't have a tag and address. Rafi checked her for bugs of the electronic kind. Don't laugh it happens.

It was a little ridiculous with all these animals, but we had room. Ari knows Harel and me so he didn't put up a fuss. He even got some big soup bones for the dogs to play with. The kitten could not be left behind because of mountain lions. Kittens are considered mountain lion *hors d'oeuvres* around here.

Everything we need for the next several days was waiting for us in a place called Hydesville, several miles south of Eureka. We left with two monstrous sport utility vehicles that were brought by the guys from the airport. Harel, Michelle, Dale, Matthew, and I went in the first with our four-legged friends. The rest followed in the second car. We kept lines of communication open.

The freeway was dark and empty, so Dale passed the time by teaching Harel and me the rules of American football and baseball. We should really have known them already because we studied American sports during our first year of training. I guess some things don't stick. Not knowing sports in America, however, is stupid thing for foreign agents. It's a way of life, here, especially on weekends.

We were already two hours on the way and close to the Montana-Idaho border when Solomon called. Something was wrong with their truck's engine, and they were stuck in a small town off the highway. They said they'd wait for us at a small casino bar called The Red Ox. It took us a while before we could turn back, but we got there a half-hour later.

Rafi and Solomon greeted us near the car. The engine's hood was open, and Rafi said something about the battery charger. Ari and Cromwell went to the bar for a coffee. Michelle, Harel, and I decided to join them, thinking it was best to leave the car to the gentiles. Dale and Matthew are all-American country boys. Fixing cars and hunting are mandatory skills.

We didn't have to look long to find Ari and Cromwell. An incredibly overweight man stood in front of them shouting something we couldn't understand. Behind him were three of his buddies, also big and half-drunk. My intelligent guess was that they were not Jewish.

We should have called Dale, but we walked to their table anyway and asked the men if we could offer any help. They ignored Michelle and me, of course, and focused their gaze on Harel, who made a point of sitting next to Ari and asking him in English if the coffee was good.

"And whutdaya think you can help us with?" one of the thugs said, stepping forward, talking to Ari.

Ari got up and stood face-to face with him. "Go and enjoy your beer and your company."

Harel stood up too, and Dale and Matthew came in about that time. Michelle must have called for them. While the men's decision-making process wasn't operating perfectly, all but the big guy decided to fade away.

The guy looked around to see where his friends were. He could have backed away from Ari, but I guess the Montanan reputation for being tough is not based on nothing.

"Fuck you and fuck your fucking friends, too!"

"Let me handle it," Harel said in English.

"No, you've had your workout for today." Ari lightly pushed Harel away.

"Come on, that's not fair," Harel begged.

"Look what you did," Ari smiled at Harel. "Now he's going to think I'm scared."

Ari was shorter than the big guy, but he's as wide as he is tall and no fat. He was really misrepresenting himself because he wasn't wearing his usual tight T-shirt—Montana is just too cold—and his oversized jacket made him look even smaller.

Without further warning, Ari reached up quickly hitting the guy in the neck with the side of his hand. The blow was soft but sharp, directly on the carotid, the artery that brings blood to the brain. The guy was on the floor without knowing what hit him.

Ari put his hands around the man's neck and said, "Did you have breakfast today?"

"Wh-what?" he asked, confused.

Ari hit him lightly on the side of his face.

"I won't ask you again. Did you have breakfast today?"

"Yes I did, I did," he blurted out.

"Good, did you like it?"

"What?"

Ari hit him lightly again, and I had to control myself not to smile. I think the rest of the patrons in the bar were watching, too.

"Yes, I liked it a lot," the guy answered, his learning curve improving.

"I didn't like mine, and I'm in a bad mood. Do you like my mood?"

"No . . . I mean, yes . . . I mean . . . I don't fucking know what to say."

"What is your job?" Ari asked.

"Construction," he answered quickly.

"Do you know a car mechanic here?"

"I'm a mechanic," one of his friends said.

"How much do you make an hour?" Ari asked.

"Hell, I'll look at your car for nothing if you show me that neck trick," the guy offered.

"I can't do that, but we'll pay you well."

Ari helped his victim stand up. The whole crowd walked outside, hoping for another rumble. Nothing happened. They were now our best buddies. Several minutes later the car was running.

Ari gave them a hundred dollar bill for fifteen minutes' work. We shook hands and headed out.

74

A small two-engine airplane took us to Arcata. The weather was foggy, and the pilot thought that he might not be able to land. This area is so foggy that the American Air Force used the area to train its pilots in the Second World War to fight in fog.

But flying further south would have meant no sleep for the night. In the end, there was a temporary break in the fog, and we managed a rough landing. The last ten minutes were so bumpy; I had to remind myself constantly that air travel is still the safest mode of transportation.

We took the fifty-minute drive to Hydesville, and all I could say about my first impression from the place was that it was dreary. The three guys waiting for us at the airport were not from Mossad, but some of our own. Marcus had come through secretly.

We were in full control now.

75

I woke up at ten California time, and spent fifteen minutes looking at the sky. The weather had turned 180 degrees. My room in the house had one big skylight window, a slanted glass roof, and a beautiful view of the sea. I tore myself away, got up and took a walk with the dogs around the house.

Whoever owns this house loves flowers. To wake up to so many different kinds of roses and scented sub-tropical bushes was just what I needed. Amazing really, what the owner had done with the property. Near the house there was a big pond filled with fish. I didn't recognize most of them except the angel fish. They were well fed and huge. I did spot some fresh-water tortoises. The best thing was the frogs, who bounced around everywhere.

The frogs, at first comforting, sent me into a spin when I thought about kissing one of them. Would Eric appear? Or would someone else? I know it's foolish to think of these things now. It bothers me that I waste my time on them. Some action tomorrow will be the best remedy.

In the house I found Rafi and Solomon oiling our new weapons. Everything looked fresh: night-vision scopes, ropes, knives, communication equipment, bullet-proof vests, and ammunition. Marcus really set us up with the delivery. I think we had all the gear needed for "collecting information."

Matthew came in the room. "Good morning everyone, there's a breakfast buffet in the kitchen, and in twenty minutes we'll all meet behind the house. We're going to get the work schedule for the next two days."

Harel was already sitting at the kitchen table with Dale and Michelle. I took some porridge and joined them. Harel was telling them about life on a kibbutz, a completely foreign concept for these rugged individualists.

"Why should I share with anybody what I earn with my hard work?" Dale was asking. "I kill myself in training, I kill myself in school, and now because of this damned kibbutz philosophy, I will have to work myself to death for nothing. Why should I be sharing whatever I make with a bum? It doesn't seem exactly fair."

Dennis and Cromwell joined us and Harel looked at Dale, then to me, and back to Dale. "On a national level, I agree with you that the concept doesn't work. But on the typical kibbutz, there are usually no more than a hundred families, and at least on ours, there are no—how did you say it—bums."

"The way I figure it, most of you here, with your training and intelligence, could make a lot of cash in this country," Cromwell said. "You wouldn't want to share it, believe me. We always hear these students talking about social justice when the very same students, once they make it, will at the most pay lip service to the old ideals."

"First of all, I wouldn't share my resources with just anybody," Harel said. "But I would share them with people in the kibbutz, people who directly or indirectly supported me when I was still a child and would have supported me if something had happened to my parents. As a matter of fact, when I was a child and one of my aunts was ambushed while visiting a friend in another village, people supported her family and gave them emotional and material support."

"What about supporting those that are less able?" I asked. "I mean, look at this country. You take the poor and the less educated and you send them to Vietnam. Then when they came back, some wounded in body, some in mind, still nobody gave a damn. The kibbutz is the ultimate opposite of this mentality."

"How do you treat your veterans?' Michelle asked.

'To begin with, the more educated and the more talented you are, the more likely you will go to combat," Harel said. "And everyone goes to the military at eighteen, men and women."

"Except for Orthodox Jews," I felt it necessary to add. "They play their little political games to stay out of the military, but it's meant their social isolation from the majority." Not that Orthodox Jews care, they live in their own world.

"And in any case," Harel continued, "there's a running joke that if a solider in our army steps on a mine, instead of shouting, "I lost my leg," he shouts "I got a Volvo."

"Volvo, why that?" Dale asked.

"Because as a disabled veteran, the nation will take such good care of him that he could afford an expensive car."

Ari came in, energized. "What's going on here?"

"Harel is trying to make us join the kibbutz movement," Cromwell said.

'If we fail tomorrow, we all won't have another choice," Ari answered.

"So, let us get down to business. I don't think they'll take four bums like us," Dale said, pondering his future.

The people who let us use the place must also own all the land in the nearby area. I guess being rich is not such a bad thing, especially on a beautiful Northern Californian day. We walked out the back door and found a big map and aerial photos posted on the brick wall of the patio. Ari usually demands that everything be done inside, but even he couldn't resist moving outdoors.

We took our seats on the yellow plastic lawn furniture. Ari stood in the center of our semi-circle with the board behind him. "In the last several days I haven't updated you about what is going on, partly because new information was pouring in all the time and there was no need to burden you. More news is coming as we speak, and I will update you if any new relevant details surface."

He looked at us, then continued, "before I begin, I would like again to offer everyone a way out. Since we've already gotten tremendous help from everyone here, I want to make it crystal clear that your walking away at this point won't change my intention of trying to help everyone who's been involved. This goes for everyone."

No one said a word.

"There is another complication, however, that all of us should at least be aware of. Not only are we going to break several U.S. laws, but I'm also not sure that the Israeli government is behind us on this matter. They definitely have no concern for anybody in this room, even though we more than made it crystal clear that you not only helped and helping us, but also saved the lives of two of our agents.

"To be honest, and I say this reluctantly, I don't think they even give a damn about what happened to Rachel. Worse, and here I can give you only my intuition, I even suspect that our government was among other governments which benefited from the activities of the organization we want to destroy.

"I will even speculate that somebody in Israel knew Rachel was up to something and also had an idea that she would be silenced."

Dennis raised his hand.

"Could you be more specific? If I end up in the electric chair, I at least want to know why." He smiled.

"You're right, I jumped ahead," Ari said. "I'm not used to talking to civilians. The story is complex and involves different stages, but I'll try to be brief.

"It began as a purely legal financial enterprise and involved into spying, perhaps even unintentionally. But when the opportunity presented itself to make big bucks; it proved to be an irresistible development.

"About fifteen years ago an old school friend of James here, an entrepreneur named John Van Engen, had an idea for building a holding company. This John Van Engen, a chemical engineer by education, owner of several small companies himself, followed Buffett by buying into only quality companies that were not too expensive. Every ten years or so, Wall Street has some favorite companies in which everyone invests until the inevitable crash happens. But, like other good investors, he religiously avoided the high-flying stocks."

"It seems that by just following this simple rule, one can make nice profits in the stock market," Solomon said, probably to make sure we hadn't forgotten his financial expertise. "And, like Buffett, he also focused on only a few companies in which he invested heavily."

"Anyway," Ari continued, "he accumulated substantial wealth, and then took his enterprise to the next level, which meant controlling the companies he invested in. He reduced the number of companies he was involved in and concentrated his substantial wealth in only five or six stocks. This naturally put him in a powerful position on the boards of these companies.

"He targeted high-quality companies, but never the biggest in their sector. As a matter of fact, he tried to take control of the smaller ones. He did this for two reasons: first, it's easier to control a small company with relatively small capitalization than a large corporation . . ."

"Capitalization?" Rafi asked.

"It's the value of the company after adding all its shares' worth," Solomon said.

"But," Ari continued, "There was another reason he wanted the power to influence events in a particular company. He did all he could to prepare the companies to be taken over. And he achieved it by installing directors, who were his men, on the boards of the companies."

"Kind of sounds like insider trading," Rafi said.

"Not at all," Solomon quickly took to the floor. "As a matter of fact, other shareholders like it because a takeover means a raise in stock value."

"So why aren't more companies being taken over if it's so great for the shareholders?" Rafi held on, pointing his question at Ari.

Ari looked back to Solomon.

"Simply because . . ." Solomon said, "simply because, many times the management cares more about themselves than the shareholders whose best interest they are supposed to represent."

"This is not supposed to be another course in economics," Ari said impatiently. "But anyway, after buying several times into companies and then letting them be bought by bigger companies, our friend accumulated more wealth. At this point, two personal things happened. He got married to a woman twenty years his junior, and several months later he became ill with multiple sclerosis."

"What a coincidence," Harel said.

"Yes we thought so too. We can also see some interesting results. But let's focus on the essentials for now. The wife and her brother took over the flourishing business. Let me point out that James here, an old and trusted childhood friend of Van Engen, was already on the board of many of his companies. The only inside information that was transferred at the time contained information regarding the likelihood of being taken over.

"At the point when Dennis joined Cromwell, this was the level of their 'criminal' activity. Let me make it very clear here, that if this is their "crime", then almost every man and woman on the boards of American corporations has committed the same crime. The laws regarding insider information are written to make the public feel better and not really to solve problems."

"The major dilemma in this regard," Dennis said, "is that those insider crimes are so intangible, you can't really prove them unless they're performed in an obvious way."

"At this point," Ari continued, "the new brother-sister team made some changes. They began to invest in biotechnology and defense companies. Many biotechnology companies are new companies, and if you buy into them before they go public, you can purchase big chunks of them quite cheaply. Those companies usually need capital.

"With defense companies, matters were even more interesting. After the Berlin Wall came down and the Cold War was over, the naïve Americans believed peace on earth had come to stay. Spending on defense went way down. Of the thirty or more defense companies, only four or five remained viable.

"At the same time, everyone on Wall Street got excited about all these high-tech companies and lost interest in the defense sector. The defense companies lost their value. Should an Internet bookseller like Amazon be worth more than the United States' entire defense companies combined? Believe it or not, for a while this was precisely the situation. The defense companies became the most undervalued stocks on Wall Street.

"For the Eureka team, it was an opportunity they didn't miss. They invested so heavily into most of these companies that they could send their representatives to the Boards of Directors."

Ari looked at us and wondered if we still followed his train of thought, then continued. "Business and investment-wise it was a good move. Ultimately, the insanity would be over and people would again buy into companies with real value. In ten years, oil in America and China will have run out and there will be only two places on earth where big reserves remain, the Middle East and Kazakhstan. Big conflicts will start, and America will have to spend way more on defense in order to secure its vital interests. Those stocks will rocket.

"But here was another opportunity to make even more money. The entire defense of this country became dependent on just a few companies, all easy to control. You put less than a billion dollars in Raytheon, for example, and you have direct representation and leverage in a company that makes most of the electronics and missiles of this country. A billion sounds like a lot, but it is very little in terms of a national economy."

"You need way, way less than half that to get a voice in such a company," Cromwell corrected him.

"But it's tricky for a foreign country to do it directly," Ari continued. "There are too many potential diplomatic risks. So our holding company offered them a service.

"As a concerned member of the board, you have the ways and means to get almost any information you want. The top scientist in the research and development laboratories will be more than glad to present you with info that shows their advances, as long as you increase their budget. For some countries around the globe this information is literally priceless.

"It didn't happen from one day to the next, but by the time Cromwell realized the advance research reports he took home to read had been copied—and delivered to other countries—he was far too involved."

Ari paused dramatically, and then stared us down.

"I'm telling you a short, very short, version of what really happened. The scheme was way more elaborate. The American government will have its hands full to prevent such a situation from repeating itself."

"Maybe we should put our efforts toward what we're actually going to do, now that we know how deep the rot goes," Harel suggested.

"We'll get to it immediately," Ari responded. "It was just essential to let everyone here know what we're dealing with and how high the stakes are. Any questions so far?"

Nobody had questions. I had some about the husband, but held onto them. I know several people with multiple sclerosis and they continue to operate quite well, at least on the mental level. But, like Harel and maybe everyone else, I wanted things to get started.

"Okay, lets get down to business then," Ari said.

"We begin with you James. Tomorrow morning, a private airplane will take you to Portland. You will take a plane back to Arcata in case somebody is waiting to pick you up. You said yourself that it has happened—rarely—but it has happened, and we don't want to take any chance. You'll rent a car as always and go through your normal routine. Lecture your class at the University; eat dinner, as always, at the mansion.

"They may or may not discuss things with you," Ari continued, "but you will hand them the latest disk you received from the research department. They will copy it as always and give you back the original. If they invite you to stay overnight, stay. If they don't, go back to the hotel and fly back to Missoula a day later. Do everything you'd normally do. We will be in touch with you."

"What if something goes wrong?" Cromwell asked.

"Not if," Ari said. "Something always goes wrong."

Cromwell looked at him, trying to figure out Ari's sphinx-like face.

"What am I supposed to do then?"

"I will tell you that now," Ari said and looked at Dale and Dennis. "You two listen carefully, too. We're dealing with people that have no scruples. They're capable of murder, blackmail, anything. But if you fall into their hands, you may survive if you convince them that not killing you will make sense commercially. I love logical guys."

"How do we do that?" Dennis asked.

"By convincing them that another country is interested in buying their services too and that they want to do it through you. You just have to guess what countries or terrorist groups aren't already paying them. There are still a lot of those."

"I don't know . . ." Cromwell said, doubting whether he could sell it.

"After we're finished here, Solomon will go with you and work out the story we've already prepared, including documentation to back up your claim if you need it. It will buy you time, and that's all you need.

"Tomorrow in Portland, you, James, are going to swallow a pill with a very tiny radio transmitter. We'll know your position at all times. It will be in your body for 36 hours and within this time frame we will get you out. That is, if something goes wrong."

Cromwell looked at Ari.

"I guess I have to trust your judgment."

I felt I could say something to ease his nerves. Nervous people can abort a mission. "James, you have not known us more than a few days. Do you feel you can trust us?"

"You almost broke my teeth the other night, unless I dreamt it, but yes, I trust you." he even managed a smile.

"I'm not famous for my manners, but do you feel you can trust *me*?" I was forcing him to get personal.

"I don't have any choice, but, strangely enough, yes I do, Yael. I just wish you could give me something a little more concrete to work with."

"I would like to take him for a short walk," I told Ari. Ari nodded in agreement.

76

Cromwell and I walked away from the group, and we sat on the grass near the pool. "James, I want you to know something about me." I got immediately to the main issue. "I'm only twenty-four, and I've already killed, lied, stole, and deceived. Take your pick. I'm arrogant, too, or at least this is what I've heard from people. I'm the most self-assured person you've ever known, maybe with the exception of Harel."

"Is this how people in Israel try to convince one to trust them?" he said, smiling.

I got a little closer to him, something that's always seen as a romantic or sexual move by Americans. People get closer to each other in most other countries, and it's no big deal.

"James, despite of the above, I'm also a nice, sensitive girl from the countryside in Israel, and I was raised with high moral ethics. I may steal towels from expensive hotels, but you know what, in things that really matter, when most people fail, I haven't.

"After years of bloody events, I can still look in the mirror every morning and tell myself that I've saved many lives and never ever let a person down who's trusted me. If something goes wrong. Harel and I will get you out—and alive! This is a personal promise. And put this deep in your head: whatever happens, Harel and I will bring you out. No country, no law, nothing will matter, we will get you out."

I'm good with these motivational speeches. I did it a lot in the army, he will perform better now, which was the only point of the conversation. Still, this little speech was not a manipulation, I meant what I say. Whatever I do, I always ask myself if I will be proud of myself in ten years down the road. And nothing can make one more proud than knowing that a life—an animal's or decent human being's—was saved because of one's action. At least, that's the way I look at things. I hope that this principle is so deep in me that even if I were born a gentile and not in Israel I'd have still stood by it. Not just play lip service like most people do.

We joined the group and Ari took charge again. "Michelle, when we go in, you stay behind on a fishing boat or on shore with Solomon and Rafi. Have some medical supplies ready in case something goes wrong.

"You two, Dennis and Dale, will provide the firepower if we need it. We hope we won't."

"What do you mean firepower?" Dennis asked. I think after we showed him what we could do, he and Dale resign themselves to our command.

"Simply be two more guns," Ari answered. "Under normal conditions, Harel Matthew and Yael can handle everything on their own. I will need to be there for any fast assessment we need. You might not even shoot once, or you might be the ones that save the day."

They looked as if they could live with that.

"Good then," Ari said. "When we go in, both of you follow us. Yael, Harel, and Matthew will lead the way. I will take care of the whole operation and you two join me. Again, I will assign tasks as the needs develop, and we may regroup if necessary."

Dale, Michelle, and Dennis left us, as did Rafi and Solomon, who had to prepare the logistics of our assault. Matthew, Harel, and I stayed with Ari and spent the next three hours planning and refining the actual attack. These ten men will not, we must assume, be as easy as the guys from Berlin.

We finished before 2:00 p.m. and since tomorrow night is the big one, we wanted to do something relaxing. There's nothing better than lounging around with your teammates, the people you need to be able to count on when hell breaks loose.

77

What we had done in Berlin was not typical in the sense that it was done without any planning. Circumstances dictated our proceedings. Usually, those kinds of actions take a lot of preparation, beginning with super high tech fun, like satellite and aerial pictures. In this case, we had rented an airplane flown by one of our pilots to get real-time photo links from every possible angle. They even arranged a fishing boat for surveillance from the ocean. The mansion stands very close to the cliffs, and despite the great electronic protection they have around the house, they apparently had never considered that somebody might come up over the cliffs—their Achilles heel, so to speak.

Not far from the mansion is a favorite spot for people who hang glide from the cliffs. Mossad somehow managed on short notice to round up some hang gliding able agents and planted them there, so the place is under observation around the clock. Hang gliding is becoming quite popular in Israel.

Ari insisted that Harel, Dennis, Dale, and I get out and enjoy the sun. Matthew, Solomon, Michel and Rafi were asked to stay behind.

I was happy for the opportunity to get outside. Harel and I had decided independently—without Naomi's and Eric's approval—to add Northern California to the list of places where we might re-settle if Israel decides to return the Golan Heights to Syria. We placed it third, after Western Canada and the Oregon coast.

We four took a two-hour hike in one of the redwood forests. I tried to think about redwoods being in Israel, but had difficulty envisioning it. Israel is so tiny for such big trees.

Our puppies were fascinated by the soft sand and the sea lions on the rocks off the shore. I like the fact that Californians are more like us in their distaste for hunting. Can you imagine what might have happened had there been an ocean in Montana? They would have hunted and killed all these beautiful animals.

Dale suggested we climb on one of the islands closet to the shore. We could walk there without getting into the water higher than our waists, just by crossing the small distance while the sea retreated. I didn't bother telling him that tomorrow night we would have to go back into the water and do even more strenuous climbing.

At the top, Harel was the first to spot whales in the distance, maybe a half mile away. They were after big schools of small sardines, diving for a long time, then coming up shooting fountains of hot vapor into the air. Albatrosses flew above, hoping to steal some leftovers.

We just sat there, enjoying nature and each other.

On the way back we stopped at the town of Arcata, also a university town. It looks a bit more sophisticated than Missoula and is far more diverse. Montana's white-ness, unaffected by the Native American population there, was difficult to handle. Not difficult, just strange. Here there's a highly visible minority of Mexicans and African-Americans.

We went back to the house in Hydesville. Rafi and Matthew had come back from town, where they brought more equipment for tomorrow, including a light, narrow aluminum ladder. They also bought a lot of vegetarian Indian food from a local organic restaurant. I love working with guys who can keep their priorities straight.

The house has a great stereo system and a great selection of compact discs. Michelle put on music from a guy I had never heard before. I think the name was Charlie Daniels. He sings a mixture of old western and fast rock. His words are funny, and he has a thick southern accent, like Matthew.

Dennis asked me to dance. He didn't wait for my answer before grabbing my hand. Soon we were all dancing. Even Cromwell decided that it was about time to come to life, and he began dancing with Rafi. Short, stocky Rafi with tall, skinny Jimmy was sight to be seen. We all gave them a hand when the song ended.

Harel danced with Dale, making up one part of the most powerful duo in the history of Hydesville, I bet. They were lifting each other while dancing, mimicking some strange combat forms. No more Jews or Gentiles, Israelis or Americans, Israelis or Montanans, we were all together, ready for what fate had destined us to do.

78

The ocean was unusually still. It was two hours after midnight when we left the old fishing boat with three dark-blue sea kayaks. They are much longer and wider than the unstable short river kayaks. You aren't locked inside, and there's plenty of room for gear. There were two people in each. After the big fishing boat let us off, it went back to the port ten miles north. If the mission were successful, we would leave through the front door.

Ari headed our small team, and Solomon, Rafi and Michelle sat in a van hidden not far from the target. The lines of communication were open.

James landed, as planned, in Arcata's airport on the noon flight from Portland. After renting the car, and later lecturing his class on ethics and accounting, he continued to visit our "widow" and her brother. This was the last time we heard from him. According to Rafi, he was still there on the second floor, hopefully alive.

From the latest reports we had, the widow is definitely the one who is running the business, not her brother. 'Widow' is just a term of endearment. Her husband is still alive, but they've placed him in a private care facility. We had seen all the photographs of the people we could expect to encounter. A motley collection of creatures that the world would do better without. Some of them had families and, as far as we could tell, no other civilians were present at the compound, which was good. The last thing we needed was to deal with children and other innocent people.

Once we neared the shore, we left the kayaks and walked in the water the remaining distance. I was glad to have our military commando shoes, which let the water out quickly, allowing the feet to stay pretty dry, as long as you wear no socks.

The dark was more of a challenge than the steepness of the cliffs, but we didn't need night vision to find our way. We had been shown very accurate close-up photos taken from sea and shore that showed us the best routes to use. Harel and I had taken a walk there earlier in the day, acting like lovers looking for seclusion.

Barbed wire was installed close to the top, but it was no match for the titanium tongs we always carry on such operations. It's always the same story. People spend a fortune on security and yet leave gaping holes large enough for any army to run through; or at least vulnerable enough for an experienced operative. And it's not just private estates. We have similar stories with the security arrangements around some of Israel's most sensitive sites. People who make security systems need to think like thieves, and it's clear there aren't many thieves in the business.

The last fifteen feet were really the only part that cost us some effort. The slope was nearly vertical, and had no rocks to steady our climb. I guess it was that feature that made them feel safe. They assumed that any sort of climbing operation would be noisy enough to arouse the guards.

We unveiled the telescopic ladder; I climbed first, while Harel and Dale held the ladder. Then came Matthew, and after he made it, we both held a short synthetic rope to help the rest come up. It took us less than five minutes.

We weren't sure if Rafi's electronic device that was placed inside James, had functioned as he promised it would. It was supposed to transmit 30 minutes of electromagnetic waves that would neutralize or deactivate, from the inside of the building, the electronic net installed in the building. We didn't tell this to Cromwell. There was no reason to burden him with details he didn't have to know.

Anyway, we decided to enter the building through the pantry window. This little storage room was added after the security system was installed. According to the security company, it was never updated. We paid quite a lot for this information—money can buy almost anything.

Using a diamond cutter, with plastic tape to stifle the sound of breaking glass, we entered through the window. I stood, gun ready, for several minutes in the silence. When I checked my watch it said three o'clock. I walked into the adjoining room, the kitchen. It was an industrial-type room, cold in the dark. Straight ahead, I saw a door with open curtains framing its window. It opened into the garden and with the moonlight outside, once my eyes adjusted to the darkness; vision was no longer a problem. I tell you, it seemed too easy.

At that point, we were all inside. Dale and Dennis, holding their Uzis, yet still looked quite unprofessional. At least, I thought, they looked damned interested. This line of work is a far cry from insider trading.

"They are most likely all upstairs." Ari whispered to me. "Before we go up, I want the downstairs rooms combed."

We needed no one at our backs. We regrouped, Dale staying behind with Ari, and Dennis teaming up with Matthew to check the big rooms. Harel and I took the small rooms. We'd considered using night vision inside, but again, fearful of being blinded by sudden light, we decided against it.

We used battery-powered torches with projectors that emit concentrated light rays. Not to be confused with lasers. Unless someone is looking directly into the room, they won't see any light. All the doors opened for us, the squeaks, although not loud, seemed like a thousand trumpets. The rooms were used as bedrooms; and the fact that they were empty didn't make me feel better.

Those were my thoughts when the first shots were heard and all the lights flicked on. Harel and I were down on the floor rolling to opposite room corners. I covered the door, Harel the window, as we shot out the three lamps. The room was to be a deathtrap, for sure, if we didn't leave at once.

"Nobody's in the corridor," Ari said through the earphones. "I want reports."

"We're okay," Harel answered.

"Matthew? Dennis?" I heard Ari quickly inquire. No response.

"Yael, Harel, come out and cover the corridor with us. You're clear. They ambushed them in the big room." Ari's voice was stable and authoritative, no sign that he might have just lost his best friend. No room for feelings.

Harel and I came out and saw Ari and Dale facing opposite directions. Dale seemed frozen. This wasn't a football game.

"Should we go into the room?" I asked Ari. It wasn't the smartest decision for mortality's sake, but Harel and I didn't have time to weigh the pros and cons.

"Can you hear me?" We heard an English accent. Whoever it was, he was using either Matthew's or Dennis's earphones. No other earphones would have been on that frequency.

"We hear you," Ari answered.

"Excellent. Our employer would like to speak with you, please enter the big room, one by one, all of you," the voice said.

"So you'd shoot us one by one?" Ari asked, at the same time signaling us to advance toward the room.

"Nobody has to die. You can keep your guns, but be careful not to point them at us when you come in. We'll give you the same courtesy."

"What about our friends?" Ari asked.

"You can talk with one of them. Here, talk." There were long seconds of silence, then Matthew's voice. "I'm all right. Dennis is wounded, and they have a gun to my head. Don't make them nervous."

Thank God they're still alive, I thought. On our first mission to Germany, we lost one of our team. I took it too much to heart, and it nearly killed me. Matthew is one of my closest friends I've ever had, and I hoped very much that Dennis' wound isn't fatal. The word "wounded" has a broad spectrum of meanings.

"Okay, we'll come in, I heard Ari say. "I will be the first one, and only I will come in. Then I'll decide if the others come in too."

"Fine by us, just walk slowly with your gun pointed down. The man who's pointing at your friend's head is, in fact, getting nervous," the voice said.

Ari looked at us.

"If something happens to Dennis, Matthew, or myself, you have the order to kill everyone in this building, understood?" He said it in slow English, making sure everyone got the message.

Another voice: "If we wanted you dead, it would have happened already. There are twenty of us here."

Ari pointed his gun downward and slowly walked to the door. Dennis and Matthew were there, not much separated from death. We really didn't have a choice.

79

(Editor's note: The following is an excerpt from Ari's journal; Yael's information on the following, important minutes were incomplete.)

As I came in, it was clear to me that it was a well-planned ambush. Dennis and Matthew didn't have a chance. It was a big library with plenty of heavy furniture to hide behind, especially in the dark.

Seven men stood there, all holding handguns or AK's. Matthew was on his knees, a gun pointed to the back of his head. Dennis was in the corner; the wood floor underneath was soaked with his blood. There wasn't enough to indicate being near death, he was clearly breathing, but I could see he needed help.

"Ask your friends to come in too, guns down," the English guy said again. "All we want is for you to talk to our employer. Then you and yours can go home."

I didn't know exactly what he meant, but he certainly meant business. It was clear to me that we had been betrayed, and I didn't think it was Cromwell. I gave Yael, Harel, and Dale directions to come in, but not to do anything without my signal. I said everything in slow English and in a tone that wouldn't further alarm our opponents. I didn't like the gun at Matthew's head.

Harel, Yael, and Dale entered the room slowly, guns pointed down. I noticed that Harel was holding the Uzi now, Yael the handgun. They had things under control without intervention, something I can always count on. That's my kids!

We stood now, guns down, against the seven of them. There was an uncomfortable silence when their henchmen seemed at a loss for words. They'd actually completed their task, and I guess it surprised them. A voice came from an intercom on one of the tables.

"I apologize that we couldn't talk over dinner, but you seem to have an aversion to front doors," a woman's voice said. "It's simply primitive, that type of behavior. But I still think we can straighten things out."

"Who are you?" I asked, knowing the answer but trying to buy more time.

"You know exactly who I am. Let's not play games. Shut up and listen to your boss."

I had no idea what she was talking about. And so we waited, all of us sizing each other up. They were all white American, perhaps one Asian, maybe another who

226

had somewhat Hispanic features. There wasn't a hint of emotion in the room. No hatred in these people's eyes, only business. They may kill you or escort you politely to the door. They could not care less. A far cry from the intense, hate-filled violence of the Middle East.

Then on the intercom, we heard Hebrew-accented English.

"Ari, can you hear me?" The speakers seemed a lot clearer now. I recognized the voice. It was the head of the Advisory Committee of the Department of Foreign Affairs.

Just a month ago, we had sat with him, the Prime Minister and Marcus, and discussed some relevant top-secret issues concerning the transfer of radar to China. Marcus and I were the only ones who vehemently objected. Sure, if we lost the deal, the Europeans would go ahead but the Americans are our only real friends in this damn world. Two hundred million dollars isn't worth anything with that in the balance.

"I hear you but I can't recognize you." I answered. In a hostage situation; gaining time is all that counts.

He introduced himself, and then added, "Since when do you do things without authorization?"

"I can't recall that in the past I ever asked for your authorization." I said. Yael and Harel were positioning themselves, I hoped, while I gave them dear minutes.

"This is not a matter of national security." He said. "This is an internal American affair; therefore it's up to the Foreign Ministry to decide on such matters."

"One of our agents was killed in Missoula and another civilian was killed in Berlin." I said, as I noticed Yael concentrating on Matthew. Harel had the guy watching Yael in his sights.

"No agent was killed. An ex-employee was killed, and an ex-employee is a civilian. The dead German is not an Israeli citizen. That is our problem, not yours.

"Besides Ari, we use the services of this company that you are trying to dismantle. After the Pollard spy case, we can't afford any other complications."

"Major countries have used their services too." I said.

"Sure, and we were less involved than others, but you know like I know that if things get to the media, Israel will be the first to get hammered. Look at the Pollard case, which got major media coverage at Israel's expense while spies working for other countries doing work that was far more damaging to the U.S., got off with far lighter sentences.

"Please, Ari, I appeal to your common sense and ask you to let it go."

He wasn't finished. "Ari, I'm sorry about Rachel, too. I was at her funeral, you know. But this is the real world we're facing, a world without justice at times. We sometimes need to sacrifice for the good of the many. I appeal to your sense of duty to Israel."

He spoke as officials always do.

"Okay," I said. "I have several conditions under which we'll walk out of here and forget what we saw and what we know."

I watched Yael from the corner of my eye. I was worried she would get into action too early.

"When we walk out of here, I want Cromwell with us."

"Cromwell wants to stay here." The woman's voice again. "Do you want to talk with him?"

"No, I want him to be brought down here, otherwise, there's no deal. We don't leave without him."

"What else do you want?" the woman's voice was business-like.

"I want $13 million to be transferred *now* from one of your many accounts in Europe to an account in Luxembourg. I can give you the number right now. It assures good retirement for all of us, and I will transfer part of it to Rachel's family and the family of the girl in Germany who was killed. Rachel's German friend will get her share too."

"Do you really assume you have this bargaining power?" the female voice on the intercom said confidently.

"For us, a million a piece is the whole world. For you, it's nothing. You give us the money, and we forget we were here. I've always dreamed about early retirement. Now, that we all lost our jobs." I wanted to lull her into thinking we wanted nothing more than to get out with our skins intact and $13 million. Most people would want nothing more than that.

"What is your account number and the name of the bank?" The women edged in. "And Cromwell is on his way down." I liked her bossiness and efficiency. She didn't try to argue or make up stories that the transfer would take too long.

"When you send him, send the confirmation of my bank receiving the funds." I told her.

Like most people in our position, we have open accounts in several countries, in case we ever need fast funds. They are established so that there are always several co-signers. If something happens to one, the money can be still recovered. The co-signer is somebody we don't know.

However, against all regulations, I had opened several accounts giving power-of-attorney to Matthew, Yael, and Harel, the only people besides my wife and Marcus I ever trusted. Governments, even democratically elected governments, take on a life of their own after a period of time. The officials take their power for granted and basic rules of morality are forgotten, or, at least, bent. I was determined that we for once wouldn't be the victims of the phenomenon.

80

Cromwell walked in the room. I didn't even look at him. My full attention was on Matthew.

"Are you okay, Cromwell?" I heard Ari ask.

"Now I am. Somebody betrayed us, but I have a transaction confirmation." Cromwells voice was clear.

"We have enough money to retire now, and we can leave in several minutes." Ari told him. He looked at the Englishman.

"And now what?"

"Now all of you, except your friend here," he pointed at Matthew. "Walk nicely out the front door and to your friends with the hang-gliding suits. Your wounded man you can take already with you. Once you are there, we will let your friend go, too."

I guess our man in Jerusalem was still on line, listening, perhaps realizing how deeply we felt we were let down.

"I am sorry, Ari. We could not afford being caught again or openly being involved in any affair in this country." He sounded genuine.

We were all alone, deserted and betrayed by the people we may sometimes criticize, but must trust, nonetheless, with our lives. But it was clear that getting us out alive this time was not a priority. Our intercom Israeli in Tel Aviv wouldn't have said what he said if he thought we'd make it out alive with millions and especially with all this useful information. We were now the sacrifice for the whole. But even if I was wrong, and they really intended to let us go, Harel and I had some business to finish.

I truly hoped that Rafi, Solomon, and Michelle had figured it out. I hoped they had driven far away from this scene. Matthew looked at me with a "we're screwed" grin and I knew he knew it, too. I had to shoot the hand that held the gun that pressed to his head. Again, only in movies does anyone shoot the hostage taker in the head or body. It would have been way easier for me to shoot the guy in the head. That target is much larger than the fingers holding the gun. But shooting in any other place could initiate reflex contraction of the finger muscles. With the finger already on the trigger, I couldn't risk that.

Another problem: The gun from the other guy had turned on me instead of Ari. A shot from me would be followed by a shot from him. I'd be dead. Regardless, Harel would finish the rest easily. I hoped Harel knew he must begin with him.

But childhood games, at least ours, maybe had their purpose. The long hours we spent as children shooting all those targets were not wasted. Did all that happen so that today I could save Mathew, a man born on the other side of the globe? Maybe.

I threw myself down, yet again, on the floor, shooting the hand at the same time. The other man shot toward me, but the bullet went through what had been my head's position a millisecond before. It missed, but I felt the heat of the shot just above me. Then I heard Harel's Uzi begin to do its magic. The others didn't have a chance to raise their weapons. Matthew was still kneeling, and I shot the man above him from the floor again, directing my gun afterwards to the others. They were already down. I shot them anyway. Presumed dead wasn't good enough.

Ari and Dale were standing frozen, realizing only now what was happening.

"Check Matthew and Dennis! We will cover the corridor," I shouted, and then moved with Harel to the exit door.

The corridor was empty, and I could hear people running above us. We flattened ourselves on the corridor's carpeted floor, covering all the doors.

"We're coming out," I heard Ari's voice tell us, this time in hushed Hebrew. They were all there. Matthew, considering the ordeal he'd just been through, was back on duty. His hair was matted with blood.

"Yours or his?" I asked him.

"Both. You scratched me. Next time try being more careful," He said with difficulty.

"Yeah, next time don't move your head," I answered while looking at Dennis. He barely could walk and was definitely in pain but still alive, thank God.

"What's up Dennis?" I asked.

"Looking for some action," He laughed, while coughing.

"The vest didn't let the bullets through, but some ribs are broken," Dale said.

"The leg looks pretty bad, but the bleeding has stopped," he added.

I couldn't look at him too long because I was watching the corridor.

"But our tough country boy wouldn't complain, eh?"

"Only because I am still trying to impress you."

That was one thing I didn't need to think about at the moment.

"Let's check the rest of the rooms here," I told Harel, "and maybe the rest of you can give us some cover, at least secure the floor that leads upstairs—there is only one stairway to the second floor."

Harel and I moved to check the rooms. They were all empty. Ari decided our next move.

"We'll regroup again. Harel, you, Yael and Matthew clean up the upstairs. Dennis and Dale, you cover from the window, in the front part of the house. I don't think they would try to leave from the rear, where the cliffs are. I'm going to stay here with Cromwell and secure the corridor. I'll join you as things develop. Questions?"

The lights were still on, but no noise came from upstairs. They were waiting for us. Even if they had turned off the lights, it wouldn't have mattered. The first light of dawn was beginning to brighten the darkness.

Matthew took the Uzi and Harel and I took handguns. On the earphones, I could hear Ari reestablishing contact with Rafi.

"Are the lines secure now?"

"Yes. I changed frequency. We're updated. Marcus himself got in touch with us and warned us, so instead of leaving; we ambushed the guys coming our way." He was pleased and proud with their performance. I bet Solomon was the one who did the actual work.

"We couldn't warn you because they blocked this frequency," Rafi continued.

"Look out," Harel shouted and shot at the same time. A body fell, slumped on the top stair.

"Give us cover," I told Matthew, and he began to shoot long barrages with short interruptions above us as we climbed the last few stairs. We threw grenades in each direction of the corridor, and as they exploded, we took cover on top of another body. This one must have died from Matthew's covering shot through the wall. Deep penetration bullets saved the day.

We searched the area thoroughly, but found nothing.

"They're gone," I told Ari trough the earphones.

"What about the roof?" Ari asked. "Dale and Dennis watched the front all the time and saw nothing."

We found the stairs to the roof, and once again repeated the drill with the grenades. Again nothing. It was good the place was so secluded, because it should have been crawling with California policemen by then. We continued carefully onto the roof's marble floor, and I immediately thought of a way to spend some of my new money. That thought was broken when we spied our adversaries from behind the roof's railings. They were running down a narrow path to the shore. In the distance, we could see a speedboat off the coast and closer, a Gumi raft waiting at the shore.

"They climbed down on an emergency fire ladder." Matthew said.

We reported to Ari as we tried to make up the distance.

"Matthew, you and I should go directly after them," Harel said, "and Yael, you cut their retreat on the shore by going down the way we came."

"Let me have the Uzi then, so I can shoot the boat when I get there," I said feeling an adrenaline rush, "and both of you be careful, because they're probably watching us now. They could see an ambush."

"That's why we're going together." Matthew said, exchanging the Uzi for my gun. "You be careful, too."

We checked again the communication between us, updated Ari, and then went our separate ways.

81

The rope from our night assault was still there, and with the morning light, the way down seemed easy. I wondered why they preferred to go all the way around and not this way. Perhaps I took our athletic abilities for granted.

Nope. A man peered out from behind a rock, and took a shot at me. I returned fire and hit him, but before I had a chance to acknowledge his death, I felt a chilly pain in the back of my neck.

"Easy now," said the first man who had ever crept up on me with a gun. "No one wants to die today."

He checked me very fast and professionally. He took everything, even my dagger, before allowing me to turn around to see him.

He was almost Dale's size, an athletic looking, and brown-haired, bearded man with sharp blue eyes.

"So where do you want me to shoot you first, in the right or left knee?"

I was scared. I'll admit it. I'd been in bad situations before, but none in which I'd had time to reflect on my own death.

"Are you scared to try it with your hands, or am I too good for you?" I said, trying to sound anything but pathetic.

He was still smiling and looked at his watch.

"My birdie, we still have ten minutes before I meet them at the boat. I think it's time for some fun. But if I win . . ."

He waved his finger as he came closer to me, using his other hand to put his gun in his belt behind his back. He grabbed my arm, turned around, lifted me on his shoulder and threw me down.

I tried to throw some sand in his eyes, but again he was too damned fast. He kicked me in the face with his steel-toes boots, and for a second, I think I lost consciousness. I found myself being raised by my hair. He turned to face me.

"I think I like you better than the other kike bitch," He said. "She cried and begged. You don't"

My eyes were full of sand, and I could barely see him. I tried to kick him, but he was too powerful for me. He blocked the kick with one of his legs, and then shoved me to the ground again. He sat on top of me with his muscular arms around my neck.

"It turns out that there is no time to play games," he said. "I think I'll break your neck with my hands, as you wished."

The pressure on my neck became tighter, and my eyes began to tear. He was killing me, and I don't recommend this method of death. I tried for a final time to lift him, but he weighed at least two hundred pounds. My vision turned to a strange mixture of light gray and black.

And then, the pressure started to ease. Gasping for air, I turned around and saw Harel standing there.

He threw me the guy's gun, as my attacker spun around to face a new enemy. I somehow caught it but couldn't pull the trigger. Harel directed his gun at the man and squeezed the trigger. Nothing, it was blank.

The rest I viewed as a spectator. Two powerful, muscular giants at each other's throats, and I was still too dazed to move. At times, the fight appeared up side down.

I saw Harel looking at me, begging me to shoot. He seemed as confused as I was. My brain was still recovering.

They were hitting and blocking the whole time, trying to determine whether brawling or martial arts technique was the better choice for the situation.

There was no pause in the action, and a lot of heavy breathing. I think the bad guy said something like, "Come on, Jew boy, and let me teach you something."

Harel didn't answer. It was the fist time I'd seen his eyes like that. I'd lived with him all my life and never once saw how cast-iron and steel his expression could be. I guess he had taken it upon himself all his life to protect us, and somebody had crossed that line today. I knew it, Harel knew it and, in an intuitive fighting way, this stranger knew it as well.

Harel approached him barely even trying to block the man's hit on his shoulder and neck. He broke through the man's defenses and bent in front of him—something we were warned in our self-defense class never to do.

The rules, I figure now, were made only for us mortals. The guy lifted his knee and hit Harel in his chest, but his leg returned back to its spot limp.

I could make out Harel lifting the man, all two hundred pounds, using his arms and his full body. When the bulk of the man was just at eye level, he dropped the whole load and pushed down with his arms. The man hit Harel's knee with full momentum and the sound of the waves nearby us were silent for a moment. I heard bone.

The man lay on the sand, eyes open, moving as if experiencing an epileptic seizure. The motions forced blood out of his mouth. Harel took his gun from me and liberated the man from life.

He helped me up, and hugged me softly.

"Are you okay?"

"I . . . don't know," I said, wishing I could formulate a better sentence. Then I nodded yes.

"I came as soon as we heard your breathing on the earphones," Harel told me. He picked up my earphones, dusted them off and gave them back to me.

"Don't lose them again. Can we go now, my dear?"

I kissed him on the cheek and hugged him.

"You're a hell of a guy."

"It's the first time you ever told me that," He said, and kissed me back.

As I regained my composure, we walked toward the water. We saw Matthew running toward the shore shooting at the two boats, but by then they were out of range.

"We're back in business," Harel reported to Ari.

"Good because we're losing them. They're already in the Gumi, heading toward the speedboat. I'll be joining you in a second.

When the three of us had almost reached the water, I heard several shots. Harel, Ari and I glued ourselves to the sand. Matthew, maybe one-hundred fifty yards away, did the same. We were on the sandy shore, easy targets. I guess we were all tired, because we should have considered the possibility that she might leave some men to secure her escape.

More barrages of bullets, this time from a different direction. On the cliffs, I saw Dennis, Cromwell and Dale standing with rifles.

"It's the second time that Dale and I have rescued you people," Dennis said over the earphone. "You can't manage without us."

"Where did you get those guns?" I asked.

"Cromwell found them; the house is full of them. We decided to make good use of 'em. It's not hunting season yet, so we thought it would be a nice opportunity to practice. From here it looks as if we got them all, but the guys in the water are too far from here."

"But they are not too far from here," I said.

I stepped in the water and lifted the Uzi, looking through the scope of the gun at the bigger boat first. It wasn't telescopic, but it was good enough for me. I had spoken a little too soon, because they were definitely at the limits of the gun's effective range. All I could do was try. I did, and it worked.

We could see a plume of black smoke before two men jumped into the water.

I gave my attention then to the Gumi boat. It took only two or three bullets to puncture the raft. The weight of the engine was enough to pull it under the water. We could see five people in the water, struggling with the waves and underwater currents.

♦

82

We went back to Hydesville to turn the clean-up over to the Mossad. It would mean the execution of a few people, and I'm thankful Marcus spared us that. I couldn't have done it. Once the threat is over, I'm no shooter.

Dennis returned to our group after he was treated at a private clinic. One of his lungs was partly punctured, and two of his ribs were broken. The wound in his leg was not life threatening, although he lost a lot of blood. He'd walk healthy again in two months, he told us.

"Too bad for all those deer and ducks," I teased him.

"Is that all you've got to tell me?" he asked me, as we stood far enough away from the group to have a semi-private discussion.

"No, you saved my life twice, and yet you're gentile. It's more than I can handle."

"I think I fell for you during that fishing trip. No, maybe before, when I saw you for the first time, at the party."

I held his hand.

"I fell for you around then too. Things you said, the way you said them and the way you were." Now I'd given him every reason to pursue more answers.

"Ari told me you're married, but that things aren't the best right now," He said.

"It isn't the best time for anything right now, Dennis. Could we just say that something special happened that I won't forget? That doesn't mean I can leave the other life I have, at least not without a fight."

I got up and kissed him on the side of the mouth, changing slightly at the last second out of some sense of loyalty to Eric.

"I like you Dennis McFarlane. I like you very much."

83

I haven't written for a month now, and I guess I've been missing it. I wonder what you'll think of all this, Marcus, especially since I want to give Naomi my notes on Montana and California.

Today was party day.

Harel and I are home for good. Last night the kibbutz had a party for us, and tonight was for our friends from the "real world." They're all staying overnight, except Marcus and his wife. Always a late-night helicopter ride for him.

Eric sat next to me for a lot of the evening, pouting I guess. I couldn't read him. Naomi told me she told him not to make a rash decision until tonight's party was over.

"How sweet of you," I said.

"Don't you care?" she looked at me curiously.

I told her I cared. I do. He can stay here, and I will be happy, I think.

"Is there something you need to tell me?" Naomi asked.

I couldn't answer. I just smiled and walked to greet Matthew and his wife Doris.

"Our kibbutz will still take you if you decide to join," I told them, my last try at preventing them from returning to Texas.

"After a few months of suburbia, we might take you up on that offer," Doris said. She hugged me.

Ari and his wife had come several hours before to introduce their six kids to the kibbutz children. Rafi and his wife Aliza, and Solomon and his wife, Rebecca, were also here. These four are all city guys at heart, but it hasn't ruined them for some reason. They do, however, still think milk comes from oxen.

And I almost forgot. Barbara Skibbe came with her little Mossad boy, Benny, the one she met in Berlin. She had a startling suntan, and I'm sure the boy is praying for a hasty wedding. Barbara didn't seem ready to go home.

In other news: Rachel's parents and brother came, still stunned, I think, by all the money they received. "I don't know what to do with it." Her mother told me, sounding ashamed. I suggested setting up a fund for students to study in America.

I also talked to Marcus and his wife for awhile. I told her, as I hugged Marcus, "He often gets on our nerves, but you've got a hell of a husband."

"Remember those words when I ask you to rejoin," He said before she could respond.

"Never."

"Never say never. In six months, I will call you."

"In six months, I might be so bored I'll be willing to listen. Who knows? Bored. It made me think of playing paint ball in Montana. I wondered about Dennis, Dale and Michelle. Cromwell, too. From what I understand, they received some good publicity from the event. "UM faculty and students help bust spy ring." Or something like that, the papers said. Even better, they got their cash from us. It will keep Cromwell living in the style of life to which he's accustomed.

The puppy's getting bigger, and Fiona and Duncan treat him like their own.

The hounds and the kitten got a very good deal out of this adventure. Dennis invited them to live at his home outside of Missoula. I hear they're doing well. I'd like to go and visit them someday.